ESCAPE
TO PARADISE

An Historical Novel

BY
EDGAR PANKRATZ, M.D.

 **FriesenPress**

Suite 300 - 990 Fort St
Victoria, BC, Canada, V8V 3K2
www.friesenpress.com

ISBN
978-1-4602-6571-0 (Hardcover)
978-1-4602-6572-7 (Paperback)
978-1-4602-6573-4 (eBook)

1. Fiction, Historical

Distributed to the trade by The Ingram Book Company

ESCAPE
TO PARADISE

Prologue

In the late fifteenth century, a former Catholic priest by the name of Menno Simons, living in Holland, became the leader of a fledgling religious group, an offspring of the Reformation, who believed that one should be baptized on the confession of faith, hence as an adult and not as a child. They also practiced the simple life, did not use the oath, and believed in pacifism, amongst other things. Through diligent work, Menno established a large group of equal-minded believers who, because of adult baptism, became known in Holland as doopsgesinte (baptism minded). Later these people would be called Mennonites. Because of persecution, many of these left Holland and moved to other parts of the world. Some moved to western Prussia, and when the Prussian King reneged on his promise of freedom from military service two hundred years later, some of them moved to the Ukraine, which was then part of Russia. Catharine the Great promised the Mennonites many freedoms and allowed them to buy large tracts of land, on which they established their colonies.

Today Mennonites are a group of people who practice certain religious beliefs, such as adult baptism, pacifism, and a simple form of life. They have a strong belief in Jesus Christ and in the necessity for the confession of sins and rebirth. Over the years they have developed a distinct culture, especially those that moved to Danzig and West Prussia, and eventually to the Ukraine. There they lived in tight communities and developed their way of life with little influence from the neighboring Ukrainian or Russian settlements. Several large rich groups of villages evolved, collectively called Colonies. During the Russian Revolution, the wrath of the communist proletariat was particularly vicious against the Mennonites because of their wealth, religious beliefs, and the fact that they were the hated Germans. Looting and murder were common. In a few instances, whole villages were massacred. In the twenties, many Mennonites emigrated to the US and Canada, but others, still hoping for things to normalize, remained in the Ukraine. These later suffered persecution, starvation, and often death. Of those that survived, some managed to get to Germany during the Second World War. From there a large group went to South America and some, especially those that were sponsored by relatives, came to Canada.

During the Second World War, many of the Germans who were born and had lived outside Germany and now lived in areas under German army control, including Mennonites, were drafted into the German army. Some had the dubious pleasure of first serving in the Russian army, becoming prisoners of war, and then being drafted into the

German army. As 'Volksdeutsche', they were not considered to be totally trustworthy and because of this they were inducted into the SS, until then a unit of volunteers. It was reasoned, and probably rightly, that this would make them think twice before becoming prisoners of war, as members of the SS were treated harshly by the allies, especially the Russians.

The folowing story, while fictional, is based on many true experiences and portrays the hardships, temptations, struggles, and discriminations suffered, and the eventual outcome for one such Mennonite and his family.

Chapter 1

Theo was sitting on a tree stump near the road in front of the house where he and Laura had lived since coming back to BC. He stared at the luger in his hand, a handgun he had taken from a German officer at the end of the second great war a long time ago, in April 1945. It seemed that the captain, whom Theo had found near the road with the luger in his hand, had deliberately ended his life, probably to avoid capture by the Russians. The Germans were retreating everywhere in the spring of 1945, and there was total chaos. It was obvious that Germany had lost the war. There were many suicides, as fear of capture by the Russians was widespread, especially among the officers.

Theo was a young man of seventeen then, almost eighteen. He had managed to get rid of his SS uniform just before his unit, or what was left of it, was captured by the American army in a small village in Germany. He and his unit had been fortunate to escape the Russians.

There had been a time when he was proud of his uniform, but it had become a danger and Theo had been happy to obtain civilian clothes from a farmer for some cigarettes and old silver coins he had collected. The Americans had no interest in a youth in civilian clothes who had hung

1

around a military unit, probably to get some food, and had chased him away.

It was all so long ago. So many things had happened since.

Theo gazed into the valley, not seeing its tranquil beauty; its rich fields, the varied farm houses strewn among the fields. He did not see the distant mountains bathed in the light of the morning sun, nor did he know what he was feeling inside him—was it despair, rage, utter hopelessness? Was he losing his mind?

His thoughts were drifting. He absentmindedly brushed a lock of hair from his forehead. It was all so very long ago, yet he could remember it so clearly: The village where he had been a little boy, where he was born . . .

The village was on the East side of a small, picturesque river. Across the river was a low range of hills. In the distance, a grove of small, scraggly trees jumped into view on the slope of the hill as if they were out of place and did not belong on the otherwise bare hillside. Between their house and the river were an orchard and a vegetable garden. A path went down one side of the garden to the river. Near the river was a large willow tree. Theo could remember this particular tree in every detail.

His father, Jacob Dirks, had planted the tree, and had lived in the village most of his life. Theo's grandparents, as many other Mennonites, had taken the opportunity to move to the new settlement when this new tract of land had been purchased by the mother colony. They had never regretted it. With some help from relatives and assistance from the old colony, they had managed to establish a respectable farm and, in time, had built a comfortable, if not large, house. Here their four children were born. It had pleased God to take one from them, but then, that was life and God's will and had to be accepted.

Jacob, the oldest, Theo's father, had worked on the farm, had married the neighbor's daughter, and had eventually taken over the farm when his father had died. Theo's parents, along with the rest of the colony, had prospered until that fateful event that not only had affected their life but the life of virtually everyone in Russia, maybe the whole world: The start of the First World War.

At first nothing was different, life went on, work on the farm went on. But then, gradually, changes began to happen. It wasn't much in the beginning: a few horses were requisitioned, then a few wagons, all properly paid for by the government. Then one day, what everyone had long feared happened: the army draft officer arrived in the village. All Mennonites knew that there was an agreement in force, negotiated with the great empress Catherine II, which gave Mennonites exemption from the draft. Yes, everyone knew that, and still everyone was afraid. Soon it became apparent that the fears had not been unfounded—the great Empress's promise was not totally adhered to. But, as everyone later said, it could have been much worse. Only substitute and medical service was asked for. Fortunately, no one in Jacob's family was of the right age to be drafted and so his family was not greatly affected. Many others were. Medical service in the army involved front line duty and significant casualties occurred. Some came home missing an arm or a leg, or with some other dreadful injury. Some never came home at all.

As the war dragged on, many items could no longer be found in the stores. Life in the village became more difficult because there were fewer men to do the work and more and more women took on the tasks formerly thought of as "men's work". There was discontent in the country. In some larger cities there had been demonstrations, some involved violence and even deaths. Then, in 1917, an event occurred that had been thought impossible by most Mennonites: The tzar was overthrown and the country was taken over by revolutionaries. Although Jacob read about these events, they seemed to him remote and somehow unreal. In the village, nothing much changed, even though great events had taken place in the country and the world.

Over the next few years, however, much did change and many hardships were endured by the Mennonite colonies. Bands of renegade army units robbed and plundered, and the rich Mennonite villages were favorite targets. By luck or providence, Jacob's family was spared, although they also suffered the general hardships that a revolution brings.

Jacob had now been married for more than ten years and even though he had prayed to God for a child, a son, nothing had happened. Just when he was ready to give up, the long wished-for miracle occurred—Jutta became pregnant. Everyone fussed and worried but the pregnancy was quite uneventful and in the fall of 1927, on September the tenth to be exact, a healthy baby boy was born. After much deliberation, Jutta named the boy Theodore, a very unusual name in Mennonite circles.

Chapter 2

When Theo turned seven years old, no one particularly noticed; his mother did not hold with parties and such, especially not for seven-year-olds. But it did not matter anyway, as there was nothing to celebrate with. Ever since the glorious state reforms and the formation of collective farms, there had been a steady decline in the economy. Even food was getting scarce. Theo and his parents still lived in the same house, but the land, the equipment, the horses and cows were now owned by the collective, which in turn belonged to the government, even though the slogan was that now "the people" owned everything. His father, Jacob, now worked for this collective, tilling the same land that formerly had been his. He had some knowledge about electricity, which he had acquired over the years because the topic fascinated him and he had read some books on it. When later that year a power line reached their village and electricity was introduced, it was Jacob who did most of the work of stringing wires to each house from the main line, which ran on poles along the street. After that he was known as the electrician, a term which did not displease him.

Theo had attented classes since the beginning of the school year a month before. His teacher had kicked up a fuss when she found out that Theo was only seven and not eight, the required age for school entry. At first it seemed he would not be allowed to continue, but after his father talked to the teacher, nothing further was said—especially since Theo did very well and always achieved high marks.

It soon became apparent that Theo was a bright boy. He not only kept up with his older classmates, but usually performed better then most. By Christmas, he was in the top ten of his class. His language skills were superb, his math was good, and his artistic abilities, except for singing, were satisfactory. There was only one problem: he could not sit still. How many times a day did the teacher say, "Theo sit still"; "Theo stop talking"; "Theo pay attention"! Even discussions with his parents did not help. It seemed that Theo's energy level was too high to be totally used up by the work in class. It wasn't that he was rude or nasty; he was just always doing something. After a while, he and the teacher came to an understanding, but throughout school and even much later at university, Theo continued to have this problem.

By the end of the school year, it was obvious that Theo was an exceptional child. Not only was he bright, he was eager to learn. He got along well with the other students and seemed to love company. He enjoyed sports but was not particularly good at any games. In spite of this, he was usually chosen first or close to first when teams were selected because he got on well with his peers and always gave his best.

While he was popular, he did not have any close friends until he was in grade three. Even then, his new and close friend was not one of his schoolmates but a Russian boy who lived just outside the village. No Russians were allowed

6

to live in Mennonite villages at that time. Theo met him by chance when his mother had missed getting the cow out in time to catch the herd and Theo had to take it to the pasture grounds later. There, he met Wanjka, the son of the herder. They seemed to hit it off right away. They were the same age, had the same interests, and seemed to like the same things. Only their backgrounds were different. This would eventually significantly affect not only their lives but also their friendship, but at this time the two boys were not aware of these differences. Had they been aware, they probably would not have cared. However, even at their young age, both boys knew of social distinctions that existed. Theo knew instinctively that he must not tell his parents about his new friend, that they would not approve; Mennonites did not associate with Russians. It was not only because Catherine the Great had specifically prohibited proselytizing, there were also marked social differences. Russians who lived close to Mennonite villages or those who came from Russian villages nearby, usually worked as servants or farm workers and were not regarded as equals. These things, however, did not at first affect their relationship. They met often, swam together in the river, and occasionally fished, but mostly they played as boys do or just sat and talked.

One of the places they especially liked was the large willow tree near the river, not too far from Theo's home. Here they often sat and talked about anything that came into their mind. In time, this became their regular meeting place.

Chapter 3

It was on one of those incredible spring days that seem to occur only in the southern Ukraine. The sky was spectacularly blue, the sun was warm, and the earth had a fresh smell. Everywhere new growth sprang forth, the snowdrops bloomed, and here and there blossoms started to open on the fruit trees. Especially beautiful were the wild pear trees that lined both sides of the village street. Theo was not consciously aware of all this natural beauty but he felt good inside. Across the fence, he spotted his friend.

"Hey, Wanja. Come here."

"Hi Theo, what's up?"

"Come here, I want to show you something."

"My old man will kick my ass if I don't finish weeding the garden."

"Aw, come on Wanja, it's important."

"Well, be quick."

"Okay, okay, look at this." Theo held out a piece of red cloth.

"So, what is it?"

"Come on you dummy, can't you see? I've joined the pioneers. The man at the school said from now on things will be different. The new government, you know, the communists, they will distribute the money and all, so that everyone will be the same, just as they have put everyone's land into collective farms. None of this poor and rich stuff no more. He said that we could help by joining the pioneers."

"Are you crazy, Theo? My dad says the Whites will come and kill you if they know you are a communist. And if the Reds even suspect that you favor the Whites, they will kill you too. It is best just not to talk about these things. So just shut up. You hear me? Just shut up." Wanjka looked over his shoulder as if to make sure that there was nobody within hearing.

"All right already! I haven't really joined, I only took the scarf, but maybe I'll keep it hidden a while. You want to go swimming later?"

"Yea, if my old man lets me."

"Okay, I'll see you at the dock."

The dock consisted of a short gangway of rickety boards, built long ago by some teens for diving. Theo sat at the end and dangled his legs into the water. After a while, he swam. The water was on the cool side and refreshing. 'Wanjka isn't coming' he thought. 'Might as well go home.'

He meandered along the river in the direction of his house and just as he approached the big willow, Wanjka came running down the path. When he saw Theo, he flopped down under the willow tree. "I'm bushed! All that weeding, and then I ran all the way here."

Theo sat down beside him. "Thought you weren't coming." He lay back and gazed through the branches at the blue sky. "Say Wanjka, what else did your father say about the reds?"

"The who? Oh yea, just to keep my mouth shut. Why?"

"Well, my dad seems quite worried. I heard him and Mom talk about not owning our house much longer and such. I couldn't really understand it, but they seemed real worried."

Wanjka gazed into the tree. "My teacher said that kulaks, like your parents, will soon be put in their place and will have to work like the rest of us."

"Listen Wanj, my parents are no kulaks and they have always worked. What are you talking about?"

"Simmer down, Theo. My teacher said that. I only repeated what he said. He also said that the collective farms are owned by all of us, at least by everybody who works there."

"You're daft. How can everyone be an owner?"

For a time the boys lay silently. They both had sensed the concern of their parents but neither had any idea how monumental the events to come would be. Wanjka watched a circling hawk in the sky. The bird flew in larger and larger circles until it suddenly dove straight down and disappeared from view. "The teacher also said we could become anything we wanted. What would you like to be, Theo?"

"Me? I dunno. Someone important: a lawyer, or a doctor. Yea, a doctor, someone who cuts up people—a surgeon."

"Yak, all that blood! I'd rather be an officer. You know, boss people around, rather than having to do everything yourself." He suddenly jumped up. "Come on, I'll race you to the house."

Theo jumped up and raced after his friend, forgetting the worries of their parents. As most young children do, he turned all his concentration to the moment. When Wanjka came near the house, he suddenly stopped. "Your father does not like me playing with you. I better cut through the gully here for the street. See you." He was gone before Theo could reply.

Chapter 4

The year 1937 started passively. Theo was ten years old that summer. Many changes had taken place since his birth; he now had a five year old sister and a one year old brother. Both were a bit of a nuisance but he could live with it. A far more major change was the loss of their farm when the collective farms were formed. The land was gone, and now so were the barn, the hayloft, and machine storage building. They had simply been moved, in pieces, to the new collective farm yard. No one had asked permission, no one had even notified them that this would happen, and of course there had been no compensation. Theo's father was now in charge of the horses at the number two barn. He worked long hours but never complained. After all, it was easier work than being out in the field.

Great changes were taking place. For the Mennonites these changes mostly made things worse, even though they were meant to improve the lot of the 'proletariat'. His mother, besides looking after the house and children, also worked for the collective farm, often out on the fields. In the new Russia there was equality, and women were expected to do their part.

German school was no more; all instruction was now in Russian. The churches were closed and all religion was forbidden. Most Mennonites had bibles in their homes and held private services or at least family bible readings. Theo's father usually read a bible passage before the evening meal as this was the only time when all members of the family were present. Theo developed mixed feelings about these sessions. He was getting conflicting messages about religion. In school it was derided and called a superstition, at play he heard jokes about it, and at home, although his parents had attended church regularly and his father read the bible, there had never been any great fuss made about religion. He told himself that he believed in God, but there was always this little niggling doubt that he could not get rid of.

At that time, Theo was in grade three. Even with the change to the Russian language from the German, he remained an outstanding student, taking first prize honors each year. His friend, Wanjka, now attended the same school and sat next to him in class. He was also a good student and there was keen competition between them. Wanjka was now allowed to come to Theo's house. In fact, it seemed that Theo's parents had totally discarded their prejudice and treated Wanjka as one of their own. For Theo life was okay; he did not go hungry, he had a good home, he had friends— what else did one need?

That summer, however, his life was drastically and permanently changed. It started with vague rumors of men disappearing at night. No one wanted to say much, but soon more men were missing, and it became common knowledge that the NKVD, the secret police, were arresting them at night and taking them away in closed trucks. Before long,

Theo's father was arrested. Several men came to the house late in the evening, searched the house, took the family bible and some letters from Canada, called his father a traitor and spy, and took him away. He barely had time to say goodbye, just a quick hug for each. Only to Theo did he speak a few quick words: "You are now the man in the family, look after them. I love you all. God be with you."

Theo tried to embrace his father but one of the policemen pushed him away. "Enough! We haven't got all day, lets go." His mother pulled him to her and held him close while tears streamed down her face. His father walked through the door holding his head high and not looking back. Theo never saw him again.

It was a difficult time. Most men in the village had been taken and the women, the old men, and the very young had to take over the work. The women adjusted best; they took over the heavy manual work on the fields, operated the tractors and other machinery, and still managed to provide a home. They became both a mother and a father to their children.

While the women adjusted best to the physical stresses, the children coped best mentally. The routine of school and play helped them get over their loss. Outwardly, Theo seemed to do as well as the others, and only his mother noticed the subtle changes: He was more subdued, smiled less often, and at times appeared even more restless than usual. He was even more determined to do well in school, but seemed to have lost all interest in sports. He still got on well with his peers but at times could be moody or even rude. Strangely, his friendship with Wanjka intensified, even though Wanjka's father, being Russian, was not taken. They would now sit under the old willow quite often. Their friendship, if anything, had moved to a more stable level. Often they would discuss their hopes and wishes for the future, their worries, and current events. It was in this setting that Theo could, for the first time, discuss the loss of his father.

"You know, Wanjka, I never knew that I loved my father, but I really did, and still do. God, I miss him. You're so lucky to have your dad still."

"Yea, I guess so, but he's been miserable lately. Sometimes I get so pissed off. You know, Theo, sometimes it appears as if he is scared or something. The other day he slapped my mom, something he never did before, but I think he had been drinking."

Theo's thoughts were still on his father. "It's been a year since they took Dad. Mom tried to see him in town, but they would not let her. She does not even know if he is still in the jail there or not. They say some men have been sent to Siberia."

"My mom heard that all the Germans will be sent to labor camps, but I guess that only means the men."

They sat silently for a while, each occupied with his own thoughts.. Suddenly Theo jumped up. "Why don't we go swimming? I feel awfully depressed. Come on."

They raced to the wharf. Wanjka could always beat Theo, both in running and swimming. On the wharf, they quickly undressed and jumped into the water naked. They swam to the other side of the river and back as fast as they could. "Damn it, Wanj! You want to kill me, I hardly made it back to the wharf."

"Aw, don't worry, Theo. I would have saved you."

16

"Yea, you little shit, you could hardly drag your own ass to the wharf. But I'll forgive you this time. Let's go home, I still have some homework to do and I would guess so have you."

Chapter 5

For some time there had been rumors of war, and on June 23, 1941, Germany invaded Russia on a wide front. There was talk of widespread bombing in several large cities but there was very little official news. According to the government radio, the Red Army was holding and would soon drive the aggressors out of the motherland.

Since it was summer, there was no school and Theo and Wanjka were hanging out near the village store, trying to listen to the conversation of the adults. Everyone talked about the war. Rumors were rife, but factual news was scarce because only the government installed radio system was allowed and the reports were all censored. But the rumors were that many cities had been bombed, that there was much damage, and that the army was in retreat. All of this, of course, was only whispered, but Theo and Wanjka had picked up enough to get the gist of it. After a while, they retreated to their favorite place under the big willow. "What will you do if the Germans get here, Theo?"

"Why should they get here? We're a long way from the front, and besides, there's the Red Army. Don't you think they'll do something?"

Wanjka looked around as if to make sure no one could hear. "I heard my mom and dad talk, and they think," again he looked over his shoulder, "they think the Russian Army is no match for the Germans, and that we will loose the war. Don't you dare repeat this to anyone, or I'll be in a lot of trouble."

"Don't worry, I'm no telltale. But your father should not say such things, at least not where someone else can hear them." Theo felt uneasy and silently wished that Wanjka had not confided in him. He was not certain why he felt this way, he would most definitely not betray his friend, but he could not shake his troubled thoughts.

"Let's go to the wharf. I saw some of the girls go there earlier, maybe they're still there." They ran toward the wharf. Even before they got there, they could hear the girls talking and giggling. The boys moved to the side of the path to hide behind the bushes. Soon they could see several girls, some were sitting on the wharf, and others were in the water. They snuck a little closer and then jumped out from behind the bushes yelling and waving their arms.

"Look at them," Wanjka laughed. "They're afraid we'll see something."

The girls had, in fact, all jumped into the water. While they were not naked, some of their attire, mostly underwear, was rather skimpy.

"Why don't you little children get lost and don't bother us?" one of the girls yelled. They were mostly a few years older and obviously more developed.

Theo recognized the one that had spoken. "What's the matter, Ann, are you afraid we'll see your boobs? You didn't mind when Mishka squeezed them in the park the other day." The girls started to come out of the water and both boys took off, laughing as they ran. They had no desire to get into a scrap with the bigger and stronger girls.

A while later, it had been two days since Theo had seen Wanjka. At first he had not thought much of it, but now he was wondering what was going on. He decided to stop by at Wanjka's house to see if his friend was sick, or at least to find out why he had not been around. Wanjka's mom opened the door. "Oh, it's you. I'll send Wanjka out." She looked upset; her face was puffy as if she had been crying. When Wanjka came out, he too seemed quite upset. "What do you want?"

"You look awful. What's happened? Is somebody sick?"

Wanjka's eyes brimmed. "My dad, He's gone."

"What do you mean he's gone? Gone where?"

"The police, they came during the night and took him away. You must have said something, or how else did they know?"

"Are you crazy? I never talked to nobody. Nobody, you hear?! Someone else must have said something."

"But nobody else knew."

"I don't care Wanj, it wasn't me. Honest!"

The boys would never know that Wanjka's father had made a few unwise remarks in other places, and one of his supposed friends had reported them to the police. They glumly walked down the street and without any conscious intent, went along the path to the old willow tree. It was early and the grass was still wet from the dew so they continued on to the wharf where they sat down and dangled their feet in the water. After a while, Wanjka got up. "I have to go home."

"I'm sorry about your dad, Wanj, but it wasn't me. I never said a thing to nobody."

"Okay." Wanjka turned around and walked away. After this, even though their friendship continued, the spontaneous relationship they had enjoyed was gone.

Wanjka's father seemed to have disappeared from the surface of the earth. His mother wrote letters, talked to the local police, and went into town to the NKVD office, but to no avail. He would never return and only several years later did the family find out that he had been shot.

Chapter 6

Theo was sitting on the front steps reflecting on the events of the last few months. In June, the war with Germany had started, then Wanjka's father was taken. In September, Theo had eagerly started a new school year, and now, only a month later, they were being relocated. All the Germans were advised to be ready for this so-called relocation in two days. Where they would be moved to, or why, was not known. Everyone was instructed to only pack personal belongings such as clothing, bedding, and dishes. No furniture was allowed.

On the appointed day wagons, driven by Russians, came to every house, loaded the packed belongings and the families, and took them to the nearest railroad station, about six kilometres away. Before they left, Theo managed to slip away for a few minutes to say goodbye to Wanjka. It was an awkward moment. The events surrounding Wanjka's father's arrest were still fresh in both their minds, and they were not sure what was going on, how long this relocation would last, or, whether they would ever see each other again. For a bit, they stood there silently. Finally Theo said, "Well, see you."

"Yea," said Wanjka, looking at his feet. Since there was nothing more to say and the wagons had started to leave,

Theo went home. His mother was frantic. "Where have you been? We are ready to leave and you are gallivanting around. What if we had gone? We could have lost each other for ever!"

"Aw, come on, Mom. I only went to say goodbye to Wanj, just a few houses away."

"Well hurry up now and get on the wagon. We're leaving. Have you got everything? Look after Sonja and Peet, I have to lock the door." She went and carefully closed all the doors and windows, not realizing that as soon as they were gone the people remaining would be in there to take away everything that was movable and even rip out some of the built-in shelves.

Theo deposited his sister and brother on the wagon, in a place where they should be safe. He then went and sat on the end of the wagon where he could easily jump off if he so desired. When their wagon reached the road to the city, a fair-sized caravan had already assembled. The wagons formed a long line that moved towards the bridge and up the hill, along the road leading to the city and railroad station. Many wagons carried more than one family. The driver on most wagons was a Russian male, the remaining travelers were mainly women and children, with a few elderly males mixed in here and there.

Theo was looking back at the village, which now lay before him in the valley, as their wagon slowly moved up the hill. He could see the river just below the base of the hill, with the gardens on the other side of the river and the houses further on, all in an orderly row. He saw the wide and now dusty street beyond the first row of houses. Theo felt a lump in his throat. All his life he had lived here; his friends, especially Wanjka, were here; and he knew all the people in the village. What would their new home be like? A despondent mood overcame him, but he was young and soon the excitement of travel and the anticipation of new places took over. He jumped from the wagon and ran ahead to see how the rest of the wagons were getting along and to fool around with some of his buddies. He found Josh Dyck on the side of the road. "Hey, Josh. What's up?"

"Hi, Theo. Want to do something interesting?"

"What's interesting?"

"Well, just up the road and a little over is a watermelon field, you know, and there should still be ripe melons there. You get what I mean?"

"Say, we could just relocate some of them melons, what? But there's got to be someone watching the field. How do we get around that?"

"Yea, we need a decoy. Any ideas?"

Theo was smiling, a caper like that was just what they needed to liven things up a bit. "What about Ann? I bet she would have no trouble keeping the guard at the other end of the field."

"That's a splendid idea, man. Let's go find her." Ann was neither hard to find nor hard to convince. Soon a plan had been worked out and off they went. The field of watermelons was not far. They soon saw the little hut set up for the guard and Ann meandered in that direction while the boys stayed out of site and made for the distant end of the field. When they saw Ann talking to the guard they crawled onto the field and each made off with two watermelons. Ann soon joined them in a gully nearby where they ate as much as they could of their plunder. Finally, Theo could eat no more.

"Boy, they were good. We'd better get back to the trek. I may be in trouble already."

The others agreed and off they went, happy that their caper had come off so easily. When Theo reached their wagon, his mother was cross again. "Where have you been again? You'll be the death of me yet! It's enough that I have to watch the little ones. I want you to stay close to the wagon from now on." Theo did not reply. What was the use? His mother always picked on him because he was the oldest. He resumed his seat at the back of the wagon and stayed there until they reached the railroad station.

There supreme confusion reigned. Refugees from several villages were arriving and there seemed to be no one who knew what to do with them. After some time, a few railroad officials came and assigned areas to each village in the large yard behind the station building. Everything was unloaded and piled on the ground and each family sat on or near their pile. They were in the middle of the yard, without shelter, not knowing what would happen next.

When the sun began to set, Theo's mom arranged the boxes and suitcases to form a little enclosure and with some blankets formed a sort of bed for the two little ones.

"Theo, you stay close. With all these people around, we could easily get separated. I don't know how we are going to spend the night. We'll have to figure out some way we can all sleep." Theo did not reply. He still felt resentment because of the previous rebuke and wasn't going to cooperate any more than he had to. He sat on one of the boxes and watched as the large railroad yard filled with people.

He was watching a small plane fly over the city when Josh came by. "They say that's a German spy plane," Josh remarked, feeling important. "It reports everything it sees to the German front, which is not far away."

"How do you know that? If that is a German plane, the anti-aircraft guns would be shooting at it."

"It's too high, that's why they're not shooting at it. And it is so a German spy plane. They are spying here because this is an important industrial city that makes war stuff." Perceiving that Theo was not in a good mood and feeling irritated himself because he could not convince his friend, he wandered off, not knowing that subsequent events would prove him right.

From where Theo was sitting, he could look along the railroad tracks and see them curve away in the distance. To the right of the tracks were the large iron works with their mighty smoke stacks and many large smelters. On the other side were some warehouses and the rolling mills where the steel was processed. Konstantinovka was a large industrial city, with many factories, and therefore quite important in a military sense. Of course, none of this was on Theo's mind at the time. He was reflecting on the events of the day, sitting on the small pile of their belongings, his mother beside him huddling the two youngsters close to her to keep them warm. With the dark starry night sky above, Theo felt an incredible sadness sweeping over him, a sense of despair, no doubt made worse by the fact that he had not eaten much that evening.

"Theo, get your blanket and come sit close to me." His mother, almost sick with worry about her children and the future, had noticed the troubled look on her son's face. "Come, if we get close together we'll be warmer."

Just as Theo got up, he heard a strange faint noise, a heavy distant hum. As he listened, it seemed to get louder. "That must be airplanes. Don't you think so, Mom?"

His mother had become noticeably more nervous, "Yes, yes, I think so. But come sit close to me."

The humming soon become a loud drone, and just when it appeared to be almost overhead, the whole world exploded into a terrifying whine that grew louder and louder until it was right on top of Theo and he could feel the vibrations in the air. Theo threw himself against his mother and clutched her coat with both hands. He had not noticed that he screamed. His mother tried to hold her three children close to her, not knowing what was happening or what to do. Immediately after the whining noise stopped, there were a series of loud explosions and the whole area where the railroad tracks disappeared behind the ironworks turned into a mass of flames that seemed to come along the tracks towards them.

"Oh God, the fire is coming this way! We have to get out of here! The Germans are bombing the city and they will surely not spare the railroad yard." She grabbed Sonja, who had awakened and was crying, and started to run toward the gate. "Quick Theo, hold Peety's hand and follow me. We have to get out of here or we will surely die."

"What about our stuff? We can't just leave it, they'll steal it for sure." Theo was so scared that he could hardly speak and it seemed strange even to him that he should worry about their belongings now.

"Hurry Theo, for God's sake, hurry. And don't loose Peety."

At the gate there already was a milling, screaming crowd trying to get out. But the gates were closed and the guards were holding the crowd back, pointing their rifles at them. Just then another wave of German Stuckas, the dive bombers that were so terrifying because of the noise they made when diving to unload their bombs, approached the city. The crowd became frantic. When the bombs started to fall, this time closer, the guards also decided to leave. In minutes, the gates were down and the people poured out into the city. Theo had lifted Peet up and carried him as best he could. They were knocked down several times but, miraculously, were not seriously injured and did not lose each other. Outside the gate, Theo followed his mother with difficulty. She seemed to know where she was headed and pushed on with grim determination. They went up a narrow street and turned into what seemed to be an alley. A few houses down the road, Jutta turned into a tiny yard and knocked on the door. It opened a crack. A husky male voice asked, "Who's there?"

"Quick, Stephan, open up, it's Jutta."

"Oh, my God, what are you doing here? How did you get here? It's such a terrible night."

Jutta waved her hand as she pushed Sonja ahead of her through the door. "Never mind, I'll explain everything to you later. Have you got some room for the children to sleep? They are tired and frightened."

Stephan, an old Russian friend, waved her in. "Of course, come in. There isn't much space, but we can bed them down on the floor in the back room."

With the help of some straw and a few blankets, they made some beds and soon the children were asleep. Even the continuing bombing, which from here was more distant and muffled, did not keep them awake.

Jutta began to relax a little. "Thanks Stephan, I don't know were we would have gone otherwise."

"You know that you're always welcome in our house, Jutta. We've been friends for many years."

"Yes, I know Stephan, and I'm grateful."

They sat silently for a while, listening for the ongoing bombing, which now seemed to be coming from the direction of the railroad station. "It's late, Jutta. I think you should get some rest too."

"Yes, you're right. If it's all right with you, I'll sleep close to the children."

"Of course, take some blankets."

Soon the house was quiet but outside, towards the industrial area, the bombing continued until dawn. When Theo awoke, the sun was shining, there was no noise, and he thought for a minute that last night had been a dream, but when he stepped outside and saw the smoke over the city he remembered.

Jutta was jumpy and hurrying everyone. Theo figured that she was worried that their possessions at the station might be in jeopardy. He helped her to get the two little ones ready, then took Peety by the hand and followed Jutta who was already on the street. When they reached the industrial area near the station, the street was closed and they had to make a detour. The devastation in the city was horrendous; several large factories were in ruins, others were partially destroyed, with fires still burning here and there. Large craters could be seen in some of the streets. When they reached the railroad yard, they found, to their surprise, that everything was as they had left it. Nothing was missing. Amazingly, neither the station nor the yard had been bombed. Some suggested that the German army had known that the refugees there were German and had deliberately spared that area.

The blankets had become damp from the dew and Jutta spread them out to dry. Then she unpacked some food brought from home, bread and homemade jam, and gave the children breakfast. Theo was restless and ate his piece quickly. "Can I go and see what Josh and the other kids are doing, Mom?"

"Well, okay, but don't stay too long, and if you see any activity come right back. Who knows when we'll be leaving and I want you here when we have to board the train." She watched him leave and called after him, "If there's some news come and tell me."

Theo sauntered along between the piles of baggage. People were standing or sitting around, and some were eating. One woman had put a few rocks together and had made a small fire and was boiling something. Eventually Theo found Josh and his family. "Hi, Josh. Where did you go last night?"

"Go? We went nowhere, we stayed right here."

"Here? Weren't you scared?"

Josh took Theo's arm and pulled him away from the others. "Scared? I was so scared I nearly shit my pants," Josh whispered. "We all crawled under the blankets and stayed close together."

They went to find some of the other kids. Quite a few people were still missing but no one had seen any deaths. Several people had been injured. There had been heavy casualties in some parts of the city—at least that was the rumor. Considering the severity and length of bombing, no one doubted that there had been much damage and many deaths. The many smoldering ruins around the railroad station attested to that.

After a while, Theo went back. His mother was talking with some other women and Sonja and Peet were playing some game. His mother saw him and called him over. "Don't go too far, I hear we're going to be loaded onto a train soon."

'Soon' turned out to be two days later. They spent two nights sleeping under the open sky, frightened all the time that the German planes would come again, but nothing happened.

Some bread was distributed the next day and later there was even some sausage and cheese—not a lot, but it helped.

On their fourth day at the railroad station, the train finally arrived. It was made up of ordinary old freight cars.

Chapter 7

The train was finally loaded. All the boxes, suitcases, and various other containers were packed away, some in cars that were used only for freight, but most of the baggage was put in the same freight cars that also had to accommodate the people. Up to fifty people were packed into one car, sitting or lying on top of their various possessions, which were piled so high that one could not even stand up except near the doors. The freight cars had only small windows, and of course, no washroom facilities. Conditions were terrible for all, but the old people suffered most. It was difficult for them to find a comfortable position; their limbs became stiff and painful from immobility, but worst of all was the lack of bathrooms. Even before the train left the station this already became evident, as some of the oldsters had to use the toilette that was in the railroad station about a half a block away. When they were moved to a siding even further from the station and left there for several hours, the problem became even worse. Old Sarah Klassen, in Theo's car, could not make it to the door in time and emptied her bladder all over the suitcases and other stuff. Everyone felt sorry for her, but it was a smelly, awful mess nevertheless. Theo moved as close as he could to the small window to avoid the smell.

When he looked out, he could see several people relieving themselves between the railroad tracks. It was easy for the men, they just stood behind a car or just turned away. The children, at least the small ones, had not yet learned to be ashamed of their bodily functions. The women had a more difficult time of it. Even though they tried to stay close to the cars, some even daring to climb under, Theo could see several women squatting with their shiny bottoms exposed. This scene would be repeated time and again on the trip east. Every time the train stopped, people would pour out and empty their bladders or bowels near the train because toilettes were mostly non-existent, and everybody was afraid to go too far away in case the train would leave.

They stayed at the siding for several more hours but finally the train began to move and continued on its way to an as yet unknown destiny. The journey into this unknown filled many with dread, but most were glad to leave the city since the frightening bombing of a few nights ago was still fresh in their minds.

Theo felt quite fortunate that he had the place close to the window. He had arranged some of the baggage so that he could lie on his stomach and look out. The train was moving east, past the now totally destroyed ironworks and what was left of the long row of warehouses. Soon they were out of the city and the train picked up speed. Theo enjoyed the scenery. The Ukrainian countryside to him was quite beautiful with its gentle hills, the meandering rivers, the autumn fields, and over everything the large blue sky. They passed several Russian villages and also one of the Mennonite settlements. When the sun had set, Theo made himself as comfortable as he could and went to sleep.

When he awoke, it was early morning. The sun had not yet risen, but it was about to. The sky in the east was fiery red, the few clouds had bright orange linings, and the land, which stretched endlessly into the distance, was bathed in a mist that arose from the shallow valleys. As the sun rose, the frost on the ground became apparent. Most of the fields had already been harvested, but here and there were still a few fields of wheat or sunflowers that had not yet been cut. Theo remembered a time when he and his father had cultivated their sunflowers. He had ridden the horse and his father had walked behind the cultivator shouting instructions now and then. It had been quite a mundane task then, but now Theo remembered it as something exceptional.

The train continued steadily on. Click-clack, click-clack, the rail connections counted the distance. Theo became drowsy and slept for a while. When he awoke, the train had arrived at a station and was diverting to a siding where it stopped. Immediately lots of people piled out, some to find a place that would serve as a bathroom, others to start a fire and cook something, even if it was only water for coffee or tea. Some got out to stretch their legs and to socialize a bit. The children ran among the adults, and when chased away they ran into the posadka, a hedge of trees planted along the railroad to keep the snowdrifts off the track during winter.

Sometimes the train would stay in one place for hours, at other times it would suddenly leave without warning and everyone would scramble to get on.

There had been hot food a few times, mainly soup, but mostly they received cold staples in very inadequate amounts. Sanitation had been a major problem from the beginning, and now there was a worse problem—lice. At first there had only been a few but now they could be seen everywhere, in the hair of the old and the very young, in the clothes of just about everybody, and, in some, sticking out of the eyebrows. Theo found that particularly nauseating. He tried to stay away from the others, but before long he too began to scratch.

The weather had turned worse. A steady drizzle had started the previous day and the rain had continued all night, and so far showed no sign of stopping. The temperature had also dropped, staying just above freezing.

It looked as if the train would stay at this little place they were at for some time, since the locomotive had been disconnected. Theo got out of the car, pulled his coat tightly together to keep out the cold, and marched along the train. He waved to a few of his peers, and then he saw Ann. "Hi."

"Hi, Theo. Where are you going?"

"Oh, nowhere in particular, just looking."

Ann was several years older then Theo and distantly related to him. But then, almost everybody from the village was in one way or another his relative. Ann fell in beside him. "Can I come along?"

"Oh sure. Let's go to the end of the train and see who we can find." They walked fast to keep warm. Even in this weather, some women still tried to keep a fire going and to prepare something hot to eat. Ann and Theo talked to several people, but soon decided it was too cold to stay outside.

Theo had just made himself comfortable beside the window when a sudden jerk suggested that the locomotive was back. Soon they were again on the main track and moving east.

The landscape now was that of endless prairie—very flat, without trees, and with a few small villages scattered here and there. The drizzly rain and gray sky produced a landscape of utter dreariness; none of the beauty that Theo had admired just a few days ago remained. He became very melancholy and turned away from the window.

They had now traveled eight days, mainly northeast, and were not too far from a largish city called Woronesh. The train was again parked on a siding at a small railroad stop, and it seemed they would stay there forever. It was another wet and cold morning, the usual fires at the side of the track were kept going with difficulty by determined women wrapped in large shawls against the cold and wet. Some boys were playing in the ever-present posadka. Theo was standing just inside the door of his freight car when he heard a faint, somehow familiar noise—an airplane, at first far away, but now getting closer. What would an airplane be doing here, far away from any cities or the front? Suddenly Theo felt very uneasy. Could it be a German plane? Now the plane was very close, almost overhead, then it seemed to pass right over the train. Suddenly there was a very loud noise, an explosion, followed in short succession by several more.

Theo felt as if the explosions had been right on top of him. He could feel the car shaking and through the open door saw something fly through the air. Although he was not aware of it, he pushed his way passed several people and jumped out of the car. All around him were screaming, running people, some covered with blood, many lying on the ground, motionless, some crawling in the mud, obviously injured. Theo turned to run toward the hedge, the posadka, when he saw the small child. It was covered with blood, its head and left arm were lying on the low signal wires. Its abdomen was ripped open and some bowel was hanging to the ground. What shook Theo most was that the child was not crying, it had a fixed glassy look on its face, but one leg was still moving back and forth as if it was trying to get up. Theo grabbed Peety, whom he must have picked up when he jumped out, stumbled over the line of wires, and ran into the posadka. As he was nearing the bush, he again heard the plane approaching. He noticed strange splashes of mud around him and heard the steady *tak tak tak* of the machine guns but kept on running. A woman running next to him, with a child in her arms, gave a strange cry and pitched forward, her face slamming into the mud. Another just ahead of him suddenly stopped and then slowly collapsed and lay still. Theo was not aware that Peet was screaming, he was not aware that his mother was beside him carrying Sonja, he could hardly breathe, his left knee felt strangely thick and sore, but he forced himself to go on until he collapsed on top of a pile of cut wheat way out on the field. Someone fell down beside him. It was his mother. "Thank God you're alive. Thank God you're okay," she cried. "Our train was bombed by the Germans! Why? Why would they kill their own people?"

She kept on sobbing. Theo just kept his head down into the wheat sheaves. He was shaking so badly he could not get up. His stomach hurt and he kept seeing the dying child on the wires. He vomited several times and after a while, he felt a little better. Only his knee was peculiarly sore.

They stayed there about a half hour but nothing further happened. Jutta made a shelter from the wheat sheaves, placed the two little ones in there, and said to Theo, "Stay here, I'll go and see what is going on." She wrapped her large, and by now wet, shawl around her shoulders and walked back to the train. After a short time, she returned with two women. One was their neighbor, Mrs. Caspers, who also had her six-year-old son with her, and the other was Jutta's cousin Greta.

"The train is half destroyed," Jutta explained. "Many are dead or wounded. The others are being rounded up to be shipped out. We will hide here until dark and then decide what to do."

They moved to a larger pile of wheat sheaves, formed a cave on one side of the pile, and all crawled in and covered themselves with some of the loose straw. Theo's knee hurt but he was so tired he soon fell asleep.

Chapter 8

The first thing Theo noticed when he awoke was that his feet were totally numb. Then he realized how cold his hands were. He blinked a few times and then opened his eyes in utter surprise. The whole world was white! It had snowed during the night and was still snowing. There was almost a foot of snow on the ground. He struggled out of his hole in the straw and stood up. It seemed that everything hurt. His feet did not want to move, his hands were like icicles, his clothes were damp and stiff—he was utterly miserable. His knee, however, hurt most of all. He looked down and saw that his pants were torn over his left knee and that there was some dried blood. He felt his knee. It was sore but he could move it well; it must be a minor injury.

The others were now also crawling out of their places. Everyone was very cold and very hungry. The three small children cried. Since no one had food, and shelter was also a priority, it was decided to find the nearest village but not to go back to the railroad station as danger was perceived there. Jutta decided that they should walk towards home, parallel with the railroad tracks, but stay far enough away so they would not be seen. Since the snow was fresh, walking proved to be more difficult than expected and, after some discussion, it was determined to find shelter as soon as possible so that they could rest for a while. Some dogs were heard barking in the distance and the conclusion was drawn that there had to be a village in the direction of that sound. Everybody agreed where the barking was coming from and they all set off in that direction, leaving the railroad tracks. Little did they know how confusing and misleading sounds were in the endless snow covered plains.

Jutta took the lead, carrying Sonja. Greta followed, than came Mrs. Caspers holding her son's hand, and then Theo with Peet, who had to be mostly carried. At first, the walking warmed them and they felt invigorated by the exercise and the expectation of shelter. If it hadn't been for the constant hunger, they could have actually felt quite good. Soon, however, they tired, their totally inadequate foot-wear allowed their feet to become cold and wet, and the little ones became so exhausted that they were forced to rest frequently. They had walked for several hours but had not seen any sign of a village or other settlement. In addition to the cold, the wet, and the hunger, all now also felt fear. Where were they? Which direction should they go? The totally overcast sky hid the sun and their sense of direction was gone. They did not even know the way back as the falling snow had covered their tracks. What to do? Since the two other women were completely distraught and almost hysterical, it fell to Jutta to make the decision.

"We can't stay here, and we need food and shelter soon if we are to survive. Therefore we will turn around and head toward the railroad, which we can't miss," she said, trying to convey a confidence she did not really feel. "Come on, everybody up, let's go."

The going was very slow, the small children were mostly crying silently and, since they could hardly walk, had to be carried. The women, each with one child, stumbled forward slowly and Theo brought up the rear, occasionally helping one or the other with carrying a child. It had stopped snowing but in the deep snow the going was tough and they left deep tracks.

After a while Jutta suddenly cried, "I see some tracks ahead, someone must have been here recently." They all hurried forward—surely these tracks had been made by humans. If they followed them, they should come to a place where people lived. But which way to go?

They decided to follow in the direction that the people who had made the tracks had gone. Buoyed by this sign of life, they set out with renewed vigor. They had now walked for several hours and in spite of this encouraging sign, they soon wearied. Jutta, who was slightly ahead of the others, suddenly stopped. She just stood there and when Theo came up to her he saw that tears were running down her cheeks. "What's the matter, Mom?"

She was so choked that she could not speak and silently pointed to the ground, where he could see a bunch of crossing tracks in the snow. At first he did not understand, but suddenly it hit him. Those were their old tracks—they had been going in circles! All this time they had gotten nowhere.

They all just stood there; silent, insignificant figures under the vast, leaden winter sky. What now? Where could they find help? Suddenly Theo thought he heard something and he strained to listen. Yes, there it was again, distant but distinct. It had to be a human voice, a young boy's. But what would a young boy be doing out here? "Did you hear that, Mom?"

Jutta nodded. "It came from over there."

"Yes, that's what I thought too," replied Theo. "Listen, Mom. Let me go and see. We can't all go, the kids are just too tired."

Jutta was reluctant to let him go alone but could see no other alternative. "Well okay, but be careful. And don't go too far, we can't lose you."

Theo stomped off, full of fear and anxiety but also relieved to be doing something positive. He walked over a slight rise and disappeared from Jutta's view. As soon as he had crossed the crest and started down on the other side, he saw a large field of sunflowers. They were dry now but had not yet been harvested. At the far end of the field, he could see a small trailer and headed in that direction. When he neared the trailer, he could see a horse and a small sleigh standing beside it. Inside he could hear voices. Theo started to run toward the door. He fell several times in the deep snow and virtually crawled the last few feet. When he reached the door, he banged on it with both fists. "Help!" he cried. "Help, we are lost! Please help!"

The door opened and a young woman and a boy looked out, utterly astonished. "Who are you? Where did you come from?"

"Please, please. Help us! My mom, Sonja and Peety, out there, and the others, out there." He waved his arm in the direction he had come from, tears streaming down his face. Now that help was likely, all his pent-up fears and anxieties suddenly burst forth. He felt immensely tired and could hardly continue to speak.

The young woman helped him into the trailer where the warmth made Theo realize how cold he was. But he could not sit down, he could not rest while the others were still out there. "Please, there are others out there, over that rise. There are small children, please help them!"

"How far," asked the young woman, "and how many?"

"Not far, over that rise. There are six. Three women and three children. Please hurry!"

The young woman looked at the boy. "I guess there must be others. Take the sleigh and follow his footsteps, Sasha. Be careful. If you see any men turn around and come back."

The boy put on his felt boots and coat and went outside.

The woman turned toward Theo. "You look half frozen. Come, move close to the stove and take your shoes off. In this weather you should wear boots, your shoes are soaked." She helped him undo the frozen shoe-laces and took off his shoes and socks. "Well, your feet look okay. No frostbite. Just rub them a bit and they'll warm up quickly."

Theo's anxiety increased by the minute and he kept glancing at the door.

The woman tried to reassure him. "Sasha will find them, don't worry. He knows his way around out there."

Theo could not sit still any longer. He got up and walked over to the small window beside the door. All he saw was an endless expanse of snow. The tears started to roll down his face again, he tried to suppress his sobs but to no avail. He looked through the window again and saw the sleigh appear at the top of the rise. With his sleeve, he wiped away his tears and moved closer to the window but could not see who was on the sleigh. He wiped the window in his anxiety but it did not help. When the sleigh came closer, he could see two people walking beside it, hanging on to its side. In the sleigh he could see several people.

It's them," he whispered. Then louder, "It's them, it's them, he found them, it's them!"

When the sleigh came closer, he pulled on his wet shoes, not bothering with the socks, and ran to the door. As the sleigh pulled up, he rushed out. "You're here, I thought you were lost." He hugged his mother.

"Quick, Theo, Sonja, she's in a bad way. Help me."

Sonja was half lying in the sleigh, leaning against Peet. She seemed to be unconscious. Jutta and Theo lifted her off the sleigh into Jutta's arms, who carried her in. The young woman in the trailer helped lay Sonja down on the cot in the back of the trailer and loosened her clothes.

"She's breathing but she's awfully cold. Help me to take off her shoes and rub her feet and hands with snow." She quickly removed one shoe and sock.

"Snow!" Jutta gasped.

"Yes, snow. We have to get her circulation going. Besides, she's got frostbite on a couple of toes."

They got some snow and vigorously rubbed her extremities.

Theo stood by the door and silently prayed. 'Dear God, please, please don't let Sonja die, please make her well. I know I have not bothered much about you but I will change, I promise.'

Sonja seemed to get some color on her cheeks and stirred a bit. The young woman smiled. "She's coming around, let's give her a little soup." She gently fed Sonja a few spoonfuls of broth. Everyone was relieved as Sonja began to look better. The others now also got a bit of food, but there was only enough to still the hunger a little bit.

Jutta realized that they could not all stay in the small trailer long and asked the young woman where they were and how far away the next village was.

"Oh, the village is only three kilometers away."

"And what is it called?"

"Krasnoje Selo."

Jutta was stunned. The village was less than three kilometers from the railroad station where they were bombed! They had walked all day through deep snow for practically nothing.

"How can we get there?"

"Well, Sasha can only take a few of you, but you can get somebody to come and get the rest. If you have money, that is."

"How much money?"

"Oh, maybe ten rubles."

Jutta dug in her pockets. "Yes, I have some money."

It was decided that Theo and one of the women should go to the village with the boy and send back a sleigh for the others. The young woman assured them that her parents would put them up for the night. When the boy was ready, Theo and Mrs. Caspers and her boy climbed onto the sleigh.

In less than half an hour, they reached the village where they stopped in front of a small hut and were asked by the boy to come in. There they met an old couple, the parents of the young woman at the trailer. Theo and the boy, Sasha, explained the situation and Theo held forth some money. The old man scratched his head, then took the money and went outside. Soon they saw him leaving on a horse drawn sleigh. Within an hour, he was back with the others. Sonja had improved quite a bit but was still too weak to walk and was carried into the house by Jutta. After the women had some discussion with the old couple, blankets were brought out. Soon a sleeping place was ready on the floor and the children were undressed and put to bed. All the wet clothes were placed near the opening of the large clay oven that took up a good part of the room. The top of the oven served as a large sleeping area; the cooking and baking was done inside the oven.

All the women climbed on top of the oven and the men, including Theo and Sasha, arranged some more floor area for sleeping. As they were all exhausted, everybody was soon asleep.

In the morning, they held a big planning session. Their hosts proved to be quite friendly and helpful. It was decided that the only sensible thing to do was to stick to the railroad tracks. There was now no question what they would do— they were going home.

For a few extra rubles, their hosts treated them to a breakfast of casha, a cereal prepared from ground barley. When all had eaten and everyone was dressed, Jutta paid the man for their lodgings and they departed. The weather had improved a little; there was no further snow but the sky was still overcast. The temperature was just over the freezing mark. 'Just right for walking,' Theo thought.

They started off, each woman holding one of the children by the hand and Theo, as usual, bringing up the rear. Soon they reached the tracks and headed west. Here walking was quite easy. There was no snow to wade through and they need not worry about getting lost. In a short while, however, the little ones tired and had to be carried. This proved quite hard and frequent stops were required. Sonja had some difficulty walking because of the frostbite of some of her toes. She tried hard, but in the end had to be carried. Utterly exhausted, they reached Korotoyak, a small city, in the late afternoon. The only thing they had eaten all day was a slice of black bread each. Jutta had obtained the bread with great difficulty in Krasnoye Selo. It was fortunate that she had enough presence of mind when they were bombed to grab her handbag that contained most of their money.

The railroad station at Korotoyak was large. In the waiting area there were several groups of people sitting or lying on the floor. Having been fortunate to arrive early, they found an empty space near the back, against the wall, and sat on the floor. In a few hours all the space on the floor was occupied by people who were waiting for trains.

When everyone was settled, Jutta and her cousin Greta went to find some food. After about two hours, they returned. They had bought a knife and a handbag but there was no food to be bought anywhere. As a last resort, they had gone from door to door begging for food. Greta had been reluctant but Jutta insisted. "If you don't come along, you won't eat either."

They went to several houses. Some had just told them to go away, but most people were sympathetic. Food was scarce and in the end, they had only a few pieces of dark bread, some carrots, a large turnip, and a squash in their new bag.

They divided the bread into equal pieces, one for each person. The carrots were given to the children and the adults ate the raw turnip and squash. After that they slept. The floor was hard but at least they were inside and it was dry and warm.

The next morning the adults discussed their situation and concluded that they could not reach home by walking. Jutta, who had by default become the leader, made some inquiries. In spite of the chaos, some trains were still running and one going west was expected to leave within a few hours. After some more discussion, they purchased tickets to the nearest large town, which was Rossosh. Jutta and Greta went begging for food again but this time came back with only a couple of beets and a small squash. By now hunger had dulled everyone's taste buds and even the children ate what was given them.

Jutta watched as the children ate in silence. How good they were! Even the little ones did not complain. Jutta's heart ached, but what could she do? She wondered if they would make it home. Maybe they should just go to the authorities and ask for help. That, however, would most certainly result in their being sent east, if not worse. They had run away from their train and would be regarded as enemies of the mother-land. No, they could not take that risk. They had to avoid the police and military at all costs. They had to try to get home without involving others. That was their only chance.

Chapter 9

There was no sign of the train until late in the afternoon. Once it was announced that it was coming, all hell broke loose. Everyone rushed out to the platform. Jutta gathered her children about her and moved with the crowd. "Theo, you look after Peety. Stay close, whatever you do, we must not be separated."

She continued to push forward. "Sara, Greta, if we lose each other we will go as far as Milerovo and wait for you there. You do the same."

"Yes, Jutta," yelled Greta over the din of the crowd, trying to stay close. "By the railroad station in Milerovo if we get separated."

The surge of the pushing crowd propelled them onto the platform and Theo lost site of Jutta. He struggled wildly to stay on his feet and not loose hold of Peet. The train pulled into the station and the crowd went wild. As luck would have it, when the train came to a halt, Theo found himself right in front of a door and the surge of the mass behind him propelled him into the car. Holding Peet, who was whimpering in fear, he stumbled up the steps and into the almost empty passenger car. He tried to get the door to one of the compartments open but the crowd, pushing from behind, forced him further along the aisle until he met up with those coming from the other entrance.

Peet was still crying and Theo did not feel so good either. When the mass of people that had pushed into the car had settled, Theo looked around and to his great relief saw Mrs. Caspers standing just inside the door of one of the compartments. He waved frantically and yelled loudly even though she was not far from him. "Where are my mom and the others?"

She waved to him with both hands. "Theo, am I glad to see you! Where's Peety?"

Theo pointed to the floor. "He's here"

Mrs. Caspers looked relieved. "Everyone is here," she motioned into the compartment. "You two stay where you are, it's too full in here."

Theo and Peet could not have moved anyway. Theo just waved and then wedged himself down into a sitting position with Peet on one side and a large suitcase on the other. The suitcase, in time, proved to be a blessing as it protected him from the feet of the people close to him, at least from that side.

'How lucky we are,' Theo thought. 'It must be God protecting us or we would surely have been separated.' He put an arm around Peet, who had now stopped crying. The train gave a lurch and started moving, at first slowly, but when it had cleared the railroad yard it picked up speed. Outside it started to get dark and Peet soon fell asleep. The train stopped several times during the night, sometimes for long periods. A few people got off and a few managed to push their way in.

After a while, Theo felt a great urge to empty his bladder but there was no way to get through. When he could hold it no longer, he turned toward the suitcase and peed on the floor. In the dark, nobody could see it anyway.

When morning dawned, they were well passed their original destination but they did not mind. The further southwest they got, the better. Because the train was so packed, no one could check the tickets. A few hours later, their train arrived at Kontemirovka. As soon as the train had entered the city, they heard the air-raid sirens wailing. When the train stopped, everyone rushed out and ran to get away from the railroad station. Jutta and her group ran with the crowd. After a few blocks they slowed to a walk, being out of breath.

"Let's go further out of the center of the city and see if someone will take us in for the day and maybe for the night," Jutta said. All agreed and they walked on a while. Soon they were on the outskirts of the city, in a district of small, old houses. After several tries, they did indeed find someone who agreed take them in for the night. The house was occupied by an elderly gent who temporarily lived there alone as his two sons had been drafted and his daughter and her child had gone to help a relative who was sick.

The first priority was, as usual, the procurement of food. The old gentleman, Sergey he liked to be called, had a few potatoes and other vegetables in his garden and was willing to sell some. There was no bread and no meat. It again fell to Jutta and the ever-reluctant Greta, to see what they could find. After about an hour, they returned with the news that the railroad station had indeed been bombed, but the damage was not great. They had found little food: some beans, a few pieces of black, stale bread, some precious sun-flower seeds, and a tiny bit of sugar.

Sergey allowed Jutta to use the stove and utensils and soon everyone was eating what seemed to them the best food they had tasted in a long time. After the meal, there was even a cup of hot tea—what luxury! By now they were accustomed to sleeping on the floor, which was their sleep-ing area here too.

When the little ones were put to bed, the adults sat in the other room sipping their tea. For a while all were quiet, then Theo spoke. "What do we do now? What do we do tomor-row, back to the railroad, or what? There are probably no trains going west anyway." He voiced what everybody feared.

"Where are you headed?" Sergey asked haltingly, not wanting to interfere. "Maybe I can be of help, I know the area. You're right, there very likely won't be any trains west, at least not scheduled ones."

"Well," Jutta was not sure she wanted to reveal their des-tination to a stranger. "We want to go to Milerovo. With the children we can't possibly walk there."

Sergey brought out an old map. "Here we are," he pointed to a spot labeled Kontemirovka, "and there is Milerovo. See how the railroad makes a big semicircle to get there? If you would follow this road here, the distance is almost half. It means, of course, walking."

Everyone squeezed in close to look at the map. It did indeed look much closer but Jutta was not convinced. "What about food and shelter?"

"There are many villages along this road and the people are friendly," Sergey offered.

"It's late. Let's sleep on it." Jutta got up and checked the children, who were all sleeping. The adults were also tired and soon everyone was asleep.

The next morning dawned overcast but warmer. The roads were dry and by mid-morning there were patches of blue sky between the high clouds. Sergey had suggested that they stay another day, and all agreed, since there was need to get cleaned up, to get their clothes in order, and to generally reconsider their options. Their recent train trip had been an unpleasant experience, but then the walk in the snow had not been a pleasure stroll either. All day they had discussions, but in the end they decided to try the shorter route on foot. The distance was about one hundred and ten kilometers and they thought they could cover it in about ten days. They would leave early the next day.

Chapter 10

Sunrise the next day found them on the road heading southwest. Everyone, even the children, was walking along the dry dirt road, eager to get home. The adults carried small packages containing to meager store of food they had managed to buy or beg. Theo was well ahead of the others. The two-day rest had restored his energy and he was anxious to move on and to cover as much distance as possible in as short a time as possible. 'I wonder what Wanjka is doing', he thought. 'I'll be so happy to see him again, so happy to get home.' He looked back and saw that he was far ahead. There was a large rock at the side of the road and he sat down on it and waited for the others. They soon caught up, each adult carrying one of the children because the little ones had tired quickly. When they caught up to him, they also sat down on the ground, leaning against the stone, exhausted.

"Let's rest here a while" Jutta said. "Theo you'll have to help us with the children," her statement elevating him to the level of adult. 'That's a switch,' Theo thought, 'suddenly I'm grown up.'

After the rest, Theo took Peet on his shoulders while the other three adults looked after Sonja and Jacob. Because the children were heavy and had to be mostly carried now, they only made slow progress, as they had to rest frequently.

It was already late afternoon when they saw the village, their planned noon stop. An hour later, they entered the village, totally done in. Nishnoje Selo was a typical small Russian village with thatched roofs covering small huts made of mud walls. There were few trees, no flowers, narrow dirt streets, and no sidewalks. Poverty was evident everywhere.

"We are not going to find much food here," murmured Mrs. Caspers. "These people haven't enough themselves."

"You may be right," retorted Jutta, "but we have to try. Let's find the Predsedatjel, the one in charge, and tell him we need help. Let me do the talking, I have an idea."

She asked directions to the village office and soon found the appropriate person to talk to.

"Comrade, we are a group of people fleeing the German hordes. We were bombed in Kontemirovka and decided to flee on foot. Now we are here and are in need of food and shelter, can you help us?"

The person facing her was short, portly, and had a perpetual smile on his face. He slowly looked at each one, then turned to Jutta. "Let me see your papers."

"Well, comrade, we have no papers. They were lost in the air raid."

"I see. Well, we have an empty house. I suppose we can put you up there, but you will have to register with the police soon." If he saw the startled looks on the faces of the three women, he did not let on. "I will see what I can do about food."

He led them to a small mud hut, similar to all the others, and unlocked the door. "There is straw in the back and there is a pot for cooking and a kettle for boiling water. Sorry, but there is no bedding."

Jutta assured him that this was adequate and he left. Soon they had a good fire going and the hut began to warm up. Within an hour, to everyone's surprise, a small horse cart stopped in front and an elderly peasant brought in the promised food. They could not believe it! There was a piece of pork, potatoes, several loaves of bread, and even a bit of sugar and some tea. They thanked the man profusely and Jutta gave him two rubles, which made his eyes light up. When he was gone, the women prepared the best supper they had eaten since they left home. As there was no pressure on them to leave, they stayed three days. In the evening of the third day, the mayor came to the hut and informed them that they had to go to town the next day and register with the police. If the police gave them permission, they could all return to the village. He assured them that, since they were refugees, there would be no problem. Transportation would be arranged and they were to be ready early the next morning.

Soon after sunrise the following morning, a cart pulled by a horse, which was led by an elderly Russian peasant, stopped in front of the hut. Jutta came out. "Is this our transportation?"

"Yes, barinja." Jutta noticed that the man used the old Russian greeting and not the modern 'comrade'. The man seemed oddly nervous and kept twisting a letter around in his hands.

"Is that letter for us?" Jutta asked.

"Well, no, I'm supposed to give this to the police in Kontemirovka. I hope I'll give it to the right person."

Jutta smiled at him. "I would be quite happy to help you. Does it say on the letter who it is for?"

"Well, well, ah, I can't read, I don't know." The man was obviously ill at ease. "If you would do that for me, it would help a lot."

His relief was obvious when Jutta took the letter. "Don't worry, I'll make sure it gets to the right place."

"Oh, thank you, thank you," the peasant bowed several times.

Jutta turned to the others and spoke in low-German, "Get everything ready and then stall him a few minutes, I want to read the letter."

She went behind the hut to the outhouse and locked the door. The letter was short: "I'm sending you a group of escapees, probably German, who are traveling without papers, and who, I'm sure, are enemies of the Soviet Union and are trying to escape to the Germans."

Jutta's hand trembled. She quickly folded the letter and put it in her pocket. When she got to the cart, everything was ready. "Let's get going," Jutta urged, "it's a long way."

Since the cart was large, everyone could ride and the journey back to the city they had left a few days before was much easier. When they reached the suburbs, Jutta said to the old peasant, "There is a lot of military traffic here today. Why don't we get off and walk the rest of the way so you won't have to go into the city?"

He was not at all opposed to this and soon was on his way back. Jutta showed the others the letter. "Our friendly fat mayor was ready to sell us out. We have to leave this place today."

They walked to the railroad station through streets full of military personnel. When they reached the station, they saw what the bombing had done. The station was damaged and several tracks were ripped up. There was no planned train service but by chance they found out that a freight train of only a few cars would leave soon. In the yard they found a train consisting of three flat cars and a locomotive with a coal tender. A number of people were already on the cars. Since the flat cars had some freight on them, there was not much room left for passengers. Jutta with Sonja and Mrs. Caspers and her boy found a place on the last flat car. Theo with Peet and Greta could not find any room and finally crawled into the coal tender and sat right on top of the coal.

By the time the train left late in the afternoon, every possible place where people could sit or stand was full. The engineer did not seem to mind the many unbooked passengers and mostly ignored them.

The train did not stop for some time, bypassing several stations. Night descended and it became chilly. Theo held Peet on his lap and Greta huddled close, trying to cover all three with her large shawl. They slept for short periods, being awakened by the noise of the train and the cold. When dawn came Theo crawled to the edge to look back. To his horror, he saw only one flat car! The other two must have been disconnected during the night, but where? Theo slid down on the coal. "Greta, Greta, they are not there, they're gone. What do we do now?"

Greta was beside herself. She frantically crawled up the coal to look for herself. When she saw that the flatcar the others had been on was indeed not there, she cried hysterically. "What are we going to do? Look at Peet, how am I going to look after him? And you, what am I going to do?" It was evident that she had relied totally on Jutta.

Theo sighed. It was obvious that he would have to make the decisions. "We will stay on this train to Milerovo, if it goes that far, and wait there. Remember what we agreed on?"

If Greta heard him, she did not respond. She was sitting close to Peet, covering him with here shawl, crying, her lips moving in quiet prayer.

At noon, the train arrived in Milerovo. It stopped on a siding outside the main station to take on water. Theo took Peet and called to Greta. "Come on, let's get off here. At the main station there might be guards."

They walked across the many tracks to the street and then proceeded to the railroad station on foot.

"We have to stay close to the station, that's where Mom will look for us," Theo said. Greta only nodded. She was totally mesmerized with fear and worry. How would anyone ever find them here? How would they ever get home? What about their immediate needs—food and shelter? Tears again rolled down her cheeks.

When they walked into the waiting area of the railroad station, they were surprised to see so few people there. They sat down on one of the benches against the far wall and looked around. Soldiers were coming and going and the few people waiting inside were mainly soldiers also.

Theo turned to Greta. "We have to make sure that Mom and the others find us here. I saw an overpass for foot passengers when we walked here. One can see all the incoming trains from there, I will go and watch there and you stay here with Peet. Don't leave here. Okay?"

Greta nodded and Theo left. He walked back along the tracks and then went up the steps of the overpass. From there he had a good view of the tracks. He stayed there for several hours but no trains came. Finally, he walked back to the station. Greta was sitting on the bench and Peet was asleep leaning against her. Theo sat down. "We have to find some place to stay close to the overpass. What do you think?"

Greta mumbled, "I don't know. What's the use?"

"Listen, you can't just mope around, you have to help me. Let's go." He took Peet in his arms and left. For Greta there was nothing else left but to follow him. They went back along the street they had come in on.

"Greta, you take this side and Peet and I will go along the other side. Stop at every house and ask if they will keep us overnight. Remember, we have no money."

"I can't do this, Theo. I don't like begging." She began to cry again.

Theo, who was close to the breaking point himself, said sarcastically, "What do you want me to do, provide a room for you at the hotel? Don't act like a silly goose. You're supposed to be the adult here." He turned and walked across the street with Peet.

After some time they found an elderly couple who were willing to let them sleep in the hallway on the floor. After they had heard their story, the woman invited them into the room and even made some tea.

Theo took Greta aside. "I've been watching the tracks. So far there have been no trains, there is probably no regular service anymore, but we still have to watch. You go to the overpass and watch and I'll relieve you in a couple of hours."

Greta turned to him as if to say something, but then took her large shawl and left. A few hours later, Theo met her on the bridge. "There have only been a few trains out, nothing in," Greta said. She seemed more settled. "I'm sorry I fell apart back there, I'll be okay now."

Theo was embarrassed and because he lacked words, he gave her a big hug. "Come and relieve me around two, I'll be fine until then. Be careful on the steps, they're tricky in the dark." He tried to hide the tremble in his voice and turned away so she would not see his face. When Greta left, he sat down on the walkway but after a while got up and walked back and forth to stay awake. Around midnight he noticed a small light in the distance. He stepped closer to the railing, yes, it looked like a train, and it was coming closer. His heart started to race, it was definitely a train. He ran down the steps and turned toward the station. He had to be there when the train arrived. When he ran onto the station platform, he could see the train a few hundred yards down the track. It was not moving. Why would it stop there? Theo jumped down to the tracks and started running towards the train. Someone shouted something but he did not stop. Before he reached the train, it started to move again and came towards him. Theo jumped aside and fell as the train passed him. As he lay there, he saw that it was only a locomotive and not a train at all. Down the track there were some noises but Theo was so devastated that he did not notice them. He put his head on his hands and started to cry.

Suddenly he heard something. He lifted his head; someone had called his name! But that was not possible. He listened. There it was again. He dared not believe it, but it sounded like his mother. He peered down the track and there was some movement, some people. Suddenly his mother, Sonja, and Mrs. Caspers with her boy were standing in front of him. Theo ran towards his mother, hugged her, and started to cry violently.

Chapter 11

Long after all the others were asleep, Theo was still awake, re-living the events of the day in his mind. It's strange how things had turned out. They must truly be under the protection of God—how else would they have otherwise survived the last few weeks, escaped in Kontimirovka, and been re-united again? Truly, miracles still happened. Theo felt an inner glow of warmth, but also deep inside he felt guilty because he had not paid much attention to God and church matters; guilty because he often had not paid attention when his father, and later his mother, had read the bible; guilty because he, only at times, rare times to be sure, had doubted the very existence of God. He vowed that he would try harder, without actually defining what this 'trying harder' meant. He folded his hands and tried to pray, but the words only came with difficulty and soon he gave up.

His thoughts wandered. It was strange that his mother had managed to persuade the station commandant to provide transportation for her so that she could be reunited with her family. After explaining the situation, she had cried and carried on until he had finally given in. "What the hell, the world is topsy turvy anyway. But all I can give you is a locomotive, no cars, and you'll have to stand in the cab or sit on the coal." She had not cared as long as they got trans- portation. Jutta had kissed his hand but he had withdrawn it brusquely.

The engineer had been quite jolly and happy to make the run. When they approached Milerovo, he thought it wiser to let them off before the station to avoid questions. Jutta had been grateful and had slipped him five rubles. Their trip had been uneventful and fast, Mrs. Caspers said.

Theo had gained new respect for his mother. She was the undoubted leader of the group, she kept a cool head, and she always came up with some workable plan. 'She's had a tough life,' he thought. He resolved to be more supportive in the future.

It was late, the day had been tiring, and eventually Theo fell asleep

In the morning, Jutta and Theo went to the railroad station, but they soon found out that no trains other than those for military purposes were operating. There were a lot of army personnel in the station, and there seemed to be a lot of confusion. Jutta thought it wiser not to attract atten- tion and they went back to the house. The weather was not too bad and since everyone was eager to get home, it was agreed that they would walk along the railroad tracks.

They thanked the old couple, gathered up their few belongings, and headed west towards their home. They walked through the city, staying close to the tracks. When they passed the city outskirts, they walked along the tracks. A short distance from the city they saw a field of carrots and pulled some out to eat. They managed to walk eighteen kilo- metres the first day and were encouraged by their success. In the evening they found an unused barn with a bit of straw in it. Jutta also managed to beg a little food in a nearby house. All were sure they would make it home soon.

Chapter 12

The next day, however, did not go as well. The day started very foggy and when they reached a small village they found out that the military were destroying the railroad by blasting the rail connections with dynamite, and that it was dangerous to walk along the tracks. What to do? They wanted to go on and decided to walk across the fields, parallel to the tracks. Soon they found out that this was easier said than done as the fog prevented them from seeing the tracks and they had to stay a fair distance away because of the blasting that sent pieces of rail flying through the air. Walking across the fields also proved difficult because some fields had been ploughed. When evening came, they had only made it to the next small village a few kilometers away. All were tired and dirty and were happy to find shelter in a shed behind a house. The owner allowed them to dry their wet clothes by the stove in the house and provided some hot tea. It was amazing how often complete strangers were willing to help them.

In the morning they woke up cold and hungry. After eating what meager food they had, they thanked their host for his kindness and left. Their diet now consisted mainly of beets, occasional carrots or potatoes and, rarely, a small piece of bread. All had lost weight, but the children had suffered most, even though they had received extra food when available. The deficiency was not so much in the amount as in the quality of the food.

After some discussion they decided they would risk walking along the tracks again as they simply did not have the strength to struggle through the muddy fields. Also, the two small ones had to be carried most of the time as they were now too weak to walk anything more than short distances. Peet struggled on but he too had to be carried at times. Their rest periods became longer and more frequent. The rail line was totally destroyed, the ankle bars holding the rails together had been blown to bits, leaving broken and twisted ends of rail.

In the afternoon a cold, drizzly rain started. When Jutta spotted an old field shed, she decided to stop there, at least for a while, and maybe overnight if the shed was dry and large enough. The door was locked but Theo managed to pry the lock off with a broken piece of rake he found beside the shed. The shed had a dirt floor but it was dry. There were a bunch of empty potato sacks in one corner and some of them still contained a few potatoes. They went through all the sacks and managed to collect a small pile. Some had been partly frozen and were beginning to rot.

Since everybody was exhausted, they decided to stay the night. With a spade found in the shed, they pulled off a wooden shelf and broke the boards into short pieces. Since they had no paper, Theo cut thin slivers of wood and managed to get a fire going on the floor. To let the smoke escape, the door was left open a bit. In spite of this, the shed, being small, was soon warm. The children were peeled out of their wet clothes and placed around the fire on potato sacks. The adults took off some clothing and tried to dry themselves by standing as close to the fire as possible. When there were sufficient embers and the fire had died down a bit, they placed the potatoes in the fire to bake. Jutta and Greta checked them frequently with a piece of wire and, when each one was done, rolled them out of the fire. It was a meager meal but it was better than nothing.

The children were tired and soon slept. The mood of the adults was somber; their prospects for getting home seemed more bleak today then ever before. The poor food, the worsening weather, the proximity of the front, and the lack of transportation were all factors against them. The children now obviously suffered from malnutrition and would not be able to walk much. The adults also were weaker and less able to carry them. The decision making had fallen totally to Jutta and she did not ask anymore what the others thought. It was obvious to her that they needed help—but they were so close! Maybe they would feel different in the morning. In spite of her tiredness, sleep came with difficulty.

Chapter 13

The night before, they had reached Artemovsk, within a day's walking distance of their home. It had taken them two days to get here after they had decided to press on and had left the shed. Theo felt the excitement rise just thinking about home. Today they would reach it! Suddenly he was wide awake even though it was early morning. When they had reached this place last night, they had found a deserted house. As some of the windows had been broken and one of the doors was open they had just walked in, too tired to worry if someone would mind. For the last few days, the places they had come through had been in disarray anyway, the government officials and the military having fled. Most of the public buildings and some vacant private houses had been looted since the departure of authority. The building they were now in had been a school but nothing much was left in it now. They had simply slept on the floor, glad to have a dry roof over their head.

Theo got up and waked over to the window. The sky was overcast and the ground wet but at the moment it was not raining. Jutta got up too. "It looks like rain again, but if we are lucky we'll be home today." She paused and looked at the others, who were still sleeping. "I'm worried about Mrs.

Caspers and her boy; they are both sicker than she admits. The little one has had diarrhea since yesterday, he really worries me."

"I know, Mom. Do you think he will die?"

"God forbid, Theo, don't even say such things!" Jutta gently reprimanded him, but deep inside she feared the same thing. She shook her head, 'We must not have such thoughts'. To Theo she said, "Let's get going early, it'll give us a better chance to make it. Wake everybody and help me get the kids ready. We will have to carry Sonja and Peet, they don't have the strength to walk anymore."

Soon they were on their way, Theo and Greta alternated in carrying Peet, Jutta carried Sonja, and Mrs. Caspers struggled to keep up with little Jacob in her arms. Their legs ached, their bodies ached, their stomachs were emptier than ever since there had been no food that morning. They were afraid to enter any settlement because of the lack of law and order.

'It's ironic,' Theo thought. 'First we run from the police and government officials, and now we're afraid because these very same people are not around.' He stopped for a moment, shifted Peet to his back, and then plodded on.

They did not make it home that night. When darkness came, they dug a hole in the side of a hay stack and huddled together to keep warm. During the night Jacob died. He had just stirred in Mrs. Caspers arms and then stopped breathing.

In the morning, Mrs. Caspers still sat there holding him in her arms. "I can't leave him here, Jutta, I can't."

"I know, dear. We are not far from home. We will take him with us and bury him there, right beside your parents." She hugged her and then turned away quickly so the others would not see her tears. 'It's silly,' she thought. 'Why should I mind if someone sees me crying? It's perfectly natural.' But she did mind. Soon they were on their way, both stirred by the knowledge that they would be home today and subdued because of Jacob's death.

When Sonja started to run a temperature and then developed diarrhea, Jutta became almost frantic. Not now, not this close to home! She walked faster and would not stop to rest until the others simply could not carry on. By early afternoon they saw the village. 'Oh God, please. Dear God, please, don't let her die, don't let her die,' Jutta repeated in a low whisper. She held Sonja tightly and walked faster and faster. She did not notice that the others could not keep up. Later she could not remember reaching her house or that she had collapsed on the front steps. When she woke up it was dark, she was in a strange bed, but she could tell that she was in her house. What had happened to the furniture? She raised herself slightly and looked around. Nothing in the room looked familiar in the semidarkness.

Suddenly she remembered Sonja. What had happened to her? She had to know right now! And where were the others?

Someone had undressed her. She could not find her clothes and just took a sheet from the bed and wrapped it around her and opened the door that led into the living room. How strange it looked; none of the furniture she had owned and lovingly cared for was there. A couple of old chairs stood around a small cheap table near the window. To the side of the oven was another chair, this one occupied by and old woman. The woman looked at Jutta and smiled.

"Come on in my dear," she said in Russian. "Come, sit down." She pulled another chair close to the oven.

Jutta remained near the door. "Where is my daughter? Where is everybody?" Her voice was full of anxiety.

"Come, sit down, it is quite late and everyone is asleep. They were all very tired. Your little girl is still feverish, but don't worry, some good food and rest will get her on her feet very quickly."

Jutta moved to the chair and sat on its edge. "Who are you, and what are you doing in this house?"

"Oh barinja, don't you remember us? We lived in the Russian settlement outside the village. When you were sent away we moved here." She smiled again.

"What about the furniture, did you sell it?"

"Oh, my goodness, dorogaja, there was nothing left when we moved in, it was all gone." She motioned to the stove. "Some tea?"

Jutta only nodded. Besides feeling weak and tired, she was still worried. "Are you sure my daughter is all right? She seemed so sick."

The woman handed her the hot tea. "Come see for yourself." She opened a door. Sonja was sleeping on some straw on the floor, her breathing was regular and easy, and she was only slightly flushed. "See," the woman whispered, "she's fine. Come, relax, we'll talk."

They went back to their chairs and sat down.

"When all of you were sent away, the people remaining came in like locusts and took away everything that could be taken away. That's why there is no furniture or anything else. We moved in a few days later; they said you wouldn't be back. We meant no harm." Seeing how tired Jutta was, she encouraged her to finish her tea and helped her to her bed.

"We'll talk tomorrow, my dear."

Chapter 14

When Theo awoke it was already daylight, the sun was up, the sky was blue and cloudless; it promised to be a glorious fall day. When he realized where he was, a wave of warm nostalgia swept over him. He was home, what a wonderful feeling!

He quickly jumped up and wanted to dress but his clothes were gone. What to do? He grabbed the blanket and wrapped it around his body, holding it in place with one hand he went into the kitchen. Sosja, the Russian woman, and Greta were sitting there, eating breakfast.

"What happened to my clothes, and where is my mother, and where are the others?" Theo blurted out.

Greta turned around and smiled at him. "You found something to wear, did you? You clothes were so filthy we took them to be soaked and later washed, so you will have to make do with the blanket for now. The others are still in bed, not feeling too well. They probably had too much good food after a couple of weeks of hunger. They should be better in a day or two. Come, sit and have some tea and bread."

Although Theo's stomach also felt a little queasy, he could not resist the food. He put three heaping teaspoons of sugar in his tea and cut himself a thick slice of black bread. Sosja laughed. "He eats well, that boy. Still growing."

She and Greta got up. "Let us go and do the wash, come Greta."

Theo finished his tea and bread and thought of getting another cup but his stomach felt more unsettled and he decided against it.

It took a few days but everyone recovered from the diarrhea they all got, presumably from the sudden rich diet and the starvation before. Theo longed to get out of the house to see Wanjka. He also missed his other friends, but they were gone on a train going to some unknown place. He doubted that he would ever see them again.

The next day around noon, Sosja came in with some startling news: The Germans were in the village. Someone had seen a horse cart and some strangely dressed soldiers at the other end of the village. There was great apprehension and not a little fear as to what the soldiers would do. They all sat in the front room looking out the window. Soon they saw a horse cart and several strangely dressed men coming up the street. The cart stopped on the street and two of the men came toward the house. There was a knock on the door. Jutta went to the door and opened it. Two German soldiers, their uniforms covered with dust, stood in front of her. They made no attempt to come in. One said, "Chleb (bread)," obviously not in command of the Russian language, and made an outline of a loaf of bread.

In perfect German, Jutta asked them how she could help. After they overcame their astonishment at finding someone who spoke German, they explained that their supply trucks had not kept up with their fast advance and consequently they had run out of provisions and were collecting one loaf of bread from every house. Jutta explained to Sosja, who was more than willing to comply, feeling quite relieved that nothing further was required and that the soldiers were not otherwise a threat.

The next day a German unit, complete with panzers and a repair facility, moved in. They commandeered several houses and also took over the school and the movie house. Sosja and her family were evicted because the commander of the unit wanted the two rooms they had lived in. "I want to live with Germans," he stated, "and, of course, I expect to be treated as family." He smiled at Jutta in a way that made Theo hate him immediately. His mother, however, seemed to be quite flattered by this attention, a fact that exasperated Theo even more.

"I'm going to Wanjka's house," he snapped over his shoulder as he stomped out of the house. 'What's with him?' Jutta wondered, but she did not say anything to him. Boys that age at times had funny moods and it was best not to make too much of it.

There was much going on in the village; Trucks were going back and forth, the panzers, big brutes, were being parked under the trees and camouflaged, some soldiers were stringing wires between houses, presumably for communication, and others were just standing around talking. No one, it seemed, was paying any attention to the civilians. After watching for a while, Theo walked over to Wanjka's house. He had not yet seen his friend and suddenly was eager to be with him again. When he reached the house, he found the door open, soldiers were walking in and out, and several vehicles were parked in the orchard. There was no sign of Wanjka or his mother. Theo walked around the back of the house. There was a guard at the back door. "Hey you, what do you want?" he called out in broken Russian.

Theo, startled, mumbled, "I'm looking for my friend."

"What? Speak up, kid."

"I, I'm looking for my friend. He lives here."

"Nobody lives here, and you're not supposed to be here. Get lost." Then slightly friendlier: "Try the house next door."

Theo left the yard in a hurry and walked over to the neighboring house. Some strange kids were playing in the yard. Theo walked over to them. "Does Wanjka live here?"

One of the kids looked up. "Yea, he's inside."

Theo walked to the door and knocked. Wanjka's mom opened the door. "Oh, it's you. Wait here." After a few minutes, Wanjka came out. Theo grabbed him by the shoulders. "Hi Wanj, it's so good to see you!" He gave Wanjka a big hug.

"Hi, Theo. Are you sure you want to associate with a mere Russian?"

"Wanj, why are you talking such rot? I came to see you, didn't I?"

Wanjka looked at him defiantly. "Well, you're part of the master race now, aren't you?" He stood there, his head bowed, kicking the dust with his foot. "That's what the soldiers told us, that the Germans are the master race. That's why they kicked us out of our house and kept most of our furniture."

Theo took a long time to answer. "Wanjka, I have been your friend for a long time, and I still consider myself your friend, but you have accused me of snitching on your father, and now you blame me for what the soldiers are doing. I think you will have to decide where you stand. When you have decided, and if you think we're still friends, come and see me." He looked at his friend sadly then turned around and went home.

Chapter 15

Theo sat at the window staring at the blizzard outside. First it had been incredibly cold, then it snowed for days, and now there was the howling wind. It seemed as if the weather was taking part in the war. Certainly for the German army, this weather was a disaster. They were not equipped for the severe cold and the masses of snow, especially now with the large snow drifts. The weather had totally paralyzed their transport system.

Theo was sitting in the kitchen, the warmest room in the house, thinking of his friend. Wanjka had not come to see him. In spite of the annoyance Theo had felt the last time they saw each other, he was still sad and missed his friend. Should he go and see him again? In the end, he decided against it, Wanjka would have to make the next move.

The door opened and his mom came into the room, accompanied by that ever-present Lieutenant Strom. How Theo hated him. It seemed that his mother and this stupid soldier had something going. It was incredible; Theo could not understand how his mother could do such a thing. 'I wonder if he sleeps with her?' he thought. 'It couldn't be, my mother isn't not like that. How could I think such a thing.' He shook his head to get these thoughts out of his mind.

"Theo, the German command has decided that we have to move to another village. There are only a few of us Germans left, scattered over several villages. Now we will be all brought together in one village. Lt. Strom says there will be a German school, just like in the Reich. Wouldn't that be nice?" Jutta smiled at Lt. Strom. "Theo will like that."

Theo was not impressed. "I like it here. Besides, the soldiers tell me that we are not true Germans but only 'Volksdeutsche'. I'd rather remain a Mennonite anyway, like my father."

Lt. Strom faced Theo and stood almost at attention. "Boy, you should not talk like that. It is an honor to be a German, even a Volksdeutscher. You haff to learn that, boy."

"It's okay, Franz, he's only a child. He does not understand these things."

Theo got up and walked towards the door. "I'm not a child, and I don't give a shit about the big Reich!" he spit out between his teeth as he slammed the door behind him.

"That one he could be trouble, liebchen, you have to watch him."

"Don't worry, Franz, he's basically a good boy. I'll talk to him."

"Ja, you do that. He is trouble, ja, trouble." The lieutenant shook his head.

A few weeks later, they moved to Ebenfeld, also a Mennonite village. All the Russian families that had moved into Ebenfeld when the Mennonites were evacuated by the Soviets were now relocated to other villages or sent to the Reich as slave laborers.

The house that Theo and his family got was about the same as their house at home, but here nobody else lived with them, so there was lots of space and Theo had his own room. The yard and garden were big, the village very much as his home village, and Theo felt he could live here. The only bad thing was that this bastard lieutenant had also been transferred here. Theo just hated him. He always hung around his mother and every time he saw Theo, he made stupid remarks. Theo was beginning to think that all Germans were crazy.

On Monday, Theo started school. He had never gone to German school and felt a little nervous at first, but it soon became evident that everybody was in the same boat. After a few days, Theo made some acquaintances and also found that school was school, German or other, and he began to relax. He had no difficulty learning what he was supposed to learn, in fact, he soon assumed his accustomed place—first in the class. His classmates were of similar, mostly Mennonite, background and Theo got along well with them, although he formed no close friendships.

Christmas came and went. There had been a kind of celebration but it was not as Theo remembered Christmas. It consisted mainly of speeches and some singing of winter songs, nothing religious. Then a soldier dressed as Santa Claus distributed a few presents. Since Theo was ambivalent about religion, he was puzzled about his negative feelings about this secular Christmas. Maybe he was more religious than he thought.

His studies were easy since he actually enjoyed school now. Since the beginning of the year all boys his age and older had to attend Hitler Youth meetings. As the meetings consisted mainly of games and sports, Theo found them to be fun. He also actively participated in the discussions that the youth leader, seemingly on the spur of the moment, initiated between events. Discussions usually were about the war and often had political overtones. Theo was quite unaware that he was gradually accepting Nazi dogma. His youth leader, however, was quite aware of the change and silently congratulated himself for a job well done. He began giving Theo increased duties, such as organizing little war games or other group activity that always had political slant. When he thought Theo was ready, he made him leader of a group.

Chapter 16

Theo took his responsibilities as group leader very seriously. He made sure his group had a good attendance record, fostered lively discussions, and made it a point to get to know each member of his group well. In short, he was a good leader, and he was noticed. If Theo was being groomed for a more important task, he was unaware of it. Although he was aware that the Hitler Youth was a mainly political organization, Theo's main interests were in sports and games.

One day, it was already early summer, one of the SS officers called him over for a friendly chat. "Theo, you speak Russian well, don't you?"

"Yes, Herr Scharfuehrer, I do."

"Would you like to do more important service for the Reich, Theo?"

"Why yes, Herr Scharfuehrer, but what can I do?" Theo felt distinctly uneasy but wasn't quite sure why.

"Well Theo," the Scharfuehrer put and arm around Theo's shoulder. "We need a translator for one of our special units, and I think you could fit splendidly into this position. Of course it would mean that you would leave home; you would become a member of the SS. Not a regular soldier because you are too young, but still—it would be an honor."

Now Theo was really uncomfortable. Leave home! This was like being drafted! "Am I being drafted?" He blurted out.

The Scharfuehrer patted his back. "Of course not. What a thought! You are too young for that. Of course if you should volunteer, it would be to your credit, and it wouldn't hurt your family either." He smiled at Theo. "You want to serve the fatherland, don't you?"

Theo felt trapped. "I have to talk to my mother," was all he could think of saying.

"Yes, yes, of course. You do that, your mother is a good German. I'm certain she will want you to do the right thing."

In the end, Theo volunteered as requested. He had not talked to his mother; she was too busy with her soldier friend and did not have any time for him anyway. Besides, it might be better to be away from home for a while and not have to be bothered by this nut, this Lieutenant Strom.

So it was that Theo, barely fifteen, 'volunteered' to join the SS as a translator. He went through a short course of military and political training and an equally short course in translation before he was assigned to a unit with special duties. His first posting was to a prison. Theo had assumed that this would be a prisoner of war camp, but he soon found out that this was a special prison, often referred to as a concentration camp. Strangely, there were not only men in this camp, but also women and children. Another thing that seemed odd was that the prisoners were moved around a lot. There were always transports of prisoners coming and some prisoners leaving, usually on foot or in trucks. It did not take Theo long to find out that most of the prisoners were Jewish, and it did not take much longer before he realized that the reason for their imprisonment was just that—they were

Jewish. Theo could not make much sense out of this, but when he made inquires he was roughly rebuffed. Since his job at the camp was to translate for some of the interrogators, he stuck to that and did not ask any further. Although he had heard from some of the guards that some interrogations were 'quite rough', he was never witness to any severe mistreatment. Much later he found out that he had only been involved in routine questioning of ordinary prisoners and that the special prisoners were 'managed' by specially trained SS personnel. Aside from the interrogations, he had no contact with other prisoners and did not develop a true understanding of the extent of suffering and death in other areas of the camp, or perhaps he deliberately refused to comprehend. In any case, he seemed to distance himself from the camp, except where his work required his involvement.

He often thought of his mother and the rest of the family. He was not terribly homesick, but did miss them at times. He had not developed any close relations with anyone at the concentration camp and therefore was not unhappy when he was transferred to another unit.

Chapter 17

Theo's new unit operated in the forests of the western Ukraine. Their specific task was to find and destroy partisans. Theo's job was to translate during the sometimes prolonged interrogations. Here Theo learned what real interrogations were like. The prisoners were beaten, starved, isolated, or otherwise mistreated if it was thought that they hid information. On the whole, not many prisoners were taken, as most of the time the partisans were killed when and where they were found and prisoners were only taken for interrogation when it was thought that useful information could be obtained.

Theo found his job depressing. He hated the brutality and the killing, but found himself trapped. He requested to be transferred to the regular army but his request was denied because of his age. He was also severely reprimanded by his commanding officer who regarded anyone who wanted to transfer from the SS to the regular army beneath contempt. So Theo stayed. He became irritable and moody, he slept poorly, he could not eat and lost weight, and eventually ended up in the hospital where a perceptive doctor, who recognized the problem, sent Theo home on leave.

Theo arrived back in Ebenfeld in November 1942. The German army had made great advances and had reached the Volga River at Stalingrad. It was expected that the war would soon be over, as the Russians could not possibly hang on much longer. At home, nothing much had changed. Lt. Strom still hung around, and in fact, he had practically moved in and spent most evenings, and many a night, at their home. Theo hated it, he hated the lieutenant, he hated his mother, or rather, her association with this person. He would avoid calling him by his name, but in the end all that hate only made Theo miserable and did not change the situation one iota.

His sister and brother had grown. Theo was surprised that he now quite enjoyed their company and he spent some happy times talking and playing with them. Although he loved both his brother and his sister, their company was not enough, no matter how enjoyable. Theo remained restless. His mother's association with the German officer did not help, especially when he stayed overnight, which was often.

In the late fall of 1942, a major change in the war occurred:- the German army sustained its first real defeat, which, in time led to the loss of Stalingrad, and eventually to Germany's total defeat.

In Ebenfeld there was at first no change. There was a bit more military traffic and more discussions about the war, but otherwise life went on. Christmas came and went very much as the year before, except that Theo had not taken part in the school activities.

The significant thing concerning Theo was that Lt. Strom was suddenly transferred to a front line unit. Since he had never been in battle, this was a major disaster for him, but there was nothing he could do to change the situation. On the appointed day, he packed his bags and left. To Theo's disgust, his mother cried. She hugged and kissed Lt. Strom until Theo could not stand it anymore and went into the house in disgust. "Make sure you look after your mother for me." Lt. Strom yelled after him. Theo only spat on the floor. Who did Strom think he was to tell him to look after his mother? Of course he would look after his mother, but not for Strom, nor anyone else.

It turned out that Lt. Strom did not have any luck. In his first battle, a bullet hit him in the head and killed him instantly. The news, delivered by some of the retreating soldiers, hit Jutta hard, but there was not much time for mourning. Because of the retreat of the army, all German civilians were also being evacuated. Theo, his family, and some of their relatives and friends were loaded unto a hastily assembled train and moved west, to a large Mennonite colony named Molochna. The village Jutta and the kids landed in was Waldheim.

Chapter 18

Waldheim became a sort of turning point for Theo. Here he left behind his childhood, what there had been of it, and in time he became a man. Some change came through his own doing, but most came about by events beyond his control. The most important was his formal induction into the SS, a cavalry unit stationed in Waldheim. Everyone, except the officers, was of the same background as Theo—namely Mennonite. Age did not seem to be considered very seriously, as Theo and several others were still only fifteen years old. 'By the time you get to the front you'll be old enough,' they were told. While stationed in Waldheim, it was actually fun to belong to the 'Shwadron', as the cavalry unit was commonly referred to in Mennonite circles. Training was only a few hours a day, and since most of the boys were expert riders already, their practices came easy. They also were expected to attend classes for a few hours, or work if they had some to do. The remaining time was their own.

These few months in Waldheim turned out to be a memorable time for Theo. He had lots of free time and made many friends, both male and female, and his social life was great. Here he had his first real girl friend, and in time his first sexual experience, which he would always later remember as a bit of a disaster. Here also he met Waldemar Epp, or Trudy, as he was commonly called. No one remembered how Waldemar had gotten his nickname, and the fact that it was a girl's name was only noticed by strangers. Right from the start, theirs was a special relationship. Although Trudy was three years older, they found that they had many similar interests. They were in the same unit, they hated their commanding officer equally, they were both superb riders, and whenever they could they would go for long rides in the country.

This ideal situation, however, came to an end when new officers, career soldiers, arrived and took over the training. Now harsh military methods were introduced, training times were extended, and free time reduced. In fact, so-called free time now was filled with classes, homework, and a multitude of other duties.

One day it was announced that the Schwadron would soon be relocated, and before long, they received their marching orders. They regarded with mixed feelings the news that they were to be used as occupation troops, maybe in Poland.

Soon the day of departure arrived. Theo had spent the two days before, when everyone had been given leave, at home. He felt a special love for his brother and sister and also his mother, but had difficulty expressing these feelings to them, and even more so to others. Even later in life, this inhibition would handicap him, and when he married would lead to certain difficulties. He was acutely aware of this inability to convey his emotions but did not know what to do about it. To make up for this, he developed a teasing, joking style of conversation.

Although he did not know it, this would be the last time he would be in this house with his family. Both Sonja and Peet had grown so! Especially Sonja, she was now a teenager, and was developing into a very pretty young woman. And Peety, how he had matured; not so long ago he had been such a pest, but now one could actually have a sensible conversation with him. Theo's feelings towards his mother were mixed, and would forever remain so. He loved her, to be sure, but he felt a bitterness about her soldier friends, of which there now had been several. He would always try to stay away when they were around and on more than one occasion, there had been sharp words between him and his mother. Fortunately, her latest friend had been sent to the front recently.

When the day of departure arrived, Theo was actually glad. There had been a tension in the air; everyone had felt it, but the cause was not entirely clear. When the time came to say good bye, he made it short. He kissed and hugged his mother, gave a hug to Sonja, and shook Peet's hand. Then he turned and left.

At the railroad station, they found out that their horses were to stay behind. Horses did not fit into modern combat, they were informed. Theo was devastated. Riding had at least made training half tolerable. He stood there talking to Trudy when one of their officers walked by. "You two, stand at attention and salute when an officer walks passed you. And remember that for the future. From now on discipline will be strictly enforced!"

When he had passed, Trudy muttered under his breath, "Bastard! This is what we can expect from now on, shit from our Reichsdeutsche friends." He spat on the ground. "Mark my word, we are in for a tough time."

Soon the train moved out. For several days and nights they traveled due west. Early in the morning, they arrived at Slonin, White Russia. The rumors about going to Warsaw seemed to have been just that. Soon they were in their new quarters, old but relatively livable military huts. Theo and Trudy had been lucky enough to be assigned to the same room.

"What do you think this is all about, Theo?" asked Trudy as they were getting their gear stowed away.

"Beats me, maybe we're here for a holiday," joked Theo.

"Listen, I haven't liked this from the beginning, and I like it less now. Something damn strange is under foot, you'll see."

The trumpet blew assembly and all rushed into the yard. When they were all assembled and lined up in ranks, the commander of the camp addressed them. "Well, I was informed to expect soldiers. What do I see? Riff-raff in SS uniforms. This is an insult not only to the Fatherland but to the Fuehrer himself, whose elite troops you are supposed to be. But never mind, you have been brought here to be put into shape and that is exactly what we plan to do." He turned to the sergeants. "Take over." And take over he did! For the next four weeks, they were subjected to the most rigorous training that Theo had ever experienced. Not only was there grueling, and sometimes cruel, physical conditioning, but in the evening there were endless classes. These consisted mainly of political instruction—'brain washing', Trudy called it.

"Just watch, Theo. Before they are through we'll all be little Hitlers."

"Are you totally nuts," Theo whispered. "Don't say things like that, you'll get us put in jail, or worse."

"Well do you believe all this crap about super-race and that nonsense about the Jews?" Trudy looked disgusted.

"That's not the point. It does not matter whether the stuff they teach us is crap or not. It's the prevailing philosophy and if we want to survive, we have to go along. Besides, how do you know that the Jews are not the enemies of the German people? How do you know that the Germans are not a super-race?"

"Now who's talking rot? But you're right, we have to play along for the time being, even if it's damn hard at times. Those bastards." Still disgusted, Trudy spat on the floor. "Those bastards."

"Well, it's getting late. Let's sleep on it." Theo turned over and pulled the blanket over his head. "Good night."

Chapter 19

It was October of 1943. Theo was now sixteen years old—of legal age for the army. What an eventful year it had been so far! Early in the year, the disaster at Stalingrad had happened. Then there had been the incredible tank battle near Kursk where the Germans had lost a very large number of their armour. Since then the whole war seemed to have gone haywire, and on top of everything, Theo's unit had received their marching orders and rumor had it that they were headed for the front.

The German army had steadily retreated and now tried to hold the front at the Dnieper River but the Russians had succeeded in crossing the river at several points. One of the small Russian bridgeheads that was becoming troublesome was just north of Kiev near a place called Lyutezh. On the first of November, Theo's unit arrived at just this place and was deployed at the northern end of the bridgehead.

Trudy, as usual, was complaining about the poor accommodation. "What a revolting situation, having to dig a hole and sleep in it. How can one sleep? How can one live in this mud?" Then came his favorite phrase: "Those bastards!"

"Relax, Trudy. You know we have to dig in. You never know what the Ruskies might do. It's best to be ready."

"Yea, yea. You're right, but that does not make me any more comfortable." Trudy resumed digging. "Those Ruskies have been damned quiet. I wonder what they are up to."

In the distance toward the Dnjeper, some dust rose, indicating activity. "See that, those Ruskies are at least on dry ground. Why do we have to be stuck in a bog?" Trudy kept complaining.

Theo looked worriedly at the cloud of dust. "We might leave here sooner than we'd like. All that activity is not for nothing. I think they're getting ready to attack, but when?"

The sun was setting in the west; the sky over the vast Ukrainian steppes was crimson. 'As if the whole world is on fire,' Theo thought. 'Maybe it soon will be'. As he continued to dig, his thoughts turned to his loved ones. His mother, Peety, Sonja—where were they now? He knew they had left what had been their last home in Waldheim. Where were they now? How would he ever find them? A deep melancholy overcame him. He glanced at Trudy. "Hey Waldemar, do you ever think of home?"

"You must be serious to call me Waldemar. Of course I think of home! Do you think I joined this lousy outfit for fun? If it wasn't for these SS bastards I'd be with my family now, instead of worrying what's happening to them."

"Don't talk like that!" Theo glanced around to see if anyone had heard, but the nearest soldiers were busy digging and were not paying any attention to them. "I swear, one of these days you'll get us killed, and you certainly are not a credit to the shwadron."

Trudy looked at him in disgust. "Cut the crap. But seriously, where do you think our people are now?"

"Well, the last I heard was that all the German villages would be relocated to the Wartegau, what used to be Poland, you know. That's where I'll look if we ever get out of this mud."

It had become quite dark. Theo pulled a pack of cigarettes from his pocket and offered one to Trudy. Smoking was a new habit for him, acquired during the long hours on guard duty. As soon as he lit his cigarette, someone yelled from another fox hole: "Are you guys crazy? Put out those bloody smokes, and don't light any more matches either."

Theo felt stupid but Trudy only grumbled. "Damned assholes, as if the Russians don't know where we are. Bastards."

Theo made himself as comfortable as he could in his hole and tried to sleep, but sleep would not come. Strangely, his thoughts kept turning to home; he thought of his father and their old home. He still vaguely remembered the farm, the barn with the animals, going out to the fields with his father. What a life it had been. Why did it have to change? He was chilly and pulled his thin summer coat tighter around him. It was already the second of November, and soon it would snow and things would get even worse.

He must have slept a few hours for dawn was already breaking when he suddenly awoke. The whole earth seemed to be exploding. In the direction of the Russians, there were almost continuous flashes, and just to the south of their own position the earth was ripped apart by multiple explosions. Huge chunks of dirt were flying through the air and at times, the hits were close enough to shower Theo with dirt. "Hey, Trudy, Trudy, the Russians, they're attacking, they're coming."

"No kidding, you think I can sleep in this racket? Seems to me they're headed south of us, maybe Kiev. But don't worry, we'll get our pile of shit."

"Will you stop your bloody clowning, you turkey? what will we do if they come this way?"

Several shells exploded nearby and Theo squeezed into his foxhole. When there was another lull in the shelling, Theo called, "Hey, Trudy, are you all right?"

"Yes, barely. Do you hear that noise?"

"What noise? Just then, Theo heard a distant rumbling. "I hear it, it must be tanks. Oh God, I hope they're not coming this way."

"Of course they're coming this way, you nut," retorted Trudy. There was some movement behind them. Theo gripped his rifle and strained to see. "Relax, trooper Dirks. It's me, Sergeant Frank. Russian tanks are attacking, stay in your holes. Our artillery will try to take them out. Some of the shells might come close, so stay down." He crawled over to the next hole. "Stay down. Our artillery will be firing, stay down."

Soon Theo heard the distant booms of the eighty-eights and the whine of the shells overhead. The impact explosions were far away, but as the noise of the Russian tanks came closer, so did the hits. Suddenly Theo saw a large dark shadow directly ahead and coming strait toward them. 'Shit, that's a Russian tank, what now?' Theo wondered.

"Trudy, are you there? Do you see that thing?" Theo could not hide the tremor in his voice.

"Keep down," Trudy answered in harsh whisper. "Maybe he will miss us."

As the black mass, which seemed immensely large to Theo, came closer, there was a loud explosion and a bright flash which seemed to come right out of the tank. At first Theo thought that the tank was shooting off its cannon, but then he saw that the tanks turret was at a weird angle and smoke was coming from under it. The tank had stopped moving. "It's hit!" yelled Trudy. "If anyone comes out, shoot."

Theo grasped his rifle tightly and watched the tank but nothing moved. In the distance, the rumbling noises continued and in the increasing morning light they saw many tanks. They seemed to move in a southwesterly direction, almost parallel to their own position.

"We're lucky again, Theo," Trudy breathed a sigh of relief. "It's Kiev they're after."

As the sun came up, they saw the Russian attack veer south. Theo's unit remained at their position until the afternoon and then they were ordered to retreat. Why or whereto, they did not know.

Chapter 20

It was now August 1944. Theo's unit had been rushed to Warsaw to quell the uprising. They arrived during the night and, under sporadic fire from the city, had been quartered in abandoned houses in a suburb. It was morning and Trudy had gone to get breakfast from the field kitchen for both of them. Theo was sitting near the broken window looking out onto the street. He was thinking back, remembering similar streets, similar broken windows, many damaged houses, many killed and wounded comrades. Where would it end?

Since their first battle experience near the Dnijepr River, there had been many engagements. Some were small, some larger, but all bloody, and most resulting in loss of life, or at least injury. Their unit had received many replacements over the last year. At least half the unit was new, and mostly inexperienced. It was amazing that he and Trudy were still together, and even more amazing that they were both still alive and healthy. There had been close calls but they had managed not only to survive but also to avoid capture by the Russians. At times this has seemed impossible, as when they had been trapped in the Cherkassy pocket and had only made it out by swimming the Gniloi Tikich in freezing temperatures. Theo shuddered. He was still suffering from nightmares about that experience, and it would be better to forget it. He heard a noise downstairs. "Is that you, Trudy?"

"Yes, but don't expect a deluxe breakfast. All they had is black ersatz coffee and black bread, and the cook said we were lucky to get that."

"Its okay, we've had worse. What's the news? Why are we here? More partisans?" Their last few months were spent trying to protect convoys from partisan raids.

"This seems to be bigger, Theo. The Poles have staged a massive revolt in Warsaw. With the Russians close by, across the river, this could get quite messy. I'm sure they'll attack to help the Poles in the city. That way they can get us between two fronts. Yes, this will get messy."

They had hardly finished their breakfast when they were ordered to advance toward Warsaw. They walked single file along each side of the street, close to the houses to avoid sniper fire, but nothing much happened until they reached the city proper. Suddenly there was intense mortar and machine gun fire. They took shelter behind the houses as best they could, but already they had casualties. As always, Theo experienced severe fright, almost panic before any action, but once the actual fighting started he seemed okay. Not that he was calm, it was more like a general numbness that seemed to obliterate any feeling and he operated like a machine. Thus, when he and Trudy were ordered to take out the mortar position, he yelled to Trudy to give him covering fire and instantly raced for a cement abutment in the middle of the street, which gave him a better view of the street. From here he could see the mortar position on top of a house down the road.

"It's in the yellow house down the road," he yelled back, "Get the tank to take it out."

A few minutes later, he heard the rumbling of the tank engine, then a few blasts and the building ahead collapsed in a big cloud of dust.

"That was easy," remarked Trudy, who had joined him behind the cement block. "We might as well go and see what's left." He got up before Theo could reply. Immediately there was a burst of machinegun fire and Trudy stumbled forward and then fell.

"Oh my God," screamed Theo as he jumped up and ran towards Trudy. "Are you okay? Are you hit? Are you..." He felt a searing pain in his left leg, everything seemed to go blurry, and he pitched forward. Through the haze he could see Trudy, lying on his back, not moving, his eyes wide open as if in surprise. His abdomen was ripped open by several bullet wounds. As he fell, Theo passed out.

Chapter 21

The first thing Theo noticed was the white linen on the bed. Strange, he had not slept in a clean bed for some time. Wonder what Trudy thought about this. Trudy! He now remembered. He tried to get up but experienced severe pain in his left leg and side. He became very agitated and called out, "Where is everybody? What happened to Trudy? I have to know, I have to know." Tears were running down his cheeks by the time the nurse came, for he did know, even before the nurse confirmed it, that Trudy was dead. 'Dead,' Theo thought, 'it's such a final thing. I will never see him again, never, never.' How could he live with this? Trudy had become more than family. Theo buried his face in the pillow. There was no way he could have described the utter devastation and hopelessness he felt. 'How could God allow this?' Theo thought. 'Is there a God? Does he care?' Then there were more tears. "Oh God, how can I carry on?"

Trudy had been his link to the rest of the world, his protector, his advisor. Theo had not undertaken anything without discussing it with Trudy first. Trudy had been his substitute father and now Theo was orphaned once again. His thoughts turned to his family. 'I wonder where Mom and the kids are.' He had to find them. He again called the nurse: "Fraulein, my family they have been moved from Russia, how can I find out where they are?"

"Oh, that's easy, Corporal Dirks. There is an agency that locates missing relatives, you just get in touch with them." She smiled sweetly as she adjusted his bed sheets.

"If you are still too weak to do this, I can do it for you. Just give me the details."

"Would you do this for me? I really appreciate it. You see, I have not seen my family for some time, and my friend . . ." He stopped, overcome by emotion. "You see . . . he's dead, he died in the . . . in the city. I could not help him." He cried. "I could not help him."

The nurse took his hand. "It's okay, Corp. Dirks, it's okay." She wrote down Jutta's last home address and other particulars. "I'll find them, you'll see. Now just get some rest." She adjusted the blanket over him and left.

After a while, Theo slept.

The next morning he found himself on a train going west. It seemed the wounded were being transferred to proper hospitals in the Reich. Suddenly Theo remembered the nurse that was going to locate his relatives. Where was she? He had not obtained the address of the agency, or even its proper name. How could he be so scatterbrained? An orderly walked by and Theo called him over. "Say, the nurses at the field hospital near Warsaw, did they stay there? Are they with us? How can I get in touch with them?"

"Sweet on one of the nurses, eh? Well, don't worry they are all here, on this transport. Which one is it then?"

Theo waved his hand impatiently. "You don't understand, she was going to help me."

"Yes, yes, they all help. What was her name?"

Theo had not even asked for her name, he had been too upset and too sick. "I don't know her name, she was blond, and slim, and… and kind of… pretty," he stammered.

The orderly laughed. "They are all pretty, but I think I know the one you mean. She's here somewhere, I'll find her, don't worry." He winked at Theo and left, laughing to himself.

The orderly was true to his word, and the next day the nurse appeared. Theo was overjoyed. Immediately he asked for her name.

"It's Gerdi," she answered. "Gerdi Schwab."

Theo repeated it several times. "Gerdi, that's a nice name. I should have no difficulty remembering it."

Gerdi laughed, then she became serious. "I'm very sorry but because of the relocation I have not been able to contact the agency about your family, but when we reach our destination I'll get right on it, Corporal Dirks."

"Please, call me Theo. Corp. Dirks sounds so formal."

"Okay, Theo. I have to go now."

In the end, it wasn't Gerdi or any of the staff at the hospital in the Reich or any agency that helped Theo locate his mother, but a patient who was also recovering, and whom Theo had seen in the dining room and in other areas of the hospital on several occasions. This time they happened to share a table in the dining area. They struck up a conversation and eventually talked about their families.

"My family was missing too and I found them through the Refugee Relocation Board in Litzmanstadt. Have you tried there?"

"No, no I haven't. Who are they?" Theo asked, not placing much hope in this new source.

"You mean you have not tried there? That's the outfit that handles all the refugees from the East. Man, if you have not tried there, you have not tried."

'Well,' Theo thought, 'what can I lose?' To his great surprise, he had a reply in two weeks. His mother, with Peety and Sonja, were in Kutno, in the new German province Wartegau, formerly part of Poland. Immediately he wrote his mother a long letter. He was all excited and waited anxiously for a reply. Soon he would be well enough to leave the hospital and he was certain he would get a few weeks of leave. How nice it would be to see everyone again! His eyes became moist. He had not realized how much he had missed everyone. Sonja and Peety must have grown a lot since he had last seen them. He tried to imagine how they now looked but couldn't. Soon he would see them.

Chapter 22

His mother and the kids lived in a small house on a quiet street. The house had formerly belonged to a Polish couple who had been relocated when the area had been declared German.

"How do you like living in somebody else's house?" Theo had asked his mother.

"Well, I don't, but I try not to think about it since I can't change things and we have to live somewhere. Besides, it's not a good thing to talk about things like that, at least not when others can hear it."

"I know," Theo replied pensively. "I've learned to be careful. Still, one thinks about it."

Theo thought that his mother had aged a lot since he had seen her last, back in Waldheim. Not so much in appearance as in her manner. She seemed more settled, more matronly. Theo found he could talk more freely with her now. Of course there was no boyfriend now, Lt. Strom having been killed somewhere on the eastern front. 'It's too bad he's dead but I'm glad he's not here,' Theo thought without much compassion.

He had been home four days. Two more days left before he had to report back—only two more days! There had been a time when service in the SS had been exiting, an adventure, but now it only represented misery and the possibility of death, and Theo hated the thought of returning to his unit. But he also realized that there was nothing he could do about it. When he had asked for two weeks leave, the commandant at the hospital had glared at him. "You are a member of the SS, you should be eager to get back into service for the Fatherland. One week at the most, even that's maybe too long."

Theo had hastily departed before the time was reduced further. His patriotism had significantly decreased over the last year. In fact, at times he caught himself thinking almost treasonous thoughts. He often thought about his home village and about his former friend, Wanjka. The chances that he would see Wanjka again were virtually zero. Theo wondered what he was doing now; he probably was in the Russian army. Wouldn't it be strange if they should meet?

His mother interrupted his thoughts. "It's been hard, you know, traveling by horse and buggy with the two kids and no man to help. Here also we are so lonesome, none of our people live in this city. I wish you would not have to leave."

"Yes, I know Mother, but there is nothing one can do about it. What worries me is the Russian advance. If it continues you will have to leave here too. How will I know where to look for you?"

"I have thought of that too. If you cannot find us after the war is over, write to the Red Cross in Geneva. I will do the same. Hopefully it will not come to that."

Theo took his mother's hand. "Mom, you know that Germany will lose the war, don't you?"

Jutta nodded her head. She was very close to tears.

"It's okay, Mom. I know things will work out." Theo hugged her. He had not felt so close to his mother for a long time. 'Who knows if I'll see her again,' he thought. Many sons did not come back to their mothers from the Russian front, but what was the use of worrying his mother about that now? He hugged her again. "It's been nice to be here for a few days. Let's go and pick up the kids from the school."

When Peety and Sonja came out of their classes, they all went over to the restaurant and had soft drinks, the only thing one could still get without food stamps. Even those were made with artificial sweetner.

The next day, his last day at home, found Theo restless. He could not understand himself; he was happy to be home with his mother, with Peety and Sonja, but at the same time, he was eager to leave. It seemed as if this peaceful time was not real; an interlude, a mirage, that did not fit into the real world of war, misery, and death that had become his true existence. 'Why do I want to get back to that?' he asked himself, but there was no answer. It was true, he had been very glad to find his family again, and he would miss them again, but now he could not really get close to them. 'Is it me?' he asked himself. 'Have I changed? Can't I love them anymore?' He knew he loved them, and he longed to express this to them, but he could not. He did not know why— maybe the loss of Trudy, who was still very much in his memory, had made him afraid of close relationships. If this was so, Theo did not consciously appreciate it, and probably would have denied it had someone suggested such a thing.

The next morning he took quick leave after giving everyone a firm hug. He had guilt feelings about the sense of relief he experienced when he was on the train. He could not understand himself.

He had been ordered to report to a new unit in Vienna. It seemed strange to him that he should have to go so far, but since he had never seen Vienna, he did not mind. He made sure his gear was stowed under the seat so that it was harder to steal, then he rolled up his coat and put it behind his head for a pillow. It would be a long trip and he might as well get some sleep while he could.

Chapter 23

The new unit Theo was assigned to was made up of soldiers from SS units whose ranks had been so depleted by casualties that they were too small to exist on their own. Almost all were veterans of the Russian front, which was much to Theo's liking. At least they would not have to bother with ignorant rookies! The new unit only had a few days of preparation and then it was shipped out, direction east.

Theo had become friendly with a young man from Berlin. His name was Horst. Although Horst was only nineteen, he had already been in combat several times. 'Why is it that I feel older than Horst when I am younger?' Theo wondered. He had no answer. Maybe it was because he had experienced more.

"Well, Theo, from the direction we are going, I would say it's the Russian front again."

Theo nodded. "You could be right."

Horst laughed strangely. "Don't worry, just stick with me and you will be all right. I'm lucky, you know, three times in combat and not a scratch. I know I will survive. You'll see."

Theo wished he had that kind of confidence, even if it was foolish. "I hope you will, and if we stick together maybe our chances will be better. At least I hope so."

Horst laughed again. He seemed to do a lot of laughing. "You have to have faith, you know. We will make it."

They settled back in their seats and lit up cigarettes. Theo looked out the window. They were passing a small village, the countryside was hilly, and there was a lot of forest. 'Not like home,' Theo thought. He hoped they would not have to fight in the forests, he felt much more at ease in the open fields. 'Maybe I have claustrophobia,' he thought. He finished his cigarette and tried to sleep.

Morning found them on a siding in a wooded area. They were ordered out and marched up and down for exercise but the officers soon tired of this and dismissed them. Apparently there would be a lengthy delay but why, no-one knew. Theo and Horst decided to take a walk around the train.

"I wonder where we are," Theo said. "We've been traveling southeast mostly. We must be out of Germany by now."

Horst laughed. "We left Germany some time ago, when you were snoring. We are either in Poland or even Romania, who knows. But it doesn't matter; it's all the Russian front. Soon we'll be fighting the bloody Russkies, unless it's partisans."

Theo stopped. "You think that's possible, partisans? I have my nose full of them."

Horst laughed again. "You're scared of them, aren't you?"

"You bet I am, and if you weren't such a fool, you would be too."

"Well, to tell you the truth I'd rather avoid them, but chances are we'll be fighting partisans before long."

Suddenly whistles blew, everyone rushed into the train, and they were off again.

Chapter 24

It was incredible, they were in Yugoslavia, of all places! Well, one thing was certain: it was the partisans. What else would bring them to Yugoslavia?

"Hey, Horst, get your ass and your gear out of the train and get ready to meet your bloody friends the partisans."

Horst was not in a good mood. "Oh, buzz off, you turkey. Who said they're my friends? Just wait until we fight them, then your shit will run thin."

This time Theo laughed. "I know more about them than you, buster, but I think you're right, it won't be fun. I hear these Yugoslavs have a guy named Tito who's as hard as nails."

"That's what I hear too, and he rarely takes prisoners."

Everyone was out of the train and they were marched off the railroad platform and down the street. The few natives on the street gave them furtive looks and then hurried away into the side streets. They were marching though a small town and there was not much evidence of war. The houses were intact—probably there was nothing of importance here and the place had not been bombed, yet. 'Our presence here might change that,' Theo thought. They marched to the outskirts of the town where they were quartered in what had formerly been a dance hall. There was lots of straw in rows on the floor, and piles of blankets.

"This looks not too bad, eh Theo?"

"I guess you're more ignorant then I thought. Don't you know that in a few days the lice will eat us alive? I guess kids don't know that, eh!"

"Cut that out, Theo. I'm no kid, and I've had lice too. The first few nights we will at least sleep in some comfort."

Theo was not so sure. "I hope you're right, I sure could use some good sleep."

They picked a place away from the main entrance and made themselves comfortable. Horst pulled out a pack of cigarettes, but before he could light one Theo said, "Not in here with all that straw, it's too dangerous."

Horst looked around. "Yeh, you could be right. I don't want to get incinerated yet. Let's go for a walk, I wanted to do that anyway."

They went out the back, past some trees to a little brook. The air was heavy with moisture and felt cold. Theo shivered. "Soon it will be Christmas again. Heaven only knows were we will celebrate it this year. Probably in some mud hole."

Horst took a deep drag on his cigarette. "Who cares about that sort of thing? I have given up on religion long ago. Christmas doesn't mean anything to me."

"Well, Horst, that's nice, then I can stop worrying what to get you."

They walked along the creek for a while in silence, then Theo said, "I'm cold, let's go back."

Horst turned around. "It's freezing." They picked up the pace, and after a few minutes Horst asked, "Do you really not care about religion and Christmas and such?"

Theo smiled. "Why, are you having second thoughts?"

"No, it's not that, but seriously, what do you think about religion?"

Theo thought, 'Yes, what do I think about religion?' Aloud he said, "It's a difficult question, Horst. I think there is a God. What or where He is, or what He does, I don't know. A lot of the Bible must be myth, that doesn't mean it's wrong. The stories, although myths themselves, might be used to explain or portray a deeper truth." He walked on quietly for a while. "There are a lot of things that bother me that I can't understand. For instance, the behavior of some Christians, some Mennonites. Although they profess to be Christians, they can still be cruel, greedy, deceitful, and many other nasty things one can think of. Conversely, many non-Christians are kind and honest, and ready to help their neighbor. To answer your question, lately I have not been very religious."

Horst laughed hilariously, as if Theo had told a very funny joke. "Well, that's certainly a mixed up answer. You have more problems than I have. I just don't bother with that stuff—no religion for me!"

'I wonder if that's better or worse,' Theo thought, but he did not say anything. They walked silently the rest of the way.

Chapter 25

It was amazing! Here they were, marching through sleet and snow and mud, seas of mud. Theo had never been so miserable in his whole life; he was wet to the skin. He could not remember when he had been dry and warm last. They had been marching for days now, always northwest. Their departure had been very sudden. They were told to be ready with all their gear in one hour, no other explanations. They had not seen the enemy, they had not seen any partisans, and there had not been any air attacks. The whole thing was a total mystery, totally amazing. Where were they going, and why?

Horst was marching silently beside him, trying to light a cigarette.

"Hey, do you have another one of those? Mine are all wet," asked Theo.

"Huh?" Horst looked up startled. "Sorry, I was think-ing. I think I still have some dry ones left." He pulled out a crumpled pack and handed it to Theo.

"Have you any idea what's going on, Theo? We've been dragging our asses though this mud for days and no-one seems to know why or where we are going."

"I know no more than you do, Horst, but that's the army for you—just follow orders. God I'm cold, sure hope we will find some dry place soon."

They smoked in silence. The rain had now turned totally to snow and the wind had picked up. 'All we need is a rotten blizzard,' Theo thought bitterly. His cigarette had become wet and was out. Theo threw it into the mud and tried to shield his face from the snow and wind. Because he was so wet, every movement brought new discomforts.

Horst interrupted his thoughts. "See that village up ahead? I bet we'll find a dry place there and maybe the bloody Sturmbahnfuehrer will be so kind as to let us rest there."

"I hope so, Horst. I don't think I can go much further." Theo was getting so tired he could hardly think.

When they reached the village, they took over as many houses as they needed. The locals vacated their houses without protest—they knew better. The house Theo and Horst were assigned to already had a fire going. Both stripped to their skin and hung their clothes around the stove to dry and washed as well as they could in a small wooden tub. Then they relaxed by the fire and smoked some of the dry cigarettes, which Horst produced from his back pack.

"It's amazing how well a few relatively minor amenities can make one feel. A good meal and some sleep and I'll be as good as new," mused Theo as he stretched in front of the fire.

"What, no woman? Are you that old?" Horst laughed.

They had to move away from the fire as others came into the house, but since they now were dry and warm, they did not mind. When his clothes were dry, Theo dressed and went to get some food. Because of the bad weather, the mobile kitchen could not be set up and he received only dry staples consisting of bread, cheese and a small piece of sausage, but it was enough. Horst had found some dry hay in the barn and soon after eating, they were both asleep.

Theo was dreaming about home and his family when suddenly all hell broke loose. There was rapid machine gun fire and glass was flying through the room. Theo wanted to get up but Horst pushed him down roughly. "Stay down you idiot, you want to get killed?"

"What's going on?" Theo yelled as he hugged the floor.

"Somebody is shooting at us, can't you tell? It must be partisans, or maybe the Ruskies have caught up with us."

After a few minutes the shooting stopped. Horst and Theo crawled to their clothes and dressed, staying on the floor. They heard shouting outside and moved to the door to see. Nothing much could be seen in the darkness, but they now heard that the shouting was in German. They ran across the street to a group of soldiers who were talking excitedly. Their platoon leader emerged from another house and barked a few orders. Sentries were posted and patrols sent out, but the partisans that had attacked them had long vanished.

The next day they got ready to leave. Their casualties had been light, three dead and about a dozen wounded, only two serious. They buried the dead and commandeered a horse and cart for the wounded that could not walk.

For the next two days they continued to march mainly due west. The weather had improved and they found food here and there in the villages, nothing special, but enough to keep body and soul together. Except for a few minor skirmishes, the partisans had also left them alone. No one seemed to know where they were going, and if their unit leader knew he kept that knowledge to himself.

"Hey, Theo," Horst motioned to Theo to come closer. "Have you noticed that we are always going more or less west?"

"Yes, that's right. So what?"

Horst steered Theo away from the others. "Don't you think that's odd? The front is the other way, unless one thinks of the other front, the western front."

"The western . . . but that's where the Americans. . ."

Horst smiled. "Is the penny dropping?"

Theo was stunned. "You think he's leading us there on purpose? To get away from the Russians maybe?"

Horst still smiled. Theo shook his head in disbelief. "He wouldn't dare. Would he?"

They rejoined the rest of the troop, both preoccupied with their thoughts.

On April 25, 1945, the few that remained of their group were captured without a fight by an American unit.

Chapter 26

Theo was sitting on the floor looking out of his tent at the endless rain. Until the previous night, there had been no tent. He and the other prisoners had lived under a make-shift shelter they had built from a few branches, some pine boughs and some sod for the roof, and a bit of dried moldy grass to sleep on. It had been a miserable existence and Theo was happy to have a dry place finally. Since April when he and Horst were taken prisoners, they had lived in a fenced-in compound that had formerly been a field. It was true, they had constructed the shelter using some branches of evergreens and other stuff, but this had only partially protected them from the elements, and anything but a light rain had come right through. The nights were still cool. What was worse, however, was the terrible food, and the small amounts. In about six weeks Theo had lost over twenty pounds, and he had not been fat to start with. They had finally been issued tents by their American captors and rumor had it that better and more food would also soon be available. Horst had gone to collect the day's food ration and was returning with a smile on his face.

"Hey, old buddy! Look what I got, some half decent food, but not much. They would not give me your ration.

You better go and get it yourself." Horst showed him his allotment, some dark bread and a piece of cheese.

Theo jumped up. "I better get mine, I'm starving." He ran off.

"What else have we been doing for the last year but starving?" Horst yelled after him.

When Theo returned he seemed preoccupied.

"What's up?" Horst inquired.

"Well, I heard this rumor, it's probably nothing."

"What's nothing? Come on, tell me."

"Some guys were talking. Apparently the Americans are going to turn over to the Russians all those born in Russia, and you know where I was born, don't you?"

"Oh boy, that could be serious. You think it's true?"

"How would I know? I wouldn't put it past the Americans to do that though. I was in the SS; the Russians will probably kill me. What am I to do?"

"First of all, keep your cool, and secondly don't tell anyone where you were born."

"But my papers!"

"You nut. You don't show them. In fact, we have to get rid of them right now, and then you say you lost them."

"And then what?"

"Well, we'll have to make up a story, convincing them that you were born in the Reich. It's lucky the Americans are lax and have not checked our papers yet."

Since Horst was from Berlin and knew the city, they decided that it would be safer if they picked an area in Berlin for Theo's home. Horst described the neighborhood, the names of the streets and other notable landmarks. After several tries, Theo remembered most things. He was still worried. "What if I forget something?"

"So you forget. Berlin is a big city, who remembers everything? Besides, you have been away for a few years, right?"

Theo was still scared.

The Russians did come. On the first day they took away over fifty, all SS. Now Theo was even more scared. The Americans now examined everyone's papers. When Theo did not produce any, he was told to come to the commandant's office the next morning. That night he could not sleep.

The next morning Horst seemed to be even more worried than Theo. "Remember the prisoner interrogations when you were fighting the partisans? This will be similar. Keep your cool, don't rush your answers, and for God's sake remember that you don't speak Russian. Be on guard, they will surely try to trick you."

Theo did not answer; he was too scared to talk. When it was time, he got up and walked to the administration building. After a short wait, he was called into the interrogation room. There were four officers, two American and two Russian. He was made to stand in front of the desk with a guard on either side of him. No time was wasted. After the camp commander had asked his name, the Russians took over. They spoke excellent German. At first the questions were general, birth date, birthplace, mother's name, her maiden name. Theo did well, he remembered all the dates and places he and Horst had discussed the day before. Right in the middle of a question one Russian turned to the other and said, in Russian, "This one we will hang." Theo understood perfectly, but this was just the type of tactic he had expected and thus he managed not to react. The questioning became more intense. The Russians, not being able to break him, became angry and abusive. At this point the camp commander decided enough was enough and dismissed Theo in spite of the protests of the Russians.

When Theo arrived back at the tent, Horst hugged him. "You're back, they let you go! What happened, tell me?"

Theo could not speak. Now the terrible emotional strain he'd been under overwhelmed him and he threw himself onto his bed, face down and just lay there.

Every day thereafter, Theo expected to be called back, but nothing happened. After a few weeks a large group, including Theo and Horst, were transferred to a work camp.

Although they had to work eight hours a day, their situation had improved dramatically. Now there was enough food and they lived in regular barracks. Best of all, there were no Russians to worry about.

Three months later both Theo and Horst were released. Horst was eager to get home to Berlin but Theo did not want to risk going through the Russian zone, and he was anxious to find his mother and the kids. After promising Horst to write to him soon, Theo headed for the railroad station and took the next train to Hanover where he knew his mother had a relative. In Hanover, he discovered that his mother and Sonja and Peet lived in the Russian zone. What to do? Finally he decided he would just go there; he had to find them. His relatives helped him to obtain some civilian clothes and he left the next day.

Surprisingly it was still quite easy to cross the border between East and West and Theo soon reached Fichtenwalde, where his family was. The reunion was very emotional. Everyone had a good cry and there were lots of hugs. His mother had found work as a secretary in the local village office and the kids went to school. They had a small but adequate apartment. Overall, things were not too bad.

Theo soon became restless. He could not find work that suited him in the small village, but also, he had been on his own too long and found it difficult to adjust being part of a family. It wasn't that he did not love them, he did, very much, and he was happy he'd found them. But there was this deep nagging that he could not explain. When an opportunity presented itself in the nearby town of Weiden, he took the job and moved there.

His wages were low, but since money did not buy much of anything, this did not matter. Being an apprentice he received food and lodging at his workplace. The food was poor but it was better than in the prisoner of war camp, and there was enough. His work consisted mainly in cleaning jobs in a printing plant, although officially he was designated as an apprentice in type setting. Soon he was given small jobs to set and, being smart, he quickly became proficient at setting type by hand. His boss even consented to show him how to use the linotype.

By sheer luck, he was able to buy an old bike and this allowed him to go home most weekends and spend Sundays with his mother and the kids. This for him was a much more manageable arrangement and the anxieties and irritability he experienced when living with his family disappeared. Life seemed to be settling into an acceptable routine.

Chapter 27

Theo worked in the printing plant for almost two years. Since it was a relatively small place, he learned not only how to set type but also had opportunity to work on the presses. At first he was only on the small Heidelberg platten press, but later he was allowed to try his hand on the bigger cylinder presses. Since he was eager and willing, he learned easily and soon was quite good at his job.

On weekends, he would go home and spend Sundays with his family. Sonja was now thirteen and was obviously growing up. At times Jutta worried about her. At the end of the war there had been a lot of rapes of German women by Russian soldiers, and even though there had not been any rapes for quite some time, Jutta still worried. But then, she worried about a lot of things. She worried about Peet, who was now nine and sometimes a bit rebellious, not that he had done anything bad so far. She worried about Theo, and always had. Most of all she worried about what the Russians might do. There was a rumor about that everyone would have to get new passports and would have to prove their birthplace, or place of residence, before the war. This put them again in danger of being sent back to Russia. Her story, that they came from eastern Prussia, would not stand up. What to do? There must be a way out. To return to the Soviet Union would mean being sent to Siberia and almost certain death. What could one do? Maybe this bit about the new passports was not true, best to wait. But if it was true then they should at least have some provisional plan. She discussed this at length with Theo and they agreed on several possible courses of action, little realizing how soon they would have to put one of these plans to use.

Chapter 28

Theo was back in the print shop working on an insurance policy. In fact, he was setting four pages in six point type by hand, because the Linotype had broken down yet again. His fingers were getting sore from handling the small letters. On top of that, he had just pied several lines of type that he now had to put back in the case and reset. When his boss called him to the phone it was a welcome break, but as soon as Theo heard his mother's voice he knew something was up.

"You need to come home now, Theo, do you understand?"

Theo understood. He walked out of the shop, not even stopping to get his things from his room, and got on his bike and left. He knew that he would not be back but he dared not to say anything to anyone.

He pedaled as fast as he could and made it home in just short of one hour. His mother had already packed a small amount of clothing. "We can only take the most necessary things," she explained to Theo. He put the backpack on his shoulders, his mother took the small suitcase, and they left for the railroad station, five kilometres away. Theo wondered how many railroad stations they had already been in. They always seemed to be associated with some form of disaster.

"We need passes if we want to use the train, Mom."

"Yes, I know. I got them."

"How?"

"I got them." She did not look at Theo.

He started to say something but then thought better of it and turned to Peet and Sonja. "Hey, you two; help Mom with the suitcase."

They got on the train to Berlin without incident, their permits seemingly being in order. At the Anhalter station in Berlin, they got off.

"We have to find a train that goes to a place near the border of the British sector. It's supposed to be easiest to get across there," Jutta said to Theo in a hushed voice. "I have some blank permits, which we can fill in with the appropriate place."

Theo was astonished. "Where did you get those."

"Well, if you must know, I traded the two sacks of potatoes and the sack of flour we had for them."

Theo was skeptical. "You were lucky to get them."

Jutta did not answer. She had been very lucky to get them. She kept looking at a small map. "We have to get to one of the villages near the border. From there we can walk across—if we are lucky."

"Do you know anything about the border, Mom?"

"Well, no. But what else can we do but try?"

"I have a friend here, in Berlin, Horst Walters, I'll talk to him." Theo had no trouble finding Horst.

"Theo, old buddy, how are you, you old bastard?" Horst grinned broadly and gave him a big hug. Theo was a bit embarrassed. "Hey, watch your language, Horst, this is my mother, oh, and the kids, Sonja and Peety."

Horst was surprised. "You always said you had a family. Shit, I'm sorry, I'll watch my language. I beg your pardon ma'am. Oh shit."

Jutta wasn't offended, she liked the bubbly young man. "It's okay, Horst, I understand."

Horst did not quite see what she understood, but as long as the old lady was not upset, it was fine with him.

After Theo had explained why they were in Berlin and what there plans were, Horst whistled thinly through his teeth. "So, you are running again. Well, you've had enough practice in the war. But I think this time I can be of some help. You see, I have this little business that takes me across the border not infrequently, and so far I have not been caught." He scratched his head. "I think the best thing would be if I come with you and lead you across. I don't think you'd find your way on your own, and it's no fun getting lost crossing the border.

Theo looked worried. "Is that not dangerous crossing with such a large group?"

Horst laughed. "Have you forgotten my luck. I'll be happy to take you across. It's the least I can do for my old SS buddy, what?" He gave Theo a nudge and laughed again. "Remember the old times, in Romania? Let's go to my place and work this out better." He took Sonja and Peet by the hand. "Come, we have to take a subway ride, but it isn't far."

Horst's place consisted of a second story room with a small kitchenette and a bathroom down the hall. They all piled in, Jutta and Sonja were offered the only two chairs, and the 'men' sat on the floor. Soon Horst had some cocoa ready and some buns. "Here, it isn't much, but you did not give me any warning."

"Not much!" Jutta exclaimed. "Where do you get such stuff in these times?"

Horst waved his hand. "Oh, its nothing, it comes with my business."

Jutta did not ask, but she could imagine what his business was. The black market was very active all over Europe.

Horst took control. "This is what we will do. First, it is late and you will all stay here for the night. I know it is cramped but we will manage. Second, I will find out when the train leaves for Magdeburg, that's where we have to get to first. From there it is only a short distance to the border. Third, I will decide when it's best to cross the border, that will probably be Sunday, day after tomorrow, but we'll see. How does that sound to you, Theo?"

"I guess it's okay, if you think that's best. But maybe we could go alone, you've done enough already."

"Nonsense, you'll just get lost and end up in a Russian prison. I'll see you across."

Jutta kept quiet. The young man seemed to know what he was doing and it was nice to let someone else do the worrying for a change.

Horst left and soon returned with the information that there was a train to Magdeburg every morning, just before ten o'clock. From there they could take a shuttle train to a village near the border.

"We'll cross there and come out of the forest near Helmsted in the British sector. It's a good spot, I've crossed there before," Horst said, pointing to a place on the map. "Now let's get some sleep. Tomorrow we'll have a day of rest, and Sunday morning we will leave."

Although they all went sightseeing the next day, the day dragged. Everyone was not only anxious to get going, but also apprehensive. Would they make it? What if they got caught? Theo could not shake an uneasy feeling that things would not work out. If they were caught they would very likely end up in Russia, and heaven only knew what their fate would be there. They spent another uneasy night, Jutta with Sonja sleeping in Horst's bed, Peet sleeping on the couch, and Theo and Horst struggling through the night with a couple of thin blankets on the floor.

Everyone was up early. They were at the station a good hour before the train left and had to wait on cold, hard benches, but finally they boarded the train and were off. In a couple of hours, they were in Magdeburg and soon found the shuttle to Hagen, near the border. Surprisingly, the train was almost full. There were several groups of well-dressed people, also some children. Theo concluded that they had been in church and were on their way home. They all boarded the train and arrived at Hagen without incident.

Horst, who had been silent and seemed pre-occupied, took Theo to the side. "Did you see those two cops on the train?" he whispered.

Theo was surprised. "What cops? I did not see any uniforms."

"Boy, are you simple. Of course they are not in uniform, but I can smell them, they are cops, you can bet your life on that, in fact you might have to." He chuckled. "I know how to outwit them. All of you go towards the village with the rest of the people and wait for me near the well by the Rathaus.

"And you, what will you do?" Theo asked.

"Oh, I will take a stroll to see if our friends follow, and if they do I will lead them up the proverbial garden path. You better get going, it's getting late." Horst gave Theo a light push and then briskly walked down the road towards the forest and border. 'What the heck is he doing?' Theo wondered. Then he saw the two men Horst had pointed out, heading in the same direction.

After about an hour Horst appeared, grinning. "I'm sure those two are still trying to find their way out of the forest. Let's go, we have several hours of walking to do and we don't want to get caught in the forest at night."

He took Peet by the hand and took the lead, Jutta with Sonja followed, and Theo brought up the rear. They left the village and, walking along a field path, soon reached the forest.

Here Horst stopped. "From here we have to be more careful. I will go ahead and I want you to follow me in single file. Be quiet, watch me, do what I signal you to do. Now, does anyone need to go to the bathroom?" Nobody moved. "Fine, then we carry on." He turned off the path and walked up a slight incline through the large trees. Everyone followed.

Soon Sonja whispered. "Mommy, mommy, I have to go, you know what."

Jutta came up beside her. "Number one?"

Sonja shook her head.

Jutta groaned. "Why now? Well, come on over there behind that tree, and hurry."

Sonja was near tears. "Here? I can't go here!"

Jutta's patience was wearing thin. "It's either here or nowhere; make up your mind."

Horst had heard the commotion and had come back. "You are making too much noise, what is it?"

"Oh, Sonja has to go."

"Well, make it quick, this area is sometimes patrolled."

Sonja disappeared behind the tree and reappeared in a few minutes. Horst was impatient. "Let's go," he whispered and quickly went ahead. They walked about ten minutes when Sonja again called her mother. "I have to go again." She had tears in her eyes. "I'm scared, Mommy."

Jutta gave her a hug. "It's alright sweetheart, it's okay, you just go behind a bush and I'll wait here."

In the next hour, Sonja had to go at least a half dozen times.

They had now walked about three hours and Horst decided to have a rest. "So far, so good. Let's all sit down, but be quiet. It's not that far anymore."

While they were sitting there, they suddenly heard a noise further down the slope. Horst motioned for everybody to lie down and then put his fingers to his lips. Soon two men appeared carrying automatic rifles over their shoulders. They were walking slowly and talking to each other, not paying much attention to their surroundings.

When they had passed, walking slowly about fifty feet down the slope, Horst whispered, "Let's go, straight ahead through those bushes, as fast and as quietly as you can. Jutta and Theo took the two youngsters by the hand and scampered up the slope. They were almost at the top when Peety slipped and caused some small stones to roll down. The noise was not great but to everyone it sounded like a thunder clap.

Horst yelled through the bushes, "Run, run as fast as you can. Keep running."

Suddenly there were several bursts of rifle fire and then a scream. All froze in their tracks.

"Take the kids and run, Mom, hurry. I'm going back for Horst, I think he's been hit."

Jutta was almost hysterical. "No, no, you can't go back!"

"For God's sake, Mom, don't waste time, run, run." Quickly he turned around and disappeared through the bushes.

Jutta hesitated a second and then took Peet and Sonja by the hand and ran as fast as she could to the border post, now only a few yards away.

When Theo emerged on the other side of the bushes, he saw Horst on the ground, trying to get up. He seemed to have some difficulty with his left leg. As Theo got closer, he saw that there was a lot of blood above the left knee. Down the slope he saw the two border guards scrambling up.

"Don't just stand there, come and help me!" Horst yelled at him. Theo got on Horst's left side and half assisted and half dragged him through the bushes and up the slope. It was evident that Horst was in a lot of pain and that he was loosing blood steadily. However, there was no way they could stop now. They had to make it to the border. Theo virtually carried Horst. They were only a few yards from the British border post when the guards burst through the bushes. One raised his rifle but decided not to shoot when he realized that Theo and Horst were practically on the border. The guards stood there a few minutes and then went back through the bushes.

As soon as Theo had Horst at the border post, the soldiers there compressed his wound with a large bandage and called for an ambulance. Although the ambulance arrived quite soon, Horst was getting very weak and drowsy. The ambulance attendants quickly put him on a stretcher, started an i.v., then placed him in the ambulance and left.

Theo watched the ambulance disappear and then went inside the guard house. Jutta was sitting on a wooden bench with Sonja on one side and Peet on the other. It was obvious that they had been crying.

With an assurance he did not feel Theo said, "He'll be all right, he's tough. We have to get into the town and find a place to stay." He found out from the German guards who were on duty with some English soldiers that transportation into Helmstedt was available and that there was a refugee camp there. Apparently there was a steady stream of people crossing over from the Russian zone.

After visiting Horst in the hospital and finding him in satisfactory condition, Theo thanked him, said goodbye, and then made arrangements for their further journey to the Mennonite refugee camp in Gronau, which turned out to be only a prolonged stop on a much longer journey that would eventually end in Canada.

Chapter 29

Theo stood on deck and watched the dock workers tie up the ship. It was amazing! He had actually arrived in Canada, he had actually made it. Even though it was two in the morning, he was not sleepy. He walked around on the deck, and when he came to the dock side, he noticed that the gang plank was out to the wharf and the gate was open. 'Strange,' he thought. 'Anybody could go on shore and nobody would know.' He stepped onto the gangway and looked around. He still could not see anybody. 'I bet somebody is watching from somewhere,' he thought. He walked to the wharf end of the gangway and again looked around, he still could not see anybody. Finally, he stepped onto the wharf and walked a few feet along the ship, still no one! 'This place is nuts, they must have some security or police around.' Finally he walked up and down the full length of the wharf several times, but nobody showed up. 'I guess these people don't care,' he thought and went back on ship.

The next day they were all processed through customs and then had to wait in a big hall for the train that was to take them to their final destination. Every person received twenty dollars for food during the train journey, and Jutta and Theo went to find a store. Sonja and Peet were instructed to stay with their suitcases and boxes and not to leave them even for a second. "There are always thieves around, and if you don't watch they will steal everything," admonished Jutta.

"Come on, Mom, let's go." Theo was impatient, not so much to find a store but to see the city in this new land.

"You two stay put," Jutta warned again and then joined Theo who was already on the street. They walked down a block where they found a small grocery store and went in.

Jutta could not believe that so much food could be just bought without food stamps, just for money, and such variety! They saw a big pile of oranges. As a child Theo had eaten oranges, but that was so long ago he could not even remember how they tasted.

"Mom, can we get some of these? I'm sure the kids would like to try them too. I don't think they have ever even seen one."

Jutta wasn't sure but Theo was already looking for a sales clerk. He found a man behind the counter, but how to ask? He could only speak a few words of English. He waved towards the oranges. "Buy, Apfelsinen, buy."

The man impatiently said something Theo could not understand. It did not sound English, not that it made any difference. Theo tried again but the man became quite annoyed. A man standing close by started to laugh. "He wants you to speak in French, this is Quebec you know." The man spoke perfect German.

"But I can't speak French, I can't even speak English. We just want to buy some oranges and some bread." Theo replied, happy to have found somebody who could speak his language.

Jutta joined them. "Would you be so kind and ask him to sell us some oranges and a loaf of bread?"

"Just take what you want and bring it to the counter. When he sees your money I'm certain his national fervor will not get in the way."

"You mean we just go and take what we want?" Jutta could not believe her ears. "Just take it?"

"There are some bags. You take what you want and pay for it at the counter here."

Jutta was still hesitant but Theo had already found a bag and was filling it with oranges. They also got some bread and a sausage and took everything to the counter. As the man had said, when the grocer saw the money in Jutta's hand, he added up the bill, gave her some change, and packed everything in a large bag.

Not until years later did Theo understand what the language business was all about.

Chapter 30

In the afternoon, they finally boarded the train and left Quebec City as the sun was setting. It was a lovely summer evening, with the air heavy and fragrant, and a slight haze forming over the river. The silhouette of the city stood out against the sky, some clouds, painted orange by the setting sun, formed a flashy background. It was a beautiful picture. Theo settled back in his seat and observed the scenery as the train left the city, but soon it was too dark to see anything and he stretched out his legs and closed his eyes. He felt nostalgic and remembered another train ride when he was a boy and the Soviets had sent them east. He knew that the outcome of the present journey would be quite different, but what would this new country be like? Judging by the customs officials, the people in this country were not very friendly, and that man in the store, he was something else! 'Well, let us hope the people at the other end of the country, where we are headed, are different,' he thought, turning his attention to the landscape as the train traveled west. But it was too dark and soon he fell asleep.

When Theo awoke the next morning, he was amazed at the changed landscape. Nothing but bush, green dense bush, with tinges of yellow and red on some trees, interspersed with innumerable lakes. Endless bush and lakes, and no houses! What a strange land this was. What would their destination be like? He imagined all kinds of scenarios, but in the end decided that he could not conjure up what was coming, and further more, he could not change it.

During the next day they passed through what seemed endless prairie. In Winnipeg they had a lengthy stop and then continued through some more flat land, at times slightly undulating, and mostly acres of grain, sunflowers and other vegetation, in endless fields. Because it was summer and dry the train stirred up a lot of dust. Everything in the car was covered with dust; he could even taste it. When it was announced that they were nearing their destination, Theo was relieved, even though he could not imagine where people lived in this vast expanse of steppe.

Chapter 31

They had finally arrived. The journey had been an adventure for Theo through such a varied and enormous country. At the station they were picked up by a man in overalls, their guarantor, who had promised that he would have work for them for a year, and that they would not become a burden to the Canadian government. After the greetings and introductions, they all piled into a beat-up old Ford.

"My son will bring the luggage in the pick-up," the farmer said, and without any further explanation started the car and drove off through a very small village and then along a paved road. Soon they turned onto a gravel road. They passed a few small houses but otherwise nothing much could be seen as it was now quite dark. After about an hour they arrived at an old but well kept-up house.

"Here we are," the farmer said as he got out.

Theo wondered where 'here' was, and why the man was so reticent, as he had hardly spoken during the trip. Was he unhappy to have them, or were all the people in this country like this?

As Theo was getting out of the car, a large, obese woman came out of the house. Beaming, she rushed towards Jutta and gave her a big hug and kiss. "I am so glad you are here, come in, come, come." She hugged Peet and Sonja and then came towards Theo. "My, you are a big one," she exclaimed as she gave him a hug. Theo felt awkward but she did not notice.

"Come, come, everybody in. You must be hungry, supper is all ready." She gently pushed Theo and the kids towards the door. What a site presented itself! Theo had never seen so much food. They all stood around awkwardly.

"Come now, don't be shy or you'll remain hungry." Mrs. Bartsch gave a big laugh as she directed them to the oak table in the dinning room.

After dinner, they were taken to a small cabin close to the main farm house where they would live. The cabin had three rooms: a large kitchen and two other rooms with beds. Jutta thought it was just fine and they could live there quite comfortably. Soon they settled into a routine. Jutta helped in the house, Sonja and Peet went to school, and Theo helped on the farm. His main job was to look after the livestock. Because he had no experience in this kind of work, he occasionally made mistakes. Mr. Bartsch would never say anything but would grumble and go and correct whatever Theo had done wrong. It was an embarrassing situation for Theo, but since any attempt at friendliness had been repulsed by Mr. Bartsch, there was nothing further that Theo could do.

He mentioned the situation to his mother, who was sympathetic, but had no solution. "These are good people, Theo, and they have helped us a lot. I know how you feel, but please try not to aggravate the situation."

Theo tried his best and in time made fewer mistakes, but Mr. Bartsch's attitude did not change. In fact, it got worse. One day Theo had reached the end of his rope and confronted him. "What is it that I have done that has set you against me?"

Mr. Bartsch was quite startled. "Against you? I'm not against you! It's your highfaluting airs that you put on, that's what's wrong, not my attitude. You think that because you're educated and I'm not that you are so much better."

Theo could not believe what he was hearing. "I never thought that I am better than anyone, that's ridiculous! And more educated, that's even more ridiculous, I have never thought that!"

"Well! Now you think I am ridiculous, do you? I have given you a home for nothing and you treat me like that?"

Theo realized that he should keep quiet but he could not contain himself. "For nothing? What about the work I am doing, and what about all the work my mother does, is that nothing?"

"You don't have to stay here," Mr. Bartsch was getting quite red in the face. "You don't have to stay here."

Theo started to say something but then thought better of it and went into the house. The next morning, after writing a short note to his mother, he left.

Chapter 32

Now that Theo had left the farm, he felt as if a big weight had been lifted from him. He felt free, totally free. He realized he had left behind some unhappy people, such as his mother and Mrs. Bartsch, but that could not be helped and he hoped that his mother would understand. Having reached the highway, he turned west, his somewhat heavy and tattered suitcase in his right hand and holding his left thumb up in true North American style.

He had walked for over an hour when a car stopped and gave him a ride to the next town. "Where are you headed, young man?" the driver of the very nice looking car asked.

"Sorry, my English not much," Theo hesitantly brought forth. "Going west, maybe Vancouver."

"Well, I can take you to the next town only." "That okay, thank you," Theo said. It was early afternoon when they arrived in the little village and he was getting hungry. Fortunately, he had packed some bread and a sausage. He was looking for a place to eat his lunch when he spotted the railroad station. 'There should be seats inside,' he thought, and waked over there. A few people were sitting in the waiting room, but there was lots of space for him and he sat down on one of the benches. A feeling of melancholy overcame him. Had he done the right thing? After all, he had deserted his family. He tried to shake off the guilt, but doubts persisted. There was no way he could go back. 'So you better figure out what you are going to do now,' he told himself.

He had heard that there were Mennonites out west in Vancouver. Maybe he should go there. In the big city, he might also find work. Yes, he would go there! After finding out that he could not afford a train ticket, he tried hitchhiking again. He walked along the highway and stuck his thumb out every time a vehicle came by, but no luck. When it got dark, he found an old shed near the road and slept there. The next morning he got a ride to the next town. He walked into a coffee shop and ordered a cup of coffee and toast. At the counter next to him sat a man who seemed very talkative. "Well young man, where to?" he asked Theo. "Who I, I no speak much English," Theo stumbled. The man laughed. "That's okay, many here like that. Where are you headed?" "Headed?" Theo looked puzzled. "Yea, where are you going?" "Ach so, west, maybe Vancouver." The man rubbed his chin. "Are you driving?" This time Theo smiled. "No, no, haf no car." The man looked thoughtful. "I drive a big rig, I suppose I could give you a ride. Would you mind riding in a truck?"

"Ach no, truck very fine."

"Well then, let's go. It's a long way to Vancouver." After they had gotten into the truck and were driving on the highway, the man turned to Theo. "I'm Chuck. Tell me your name and why you are bumming around on the road."

Again Theo looked puzzled. "Bumming round? I don't understand. Ja, ich Theo, that my name."

"Well Theo, I guess I will have to keep it slow and simple. You know, walking here, not doing anything."

"Ach so. Ja, long story that iss."

"Go ahead, tell me. We have time." With some difficulty, and using his hands as an aid, Theo told him.

"Wow, that's some story. And now you're at loose ends, eh? Well, I am on my way to Vancouver, and if you want I'll take you there."

It did not make much difference to Theo were he went, and Vancouver was probably better than other places.

"You think I can find there work?"

"Who knows, but more likely there than anywhere else."

'My luck is improving,' Theo thought and began to relax. They talked about this and that, while Chuck patiently taught Theo some English. Theo was warming to this man, who seemed to have taken a liking to him. After a while, they saw mountains in the distance.

"See that?" Chuck pointed. "Those are the Rockies, some of the biggest mountains in Canada are found there. We will go past some of them."

"They looks beautiful," Theo exclaimed as they came closer, truly impressed by the grand vista before him.

When it got dark they pulled into a motel. "We'll get a unit here and tomorrow we will continue to Vancouver. We should get there in the afternoon," the truck driver said.

Theo got all flustered. "I have not much money. Can I sleep in truck?"

Chuck laughed. "Not to worry, we sleep in the same room. The motel is on me."

"On me? What does mean?" Theo looked puzzled.

"It means . . . oh hell, never mind. Come." Chuck jumped out of the cab and there was nothing left for Theo to do but to follow. After they had registered they went to their motel unit—a very nice big room with two beds and a big bathroom, which Theo eyed with great interest.

"Go ahead, have a bath if you want. I have to look after the truck and fill up. Be back in five." Chuck waved and went out the door.

"Can't understand what he mean, but bath sound good," Theo muttered, already undressing.

After supper, for which Chuck paid, they walked back to the motel. It was a balmy, peaceful prairie night, with the big sky full of stars—just the type to put Theo in a melancholy mood and reminded him of his childhood and their village in the Ukraine. He could not remember ever feeling more lost than he did in this vast seemingly endless land. Maybe he should have stayed on the farm and put up with the abuse. Well, it was too late now and he would have to find some way to fend for himself. What a dope he had been. He should have guessed what he was letting himself into. Well, he would have to reign in his emotions and be more careful in the future.

Both were tired and when they arrived at their unit, they went to bed. After a while, Theo fell asleep and only awoke when he heard someone moving around. He sat up, startled. "What the ..." then he realized where he was. He sat up, rubbing the sleep from his eyes. He could hear Chuck in the bathroom and quickly jumped out of bed and dressed. What would today bring? They would probably reach Vancouver— and then what? After they had eaten breakfast, which Chuck again had paid for, they were on their way. After a while, they came to a range of quite high mountains. 'Must be the mountains I saw earlier,' he thought. Just as Theo thought things were finally going his way, the truck's motor started to sputter, and Chuck could just get the rig off the road when the engine stopped.

Chuck punched the steering wheel with his fist. "What damned luck." He climbed out of the cab still swearing. "I must find a phone. No use you hanging around. Try to get another ride. With luck you might reach Vancouver yet."

Theo did not want to leave Chuck at first, but Chuck convinced him that it was best. "You can't help me here, in fact, you would be an additional problem, so you might as well go."

It did not take Theo long to get another ride with a pleasant elderly couple, but they only took him as far as Revelstoke. It was already getting dark, and Theo was tired. He did not want to spend any money on lodgings, so he found a secluded spot under a tree near the river and slept there. He awoke early, stiff and cold. During the night he had heard trains going by not too far away. 'Maybe I can hop a fright there,' he thought. As he was getting his things together, he heard another train coming. He ran in the direction that the sound was coming from and saw the train as soon as he came over the river bank. As luck would have it, the train slowed at the curve, and Theo managed to get onto a flatcar. It wasn't the best travel mode, but since it was not raining, it was okay.

Chapter 33

By luck (or was it God's providence?) he arrived in what he thought was Vancouver some sixteen hours later. He had not eaten for about twenty-four hours and felt almost sick from hunger. When the train slowed and he saw houses, Theo jumped off and walked to the nearest street where he found a small store and bought some bread and cheese. After he had eaten, he asked for directions at a gas station. He found out that the place he was in was called New Westminster, and that Vancouver was ten to fifteen kilometres away. Fortunately, there were busses and soon he found himself in the large city he had heard so much about.

It did not take Theo long to get his bearings in Vancouver. The YMCA, to which he was directed by another friendly gas station attendant, provided a good and cheap temporary place to sleep. He bought some more food in a corner grocery: Bread, a sausage, some milk, some fruit, and mostly ate in his room. Even so, he realized that he would have to find work soon or his money would run out. Through the phone book he found out that there was a Mennonite church in Vancouver and decided he would go to church there on Sunday. What better way to make some contacts? Maybe there would even be a Mennonite business-man who would give him work. It was worth a try.

Theo did not find a job that Sunday, but he did meet some young people who eventually became his friends and he did, after a while with their help, find work. It came just in time too, as funds by now were very low. The job was nothing grand, mind you, just some manual work, but it brought in badly needed cash. While looking for work he experienced some unpleasantness, to be sure. At one place, he was told that there was no work there for lousy, bastard DPs, and at another that Germans were not welcome.

When he received his first pay, he rented a basement room. A small room it was, but what a luxury. His own place!

He wrote his mother and asked her to come to Vancouver where the opportunities for work were much better than in the prairies. At first she was reluctant, claiming that she first had to fulfil their obligations to the Bartsches. In time, however, Jutta, with Sonja and Peet, did settle in Vancouver. She found work, at first as a domestic, but later obtained a job in a small bakery. Theo visited them often, but he continued to live on his own.

Because he was restless and found his job not terribly fulfilling, Theo started to take night school. To begin with, it was just a class in English. Then, at the suggestion of his teacher, he enrolled in a program to complete his high school. In the meantime, he found a job in a printing plant, where the work was much more stimulating. To top it all off, he found a girlfriend! Needless to say, his night school began to suffer somewhat but his social life improved dramatically. Theo was sort of in love although his affection wasn't all that strong. He was not very emotional and maybe he was not capable of stronger feelings. He certainly had difficulty expressing them. One evening he simply said, "We should get married." Laura said, "If you think so."

Laura's family had also immigrated to Canada after the war, and also came from a Mennonite colony in the Ukraine. This immediately gave them something in common, although they did come from different areas in the old country. They both liked to socialize and soon had a small circle of friends—mainly young recent immigrants of Mennonite background.

Similar to Theo, Laura had only a minimal amount of education, but she was younger than he and had enrolled in the local high school. She went to school for two years but did not complete high school because it was thought more important to earn some money and pay off the "Reiseschuld"—the money they owed for the trip from Europe.

At age sixteen, Laura had left her family and had gone to Vancouver, where she worked as a domestic, since she had no other training. She lived with an 'English' family and on her day off would go to the "Maedchenheim", the girl's home run by the Vancouver Mennonite Church. Here a number of girls congregated, had fellowship, and exchanged news. This was also where the boys showed up—not inside the home, this was not allowed, but on the street, waiting for the girls to come out. This is also where Theo and Laura first met.

Once they decided to get married, things progressed quite fast. There was no objection from their respective parents, and Laura's mom organized everything very efficiently.

The wedding was a traditional Mennonite type wedding with a church service, then lots of food, which was served in the church basement. There was no honeymoon because of a shortage of funds. They moved into a small apartment they had rented before the wedding.

Since both worked, they soon saved enough money for a down payment on an old house. Laura was thrilled. Theo was happy too, but lately his restlessness had returned and prevented him from fully enjoying their success. He could not quite understand why he felt the way he did. He wasn't unhappy and yet something seemed to be amiss, something was lacking. Try as he might, Theo could not fathom what it could be. For want of a better solution, he spent more time on his night-school and correspondence courses. As usual, he did quite well. He finished all his grade 10 courses and was now ready to start grade 11. If he continued at this rate, he could finish high school in less than two years, maybe even in one year if he worked extra hard.

He had, of course, not counted on any diversions. When Laura told him that she was pregnant, he knew that his plans would be altered. He was happy and excited about the pregnancy. He had all kinds of images about himself and his son. Theo could not remember much about his relationship with his own father and therefore assumed that it had not been close. Right there he resolved that he, Theo, would have a close, understanding, and lasting bond with his son. He would see to that. It never occurred to him that the child could be a girl. The expectation of a child made Theo work extra hard and by the time Sarah was born, Theo was close to finishing grade twelve. The birth of the child was for Theo a very happy event. When Laura reminded him that he had wanted a son, Theo vehemently denied ever having thought that.

"I can't understand how you can say that sort of thing, Laura. I know that one can't predict the sex of the child anymore than one can decide beforehand what sex the child should be. I don't know why you would think me that ignorant."

Laura laughed at his indignation. "Oh Theo, stop carrying on like that. You're just an old grouch. Come and give me a kiss."

"Oh, all right. But whatever you say, I think it's best to have a girl first, so there." 'She's a sweet one,' he thought as he headed for his little study to work on his courses. Lately the old thoughts of becoming a doctor had surfaced again. He remembered his friend, Wanjka, and the discussions about their future under that old willow. 'I wonder what Wanjka is doing now,' he thought. 'I wonder if he's even alive.' So many people had died in the war, especially young men. He remembered Trudy and became quite melancholy. It was strange that he still remembered him so vividly. He turned to his studies and worked late into the night. When he went to bed, Laura was already asleep.

Chapter 34

Now that he had made the big decision and had enrolled at the university for pre-med courses, he was plagued by doubts. Had he made the right choice? Laura was again pregnant and his mother had called him a fool for giving up a good job and going on a wild goose chase, as she had called it. Only Laura encouraged him. "We will manage somehow, with God's help."

Theo wished he had her simple faith and trust in God. Although he had been baptized and had joined the Mennonite church before their marriage, he had many doubts and was not as strong a Christian as Laura. In fact, if it came right down to it, he was probably no Christian at all. For Laura's sake, he attended church at times and accepted her statements about God and the church without argument. He marveled at Laura's deep and unquestioning faith, and in comparison, felt inadequate.

Now that the decision to go to university had been made, he was eager to get going. He could hardly wait for classes to begin. It had been so long since he had attended a regular class, he could not imagine what it would be like. The grade thirteen he had taken at night school last year allowed him to register in second year at university. He had picked his courses as recommended for pre-med, bought some books, and had the schedule for his classes—he was all set. With some unease he was aware that taking pre-med did not guarantee acceptance into a medical school. Even doing well in pre-med was no guarantee, but there was nothing more he could do. He was determined to give it his best shot, the rest was in God's hands, as Laura would say.

During the summer, Laura was delivered of her second child. It was a boy and, after some prolonged discussions, they named him Paul Jacob. Even though Theo was immensely proud, as usual he had difficulty expressing his feelings and Laura complained that he showed little interest in the baby.

Soon the day arrived when Theo, with some trepidation, attended his first class. Doubts assailed him. Would he make it? What if he would not? All that wasted time and money! How young all the other students were. All day he had doubts and anxiety: Could he do it? Was his patched-up previous education enough? He brushed these thoughts aside and again decided to try as hard as he could. He certainly would not give up easily. The classes he had selected were a mixture of those courses required for pre-med, such as English, chemistry, and zoology, and some others he thought he could easily pass, such as Russian, German, and, for fun and interest, mathematics. On his first day of German, his teacher discovered that Theo had some knowledge of the German language and promptly transferred him to a higher class. No amount of arguing helped. He was stuck with a German philosophy course, which would in time prove to be his most difficult subject. Strangely, no one cared that his Russian was quite fluid, and that he was enrolled in a beginner's course. Theo was happy to be left with at least one easy course, because this, in part, allowed him to end up with an acceptable grade level at the end of the year, as his perfect mark in Russian made up for his rather average grade in his German course. Even so, he had hoped for a better overall grade, as acceptance into medical school depended very much on good marks.

With Laura's encouragement and reassurance, Theo managed to adjust to classes reasonably well. The first few weeks were hard, especially when he found out that grade thirteen night school was in no way comparable to first year university and that he was not well prepared for entrance into second year. With grim determination and long hours of study, he soon caught up and, in many cases, surpassed the other students.

His biggest problem turned out to be money. Laura had started work, but with two small kids she could only work part-time. Without any special training, she could only command a small wage. Theo continued to work as much as he could. As a printer he had no difficulty getting work, and having in the past made some friends in the industry, he easily got good work at times that suited his scedule. However, with all the work he tried to squeeze in, there was never enough time, even though he had tried to arrange his classes so that as much of the day as possible was left for work.

There were some gaps in his timetable during the day, which Theo tried to use for study in the library, but the library was usually full and with the many students around he often found concentration difficult. He found that he could study much better at home where he had a quiet room and where Laura made sure that the kids kept quiet and did not bother him. After a while, he found a job where he could work afternoons. He started at four and worked until midnight. When he got home he would study for an hour or two and then go to bed, totally exhausted.

"You are driving yourself too hard. How long can you keep this up?" Laura would say to him with a worried look. "Look at the time, it is way past midnight."

"I'm sorry, Laura. I know I neglect you and the kids, but I have to do this, I have too!" He hugged her silently. She was a peach; he began to realize that without her total support and help it would not be possible for him to reach his goal.

During the summer break, Theo worked full time and took overtime or extra work at other shops when he could get it. They managed to get a few free days and went camping. It was a huge success, and everyone, especially the kids, enjoyed themselves and came back home in good spirits.

In September, Theo started his third year of university, hopefully his last pre-medical year. If he had to take another pre-med year, there would be even more financial difficulties. He had to make certain that his marks were good enough to be accepted into medical school. He cut back the number of hours he worked, but this of course reduced his earnings. It was a difficult balancing act. Sometimes Theo had great doubts that he was doing the right thing. What if he did not get in? What if later he did not make it through med school? When he mentioned his worries to Laura, she would gently scold him. "Don't be silly, we both know you'll make it. You're just wasting time and energy with your silly worries. Come and give me a hug." They would embrace and Theo felt encouraged by Laura's faith in him. In her quiet way, she was a tower of strength and he again knew that without her help he could not possibly make it.

Theo applied to medical school at the beginning of the term, but he knew that there would be no answer before December, and it could be as late as next August before he would know if he was accepted or not. To be on the safe side, he applied to three different universities, but his preference was Midwest University, a small university in an equally small western town. It was a compromise; life would be cheaper than in a big city, and there was work available for both, but the medical school had only a fair reputation.

It was a great Christmas present when on the 23rd of December the letter, informing him that he was accepted at Midwest, arrived. At least it was a present for Theo; Laura had mixed feelings about moving. She did not like to leave the friends they had made, and most of all, she knew she would miss the church, but if it had to be, it had to be. She would move and make the best of it.

The rest of the term went quickly. Theo maintained his good marks and was assured of a place at Midwest. During the summer, he again worked as much as possible, taking off only a few days for a much needed camping holiday, which the kids enjoyed immensely.

Finally moving day arrived. Laura had already rented a small house through a rental agency. Theo wasn't happy to rent a place without seeing it first, but since they could not afford to go there just to look, they would have to take the risk. As it turned out the rental agency described the place quite accurately. It wasn't big and it wasn't new, but it was adequate, and the nice little back yard was a bonus.

They had a few days to settle in before Theo needed to register. On September 4, 1957, a Monday, Theo registered in medical school at Midwest University and thus started a new career. He was almost thirty years old, the oldest student in his class.

Chapter 35

The first day was filled with meeting some of the faculty and getting lab group assignments and an orientation, but on the second day, the real work started. The morning was filled with anatomy and physiology classes and the whole afternoon was reserved for the dissection lab. While the classes were remarkable for the large amount of material presented, it was the dissection lab that made everyone a bit anxious. What was it like to cut up a human body? Where did the bodies come from anyway? And what if it was someone you had known in the past, or a relative even? Imagination ran wild. In the afternoon the time had come to separate the men from the boys as Theo's new friend and classmate, Walter, put it.

"I hear that each year a few quit because they can't take the lab," Walt said as they walked toward the lab building.

"You mean they just leave because of that? That won't happen to me." Theo could not believe that someone would just quit like that. He certainly would not, not after all that work and worry.

Walt was not quite as certain. "Well, I don't know. I hope I'll be okay. Anyway, here we are, soon we'll know."

They entered the large clean dissecting lab with its strong smell of formaldehyde.

"What's that awful smell?" Walter wanted to know.

"It's the stuff that's used to preserve the bodies," Theo whispered as the instructor came in. "And it's not awful, it's a nice, clean smell."

Walt stared at him. "You must be batty. Clean smell, my ass." He wanted to say more but the instructor demanded their attention. "Good afternoon, gentlemen. My name is Dr. Truber. I will be your main instructor, but others will assist me or will give special demonstrations in the dissection of certain organs, such as the brain, for instance. You are expected to behave as gentlemen at all times. Those that cannot do so are really not welcome here. Any questions?"

No one moved. After a brief pause, he continued. "Well, no need to waste time. Open your tables please."

Slowly each group of six students opened the metal covers of their dissecting table. On each table lay a body, face down, arms at the side. Some were female but most were male. Dr. Truber let his eyes sweep the room. No student moved. Most had a somber expression on their face, but some looked pale, almost green. Dr. Truber smiled. The discomfort of the students gave him a certain sense of superiority. Not that he had an inferiority complex, not at all, but it was evident that, for the time being at least, he was the only one in the lab that was completely at ease. He gave a small cough to gain the students' attention. "Well then, gentlemen, before you is a body in the prone position. You will start your dissection at the upper back and expose the large muscles of the back: the Trapezius and the Latisimus dorsi on each side. If you can expose even a part of these muscles today, you have done well. Please note the fatty layer under the skin, even in thin individuals, and the small nerves, the thin white strings, as they emerge from the muscular layer on their way to the skin." He slowly walked along the tables, stopping here and there and encouraging the students to start.

In Theo's group there were only five, three other male students and one female. One of the students stepped up to the table and mumbled, "I guess we should start," but he made no attempt to do so. All had come a little closer and were staring down at the thick, somewhat tanned skin of the body of a middle-aged male. 'Wonder who he was,' Theo thought. He had a strong urge to ask the instructor, but didn't as they had been told that the bodies must remain anonymous, and any attempt to find their identity would be frowned upon and might bring unpleasant consequences, such as suspension. It occurred to Theo that he was probably the only one who had seen a dead body before. As no one seemed eager to start, Theo picked up the knife and made an incision in the skin as they had been instructed in the lecture that morning. As soon as the first incision was made, everyone came to life. They all peeled off bits of skin, showing each other various structures. 'It's a good group,' Theo thought, 'I've been lucky.'

The next day Theo heard that two students had quit. Apparently they could not stomach the dissections.

Soon Theo was totally immersed in his studies. There was so much to learn, so much to memorize, even though the first year consisted of only three subjects: anatomy, physiology, and biochemistry. Each of these, of course, also included extensive lab work.

As money was always a problem, Theo had to squeeze in some work at the local print shop. Fortunately, the pay was good, but it was difficult to arrange his schedule so that he would have adequate time for study. Laura was a tremendous help; not only did she work, but she made his study time easier by keeping the kids quiet and out of his way. When he had time to think about the kids, Theo would feel guilty, thinking that he did not spend enough time with them. Since he did not know how to change things, he would just try to suppress any thoughts about this problem, but he could not always do so, and then he would become irritable. Laura suggested that he talk to the children and explain why he could not be with them much, but Theo's reluctance or inability to express his feelings made it impossible for him to do so.

In the end, the year went reasonably well. While Theo did not get the first class he had set as his goal, he did place in the top ten.

During the summer, Theo found more work in the local print shop and also some part time work in the neibouring town. For a while he worked twelve, and sometimes sixteen hours a day, but the stress proved too much and after five weeks he gave up the part time job. As in past summers, they took a few days, a long weekend, for a holiday. When September arrived, Theo was happy to start second year.

Second year was not that much different from first year. Instruction was mainly in the classroom. Only near the end of second year were a few clinics held in the hospital.

The summer was again mainly work. One significant event was the visit of Theo's mother. Days before the visit, Laura had baked and cleaned and worried. 'Will everything be okay? Will your mother be satisfied?' Theo laughed. "You fuss like an old hen. Relax, Mom is not a dragon. Everything will be fine." But Laura still worried.

In the end, the visit turned out to be quite pleasant. The kids were happy to see their Oma, and Oma was happy to see them all.

Chapter 36

The summer was drawing to a close and Theo prepared to start third year, the year when much more practical work would be done, and most of his time would be spent at the hospital. There would still be classes and lectures, but they related more to clinical matters such as diagnosis and treatment. Furthermore, there would only be two weeks off, and those not necessarily in the summer. In third and fourth year they were classed as Student-Interns and were, as a courtesy, called doctors, although they had not yet graduated.

Theo was eager to get started. Even though the last two years had gone well, they had consisted mainly of science such as anatomy, biochemistry, physiology, pathology, pharmacology, and some classroom instruction in clinical subjects. Only at the end of second year, had there been some practical clinical stuff, and the odd patient to look after. This year he would actually be assigned to wards and see patients.

He looked back at the summer just passed. Laura and he had worked most of the time, but even though they could only squeeze in a few days of camping, this time off had been great fun. They had gone to a lake, the weather had co-operated, and the kids had been good. Theo had a warm feeling in his chest when he thought about his children. 'I have been really lucky,' he thought, 'they get so little, and yet they're happy, and Laura too. Without her I would not make it.' And, of course, his mother's visit had been great.

He shook his head. 'Enough of day dreaming!' He had to get ready for tomorrow, when he had to be at the hospital by seven in the morning.

Theo arrived at the hospital early. Soon others came and he was happy to see and greet some of his classmates. In spite of his eagerness to see patients, the day was mainly spent in the classroom. They received their assignments and schedules and in the afternoon went to their assigned wards for orientation. Theo started in pediatrics, then after two month, he would move to surgery, a subject more to his liking.

The head nurse took them around the ward. She was a plump, jolly type, well suited for a kids ward, Theo thought. The ward was large, with two big areas of twelve beds each, and several rooms containing either two or four beds. Three rooms with only one bed were used mainly as isolation wards.

There were several children with cancers, including leukemia, a whole bunch with croup or pneumonia, and others with weird hereditary diseases. Theo found pediatrics depressing and had long ago decided to specialize in surgery, but for now that was far away. For the next two months it had to be pediatrics.

He noticed a cute but somewhat pale girl of about five or six years in one of the beds. "What is the matter with that one?" he asked the head nurse, who had informed them that she liked to be called Mrs. Stoker.

"You mean Jenny? She has leukemia, she's not doing well. The large towel on her arm is to warm the area so that the veins will dilate. We're having difficulty getting an i.v. and she needs a transfusion."

Theo was sorry he had asked. "Thank you," he mumbled.

They continued on and saw several other equally horrible cases. 'I'm lucky my kids are healthy,' Theo thought. He was glad when it was time to go home.

The next day Theo familiarized himself with his patients. Five children were assigned to his care. He had to do a complete history, write daily progress notes, and work out a plan of investigation and treatment, which had to be discussed with the attending doctor in each case before any action was taken.

Of his five patients, three were routine asthmas or pneumomias, and the other two were quite complex cases. The two year old with multiple fractures at various stages of healing was obviously a battered child that had been there for three months and still was not totally recovered, and probably never would. He would retain the weakness now present on his right side and could also remain somewhat retarded. Theo examined him carefully; the previously described weakness on the right side was unmistakable. The child seemed lethargic and never seemed to smile or cry. Again, Theo had to think of his children. So many things could happen to a child; he should thank God that his children had so far been spared. 'What crazy thoughts I am having.' He shook his head. 'I better concentrate on my work.'

The other unusual case Theo had was a six-year-old boy with a large raised, very purplish area covering a large part of his right face. In addition, the child was grossly retarded, or rather severely mentally challenged, as the new terminology went. Collectively his abnormalities were called Sturge-Webber Syndrome, a congenital condition. He was admitted here because of pneumonia, which did not yet seem to respond to treatment. There had been debate earlier on whether this child should be treated at all, or whether one should let him die. When someone pointed out that the withholding of antibiotics would not guarantee that the child would die, and that his handicaps might get even worse if his lungs were also damaged, it was decided to give him full treatment.

Theo was ready to go home when an urgent admission, a five-year-old girl, arrived on the ward. Since nobody else was around, Theo had to do the admission history. Even with his lack of experience, he realized that this child was seriously sick and called the attending doctor, who informed him that a pediatrician was on the way as the suspected diagnosis was meningitis. Dr. Hardy, the pediatrician, arrived a short time later. Theo introduced himself and together they went to see the child.

"What do you make of this case?" Dr. Hardy asked.

"Well sir, the admitting diagnosis is meningitis."

"Yes, I know that," Dr. Hardy said impatiently. "I want to know what you think."

"Well, ah, the child is very sick." Then suddenly he remembered the blotches on the girl's skin. "It could be meningococcal meningitis, sir."

"Yes, very good, Dirks. Supposing it is?"

"She, ah, could die, sir?" Theo was now on very shaky ground as this was the first case of meningitis he had ever seen.

"Your damned right she could die, Dirks. In fact she is very likely to die, and soon." Theo was shocked at this abruptness but kept his mouth shut.

They had arrived at the little girl's bedside. She now looked a lot sicker. The skin blotches were much more pronounced. An i.v. had been started and antibiotics were being administered.

After a quick examination of the child, Dr. Hardy walked back to the nursing station. Theo, not knowing what was expected of him, followed. After writing some orders on the chart, Dr. Hardy turned to Theo. "I want you to remember this case. This is a classic case of Meningococcal Meningitis. Only very early treatment with large doses of antibiotics can help. Even then the prognosis is bad." He was silent for a moment, then said quietly, "This girl is not likely to survive. Do you have children?" When Theo nodded, he continued. "Wash your hands carefully, and change your clothes before you touch your children, this condition is very contagious." He got up. "I have to go and talk to the parents." 'I guess he is not so bad,' Theo mused. 'I've judged him prematurely and wrongly.'

Even though Theo had realized that the little girl was very sick, he was still shocked. He felt he could not go home before he knew the outcome. He phoned Laura to tell her that he would be late and then returned to the girl's bed. She was visibly worse. When the parents arrived Theo returned to the nursing station and tried to study, but could not maintain his concentration. At 19:40 hours the little girl died. On his way home, Theo again remembered Trudy's death. 'It is strange,' he thought, 'that at times like these I always remember him.' He wept.

Theo was happy when the rotation in pediatrics was over. It had been difficult for him. Every day there was a new tragedy that most of the time could not be resolved. He found it very stressful to see children die. It seemed that he was less able to deal with this than some of his colleagues, who seemed to take a child's illness or death in stride. Was he too sensitive? In any case, he was happy to move on to his next rotation—surgery.

Chapter 37

Christmas was over. They had found enough money to visit Theo's mother. Sonja and Peet had been as happy about the visit as had Theo, Laura, and the children. They had all spent a quiet but very nice Christmas Eve, and had gone to church on Christmas Day. On Boxing Day, some of their old friends had dropped by, and then it had been time to go back. Since Theo was now on the surgical rotation, he only had a few days off and was due back at the hospital the next morning. He arrived at the hospital just in time for morning rounds. The first case at rounds was a forty-nineyear-old woman with recurrent cancer of the bowel. She lay in bed, staring straight ahead, apparently not aware of her visitors. She was emaciated. Her abdomen, even seen through the covers, was visably distended. The attending doctor, Dr. Greyfield, waved off the student who was about to present the patient's history and motioned for the other students to follow him. They continued their rounds and saw several more patients, and some students were asked to present and discuss these cases. When rounds were done, they all went to the small classroom on the ward.

"Tell us about your patient now, Chris," Dr. Greyfield said when they were seated. "From the beginning, but make it brief."

"Well, sir," Chris was fumbling with the chart, "she had surgery six months ago, carcinoma of the sigmoid, with some positive lymph nodes, and now she's full of cancer."

Greyfield smiled. "That's certainly brief, Chris, but it'll do for now. What happens now?" He was looking at Chris.

"Well, she's terminal, sir."

"So?"

Chris was obviously uncomfortable. "Nothing can be done, sir."

"Well Chris, pretend you are the attending doctor and have to write the orders, what would you write?"

Chris squirmed. "I don't know sir."

Greyfield looked at the others. "Anybody?"

Silence. "What would you do, Theo?"

"Well sir, if it has been determined that no treatment would help, then the only thing left is to keep the patient comfortable."

"How?"

"Control the pain and maybe some sedation." Greyfield looked at the others. "Any comments, Sheila?"

"Well, ah, the analgesics might not work."

"Yes, that's true, depending on what is used, right?"

"Ah, yes sir."

"What would you use, Sheila?"

Sheila was by now wishing she had kept her mouth closed. "Well, sir, something strong, maybe morphine."

"How much?" Dr. Greyfield was certainly persistent.

"Well, ah, well, I don't know sir."

"That's okay, Sheila, I guess at your stage in the training that wasn't a fair question, but you are right, most likely narcotic analgesia would be needed."

"What about addiction?" The questioner was Brad, a quarrelsome type, not much liked by the staff, nurses, or other students.

Greyfield looked straight at him. "What about it?"

"The patient could get addicted."

"So?" Greyfield shared the dislike and wasn't going to let Brad of the hook so easily.

"Well, that's not good." Brad never used the common courtesy of saying 'sir' to a staff man.

"Why not?" Greyfield now was annoyed and the questions were becoming short and crisp.

"Well, well..." Theo came to Brad's rescue. "Would it matter, sir, if the patient became addicted, since she's going to die soon anyway?"

"I wasn't asking you, Dirks, but you're right. The patient will require pain relief until she dies, and in ever increasing doses. Since you seem to have the right answers, I want you to take over her care. Work out a plan of management, and then discuss it with me. That's all for today."

'Me and my big mouth,' Theo thought, but actually he was glad for this opportunity to be involved in patient care. He reviewed the chart and then went to see the patient. She was still lying in bed in the same position. Theo sat down on a chair near the bed.

"How are you today?" He asked just to make contact. To his amazement the woman responded by moving her head from side to side.

"Do you have pain?"

Again the same response. Now what? Suddenly it struck him that she might not understand him. He went to the nursing station. Fortunately a nurse, not too hostile to students, was there. "Say, Nancy, that patient in 305, bed three, what do you know about her?"

"Not much really, I work on the other end." How many times had Theo heard that answer already? It seemed to be a standard reply. He sighed. "Who looks after her?"

"Well, Madge works on that end, ask her."

"Do you know if the patient understands English?"

"Oh no, not a word, she's Hungarian, or something like that."

'Well, wonders never cease,' Theo thought. 'A nurse that knows something about the patient.' Just at that moment a buzzer from room 305 went. Theo looked at Nancy but she seemed not to have heard.

"Aren't you going to answer that?" he asked.

She did not even look up. "Not my room."

'Might as well go and look myself,' Theo thought, and went to room 305. One of the other patients pointed towards the bed with Theo's patient. Theo immediately saw what everyone was staring at. Right in the middle of the blanket, over the distended abdomen, was a large red area. 'My God, she's bleeding,' Theo rushed over to the bed and quickly pulled the drapes around the bed, and then removed the blanket. In the middle of the abdomen was an irregular, bloody area where the tumor had eroded through the skin. From the middle of the tumor there was steady oozing of blood. Theo raced back to the nursing station. Nancy was sitting there doing her charts. Theo was glad she was still there. "Come quick, this woman is bleeding, come, come."

He raced back. The woman was staring at him, sheer terror in her eyes. Nancy came in at her regular pace. "Oh, it's her, there's nothing we can do, she's terminal. Besides, there is a 'do not resuscitate' order on her chart." She turned around and left.

Theo noticed that the bleeding had increased. The woman lifted her right arm towards Theo as if to plead for help, but she was too weak and the arm dropped to her side. Theo felt so helpless. He ran back to the station and phoned Dr. Greyfield. When the receptionist answered, Theo almost shouted, "Dr. Greyfield, quick, it's an emergency."

Dr. Greyfield came to the phone. "Yes?"

"Oh, I'm glad you're there. The patient in 305, the one we talked about this morning."

"Yes?"

"She's bleeding, she's bleeding a lot, what shall I do?" By now Theo was getting almost hysterical.

"The first thing you must do, Theo, is to calm down. You can't fall apart every time there is an emergency. Then I want you to go and make sure the patient is not in pain. Give her whatever is necessary to keep her comfortable."

"But, but, she's going to die, she'll die!"

Yes, Theo, she'll die." He hung up.

Theo stood there a second then raced back. The bleeding had increased and the woman looked very pale. Her eyes still showed the fear but they were getting dull. Instinctively Theo took her hand; the pulse was thready, the hand cool. Theo could feel the slight pressure as she hung on to his hand. There was now a steady flow of blood. Theo did not know how long he stood there, but after a while, a nurse came in and gently freed his hand. "She's dead, Dr. Dirks."

Chapter 38

It was again Christmas; hopefully this would be Theo's last year in medical school. Last Christmas they had spent with Theo's mother in Vancouver, but this year it was different. They could not afford to go anywhere; they could hardly afford the bare necessities, such as rent and food. They spent only twenty dollars for the children's presents, and even that required adjustments. Not that Sarah and Paul had minded, the children had seemed quite happy with their small presents, but Theo felt guilty.

Laura, who noticed, had said, "Don't be silly. Look at them, do they look unhappy?"

Theo had to admit that they did not. "I know. But I should be able to give them more."

"They are happy, what more can you give them?"

Theo smiled at her. He did not want to tell her that he had other worries, that there wasn't enough money to last to the end of the next semester. He would not finish until the end of May, and he could not take a job now. He could not risk failing fourth year, not after all they had gone through. Laura was working only part time, but her income was just not enough. They could manage for a few more months. He tried to put his worries out of his mind and concentrate on the present. "Hey, you guys, it's a beautiful evening, why don't we all go for a walk and look at the Christmas tree in the square?"

The children were instantly ready and ran to get their winter coats.

Laura turned to Theo. "We will manage somehow, you know."

'She reads my mind,' Theo thought, 'but then, she's always known what I feel.' He gave her a squeeze. Suddenly he felt better.

After the New Year, he started a new rotation in obstetrics and gynecology. The gyne part did not worry him but obstetrics made him, and a lot of other students, apprehensive. So many things could, and often did, go wrong. After all, one had to look after two patients: the mother and the forming baby, the fetus. Well, it was only for six weeks. Then six weeks of psychiatry and one month of emergency and he was done, except for the dreaded exams.

As in the other specialties, the day started with rounds at seven a.m. sharp. Especially in B3, where Dr. Anne Brooke, it was said, reigned with an iron hand.

Theo was on the ward early and greeted Sheila, Chris, and the others as they came in. Dr. Brooke arrived at exactly seven o'clock. "Is everyone here? Good. A few rules, which I expect all of you to obey: No smoking, no chewing gum, patients are to be treated with the utmost respect, and no orders to be written without prior discussion with the attending doctor. Understood?" She did not wait for an answer. "Good, let's go."

As on other services, rounds on the first day were easy. Only routine cases were presented, usually by a bored first year resident. Then the students were assigned to certain parts of the ward. Before she left, Dr. Brooke called Theo. "Dr. Dirks, you will present a case at rounds tomorrow. Something enlightening, please."

Theo was, well, pissed off would describe it nicely. Why was he singled out so often? Was it his age? And what was an enlightening case anyway? There was nothing to do but to find something interesting. He looked through the cases assigned to him; nothing enlightening there. What now?

"Hey, young man, you look as if you have lost your last friend." It was one of the nurses on the ward. Theo had noticed her earlier because she had been friendly to another student.

"Well, not yet, but I will lose something if I don't come up with a case by tomorrow." Theo looked at the ceiling in mock anguish.

"What kind of case?" Sandra, the nurse, showed mild interest.

"An enlightening one, whatever that is!"

"Ah yes. Dr. Brooke, right?"

"Right."

Sandra thought a few moments. "You know, there was a patient admitted a few days ago. I think she went to the medical floor. She had something weird, and she was pregnant. You should check it out."

"Right now I'll try anything. How do I find her? Do you have a name?"

"Oh, sure. We'll just look in the admissions book." She leafed through an obviously much-used ledger book. "Yes, here she is. She went to north seven. Her name is Forder, Pat Forder, see?" She held the book under his nose.

Theo wasn't overly excited but it wouldn't hurt to check it out. He went to the medical ward, found Pat Forder's chart, and sat down in a quiet corner to go over it. Almost immediately, he knew that he had hit pay dirt. This was a most unusual and fascinating case.

The story was that the patient had been admitted about four days ago because of severe anemia and pregnancy. The cause of the anemia had as yet not been ascertained. That the anemia was severe was evident from the tests performed in the hospital. These suggested a quick and significant loss of hemoglobin, most likely a massive bleed, but there was no evidence of that. After reading the chart, Theo concluded that certain information was lacking and he decided to talk to the patient.

He went to her room and introduced himself. "I'm Dr. Dirks. I am a Student-Intern, would you mind if I talked with you a few minutes, please?"

Mrs. Forder seemed pleased to have some company, she smiled. "But of course you may talk to me, Doctor. Please sit down. What do you want to talk about?"

"Well, I would like to ask you some questions, Mrs. Forder."

"Yes, of course."

"Tell me when you first got sick, Ma'am."

"You mean with this anemia?"

"No, no. When did you first not feel well?"

"Ah, that's some time ago. When I started to have head-aches, not severe mind you, but bad enough."

"What did you do?" Theo was getting impatient, but he did not want to upset the patient. "Did you see someone?"

Mrs. Forder looked surprised. "Yes, of course I saw someone; the headaches drove me to it."

"Who did you see?" Theo asked patiently.

"Why Dr. Slevski, my regular doctor." The emphasis was on 'regular'.

"Yes, and?"

"Well, he treated me of course."

"How did he treat you, Mrs. Forder?"

"Why he bled me."

Theo was stunned. "You mean he really bled you?"

"Why yes, every week, until I was admitted."

It was unbelievable that in this day and age phlebotomy (opening of a vein) was still used in the treatment of headaches. He had certainly hit the jackpot. After completing the history, Theo went home. It should prove to be an enlightening day tomorrow, how enlightening even Theo did not suspect.

The next morning, after rounds, the group filed into a small classroom on the ward. Dr. Brooke was all business. "Alright Dr. Dirks, present your case. Concisely please."

Theo presented as concisely as he could, but could not hide his satisfaction at having found something interesting. There were a number of questions from the students who also seemed to find the case interesting. Dr. Brooke did not show any reaction. "So you think this is a worthwhile case to discuss, Dr. Dirks?"

"Yes I do," answered Theo, not sure what she meant.

"I see," Dr. Brooke seemed to see something fascinating on the floor. Without looking up, she asked, "And what about the rest of you, what do you think?"

They all agreed with Theo that it was an interesting case.

Dr. Brooke still stared at the floor. "I see," she repeated. "Well, I don't agree, and furthermore I resent this deliberate attempt to smear one of our staff members. In the future you will restrict yourself to the facts Dr. Dirks. Do you understand? The medical facts!"

"But these are the facts," Theo blurted out, not comprehending what was going on.

"Dr. Dirks, I will not argue with you. On this ward what I say goes. Do we understand each other?" As usual, she did not wait for an answer but got up and left.

At first there was an embarrassed silence, then Chris said, "She's a bitch."

The others agreed. "Yes, Theo. Forget it."

But how could he forget it? He thought he had done a good job, and now this. What was going on?

Theo did his usual work, which consisted of new admission histories, phone calls to the attending doctors to discuss orders, and rounds on his patients. He was still troubled by this morning's episode and decided to speak to the head of obstetrics. He phoned and was advised that he could see Dr. Stronge in about an hour. He went to the faculty office early. After waiting twenty minutes, he was ushered into Dr. Stronge's office. Dr. Stronge, who was sitting behind a large oak desk, motioned for him to sit down. "What can I do for you, Dr. Dirks?"

Theo felt uncomfortable and wished he had not come, but since he was here, he related what had happened this morning.

Dr. Stronge looked at him over his glasses. "Ah yes. Dr. Brooke mentioned something about that to me this morning. Her version was somewhat different. What exactly would you like? Are you laying a complaint?"

"Oh no, sir," Theo protested, "I just want to say that I feel I did nothing wrong."

Dr. Stronge scratched his head. "I see. You know, Dirks, the attending staff take criticisms of one of their own very personally, but I can see your dilemma. Why don't you forget the whole thing and I will make certain that this will not go against you on your record."

There was nothing left for Theo but to agree. He left the office with mixed feelings.

Among other things, in his treatment plan he had suggested that Mrs. Forder receive iron replacement by mouth, but the patient's doctor decided to give the total calculated requirement all at once by iv. Theo could not help but feel somewhat vindicated when Mrs. Forder developed almost every complication ever recorded with i.v. iron replacement, although he did feel sorry for the patient and visited her every day. In the end, she did recover and eventually she delivered a small but healthy baby boy.

Theo found deliveries fascinating but somewhat scary. There was a lot of fussing, the patient experienced pain, and sometimes there was reason for worry, but in the end there was this incredible event called birth, when suddenly there was a fully formed, squirming new beautiful life. It was incredible. Try as he might, Theo never could get over the worrying part, and even in later years, when a delivery was near his pulse would beat a little faster, and there always was a feeling of immense relief when the delivery was over and things had gone well.

Chapter 39

Theo knew that he had to do something very soon or there would not even be money for food. With a heavy heart, he decided to talk to the dean of student affairs who was responsible for loans and other financial assistance. Theo had already obtained a loan at the beginning of the year and thought that his chances of obtaining another were slim, but what could he do? His mother had refused any financial help and had only made him angry when she reminded him that she had advised against 'this reckless undertaking.' It still rankled when he thought about it. He knew that she did not have a lot, but she could have given him a small loan. He would have paid her back. Well, she had refused so he had to look elsewhere. He made an appointment in the hope that he could obtain another loan from the university. If there was no help there, then he did not know what he would do.

Two days later he was sitting in a nice, but not ostentatious office, facing Dr. Chalmers, the dean for student affairs. Theo had presented his case. Dr. Chalmers was leafing through Theo's file and seemed to study the pages intensely. Finally he looked up. "You have only a few months to go before you graduate?" It was more a statement than a question. Theo nodded.

"Well, it would be a waste to let all that go down the drain, right?" By 'all that' Theo assumed he meant all his past studies. Again, he just nodded. There did not seem to be anything else to say.

"Well," Dr. Chalmers said, deep in thought, "well, it would be a waste." He was silent for a short time, then turned to Theo again. "The university has some resources for just such situations. Did you know that?" He smiled.

"No sir," Theo muttered.

Dr. Chalmers got up and walked around his desk. "It is time that you go now, young man." Theo's heart sank. "But what do you say we give you a six hundred dollar scholarship and a four hundred dollar loan?"

Theo was speechless. A few moments ago his world seemed to be falling apart, and now—salvation. He could only mumble, "Thank you, thank you, sir." Then he dashed off to tell Laura about this miracle.

At the supper table, he told the story for about the fifth time. Laura smiled, she also had known that they were in financial trouble, and knew how important this assistance was to them. Sarah however, had heard the tale often enough. "Aw, papa, can't you talk about something else? Money is so boring."

Theo was momentarily startled, than he laughed out loud. He picked Sarah up and hugged her. "You are absolutely, totally right, my precious. Let's all clean up the table and then play a game."

"Me too," piped up little Paul.

They had enjoyed a nice, and rare, evening together, but now it was morning and the realities of the day were to be dealt with. Theo was finishing obstetrics and gynecology with apprehension. He had worked hard, but Dr. Brooke had remained distant, and Theo feared that she might in some way cause difficulty. Well, in a few days he would start psychiatry and then all this unpleasantness would be behind him. Hopefully he would not encounter the same problems there. Although psych was not Theo's favorite, at least not from the lectures, it remained to be seen whether in real life it was more palatable. Maybe once he saw some patients his attitude would change. He went through his routine on the obstetric ward quickly and finished early. He decided to use the remaining time to study in the library and get a head start for his psychiatry rotation.

Theo's stint in psychiatry went without a hitch, and while the one month in emergency was a busy one, it also went well. There were two weeks left before the final exams, on which everything depended. It was strange that one could study for four years, but in the end everything was decided by a few exams. Fail those and all that time spent would mean nothing. Well, he had worked hard, too hard to fail now.

Finally the long awaited day had arrived—graduation. The exams had been tough, especially the oral exams in obstetrics. Dr. Brooks had fulfilled Theo's worst fears and had tried to fail him. Fortunately, when her recommendation was reviewed by the faculty committee, his excellent performance in all other departments proved to be his salvation and Dr. Brooks recommendation was not supported. For Theo, however, there had been several days of anxiety and a lasting bitterness.

Theo looked at his classmates, all wearing black gowns with bright red trim, eager to walk to the stage and receive the diploma, which pronounced to those who cared to read it that they were now doctors. They all lined up in alphabetical order and waited their turn. The Bachelor's and Master's degrees were awarded first, and the Doctor's degrees last. Finally it was their turn. Theo watched as the first of his classmates walked unto the stage, went down on one knee in front of the Chancellor, and received the diploma. For Theo it was a very emotional moment. As he walked off the stage, he looked into the auditorium but the crowd was too large and he could not find his family.

When the procession was over, Theo went to find Laura and the children. His mother had also come, but Peet and Sonja were not here. It was a nice sunny day and most of the visitors had left the auditorium and were in the mall. Theo walked through the crowd and finally he spotted his family standing apart and looking just a little bit lost. Theo rushed over and hugged Laura. "We did it, Laura, we did it!"

Then turning to his mother, he asked, "What did you think of the ceremony, Mom? Impressive, was it not?"

Jutta agreed. "Yes Theo, very impressive. And now you are a doctor. Isn't that something, Laura?"

Laura also agreed. "Ja, Mama." She remembered how unhappy Jutta had been when Theo had given up his job to go to university, but she wisely kept these thoughts to herself.

Sarah was getting restless and tugged Theo's sleeve. "Papa, Papa, you said we would go to the restaurant after. When is it after?"

"Yes, precious, you're right, let's go, and when we're there I have some news for you."

They all wanted to know what the news was, but Theo would not tell them until they arrived at the restaurant and were seated.

"Well Theo, what news?" asked Laura although she had a good idea what it was.

Theo beamed. "I have been accepted into the surgery residency program."

The only one startled by this news was Jutta. She only asked one word: "Where?"

"Oh, here." In his happiness, Theo did not notice his mother's disappointment. Jutta had hoped Theo would return to Vancouver.

Chapter 40

Theo had been lucky again. Not only did he get a surgical residency at Midwest, he was also assigned to Dr. Feber's ward, three west. He soon found out that being a resident was quite different than being a student-intern. He was now responsible for assigning patients who required admission histories to the students, in addition he had to do the histories on emergency admissions himself when he was on call after hours. Then there were the assists in the O.R., daily morning rounds, calls from the nurses regarding orders, minor or major problems with post-operative care, and a host of other things that needed looking after on a surgical ward.

Another large difference from his student days was the fact that he was now on call. Every third night Theo had to stay in the hospital and see patients in the emergency department if a surgical consult was required. He had backup, to be sure, but he now had to make decisions based on his own initial assessment. Only then did he call the chief resident or a staff man, depending on whether the patient was paying for his or her care or not.

Non-paying patients or those without insurance, called staff patients, were cared for mainly by the residents, with one of the staff surgeons supervising the care.

Theo loved staff patients. It gave him more freedom; he made more decisions and was more involved in the treatment, even though he had to discuss everything but the minor stuff with the chief resident. Theo soon found out that the chief resident had control of the ward if he had the confidence of the head of the service, in this case the surgery service. He could even overrule staff doctors in certain situations. Theo also soon found out that not all surgeons were equally good, in fact, some were only mediocre. It puzzled Theo, even many years later, why these surgeons not only were tolerated, but often were actively protected by the others. One surgeon on Theo's ward, Dr. Barstein, was noteworthy for the fact that he seemed to have more complications than any other surgeon on the service. Mark, the chief resident, had instructed Theo that Dr. Barstein was to be assisted by a senior resident, always. He had not explained why. Unfortunately, Theo soon found out. He was on call one quiet Sunday afternoon when Dr. Barstein called. "Dr. Dirks, a patient of mine is coming into the emergency. I want you to see him and call me."

Theo asked for the name of the patient and promised to call. After a short time, he went to the emergency department to see if the patient had arrived. She was not there yet but did arrive a short time later. Theo asked the usual questions and then examined her. Since the patient seemed nervous, Theo asked a nurse to be in attendance when he examined the patient. It looked like appendicitis but he was not certain. He called Dr. Barstein. "Sir, I've seen Nancy Kline. It could be appendicitis but I'm not sure."

"Well, Dr. Dirks, I'm sure. Arrange for the O.R."

"Should we not ask someone from gynecology to see her, sir? She could have a pelvic infection."

"Are you questioning my judgment, Dirks? Just do as I tell you. Those guys from gyne don't know anything we don't know anyway."

"They could do a laparoscopy, sir."

"Just do as I tell you."

"Yes, Dr. Barstein." 'What can I do?' Theo thought. "I'll call you when the O.R. is ready."

He called Mark but there was no answer. He tried to reach the senior resident on call but got the message that he had just started emergency surgery and would not be available for some time. The message from the senior resident, via the nurse, was that Theo had to manage as best he could.

An hour later he met Dr. Barstein in O.R. five. The patient was already in the theater and the anesthetist was putting her to sleep. They scrubbed their hands in silence, Theo not knowing what to say and Dr. Barstein apparently not in a talking mood. When they walked into the O.R. the patient was prepped and draped. They gowned and gloved, then Dr. Barstein walked to the patient's right side.

"You'll assist me, Dr. Dirks. I know you're just a junior, but if you try hard you'll be all right."

'You pompous ass,' Theo thought, but did not say anything.

Dr. Barstein made and incredibly small incision, more or less at McBurney's point in the right lower abdomen.

"One has to be careful with incisions in women, Dr. Dirks, they are very vain."

There was some bleeding but Dr. Barstein ignored it and tried to bore his way through the muscle layers with his fingers. When this was not successful, he enlarged the skin incision. He hurried and the incision became angulated. He tried again to separate the muscles but again was unsuccessful. He enlarged the incision again, the other way. It looked now like a ragged zigzag. 'This woman better not be vain,' Theo thought as Dr. Barstein plunged on. Eventually they managed to open the abdomen. The appendix was normal and there was pus in the pelvis.

"Remember this, Dr. Dirks, appendicitis is very difficult to diagnose, especially in women. One can never be too careful. We might as well remove the appendix and then I want you to close. I have an urgent appointment. The nurse can assist you. Make sure you do a good job."

When Barstein had left, Theo muttered, "How can I do a good job with this mess?"

He began by clamping all the bleeders and tying them, then he closed the wound in layers as he had been tought. There wasn't much he could do with the irregular incision, so he closed it as best he could, but it still looked messy.

The next day the patient's temperature increased in spite of antibiotic treatment and two days later her abdomen became distended. When Dr. Barstein made rounds he said to Theo, "I want you to arrange a gynecology consult, Dirks. One can never be too careful with these women, you know."

When the gynecology resident arrived, Theo gave him the chart and took him to the patient, then he waited in the chart room. The gyne resident returned shortly. "Hell, what has happened to this woman? She comes in with a simple P.I.D. and now is at death's door. What happened?"

Theo explained.

Herb, the gyne resident, shook his head. "You did take her appendix out?"

"Yes."

"At least we don't need to worry about it, or do we?"

"No. The appendix is gone. What do you think is going on?"

"It's a total fuck-up, that's what's going on! I know she has peritonitis, but there's something else, I can feel it. You better get your chief resident. This case is trouble, major trouble."

Theo already knew that. With a heavy heart he called Mark. "You know that case of Barstein's? She's gone sour. Can you come and look?"

Mark came. "Christ, Theo, I told you not to let Barstein into the O.R. without a senior resident. What happened?"

Theo told him.

"Well, I guess you got caught. Let's go and look."

It did not take Mark long to see that the patient was gravel ill. He quickly walked to the phone and phoned Barstein. "Your patient from Sunday, she's needs to be opened."

"Now, now, Mark, lets not be hasty. We should do some tests."

"Look, Barstein, this patient will not stand any further fucking around, she needs to be in the O.R. soon. Furthermore I think you should get some help."

"Mark, I will not stand you talking to me like that."

"Oh, cut the crap, Barstein." Mark could be quite direct at times like these. "Shall I call Feber or will you?"

"I will call Dr. Feber, but you are overstepping you boundary. I will discuss that with Dr. Feber."

"You do that, Barstein." Mark hung up.

"You were quite rough with him, Mark. Aren't you worried about your residency?"

"Look Theo, this woman's in danger of dying. That's what's important. I want you to arrange for an O.R. stat. I'll wait here for Feber. Go on, hurry!"

When Dr. Feber and Mark arrived in the O.R., Theo was already there and the patient had just been wheeled into the theater. Theo informed them that it would be a few more minutes and Dr. Feber said, "Let's go to the doctors' lounge and discuss this case a little more. Theo, tell me what happened on Sunday, from the beginning."

Theo related the events as he remembered them, for about the fifth time.

Dr. Feber thought a few moments, "Who did the actual surgery?"

"Dr. Barstein, except for the closure. I did that."

"What do you think is going on now, Theo?"

"Well sir, she has peritonitis, but there must be something else or she would have responded to the antibiotics."

"What else?" Dr. Feber asked as he got up to go to the O.R.

Theo tried to keep up with him, "I don't know, sir."

"What do you think, Mark?"

"She has a distended, silent abdomen, sir. She must have perforated something, probably bowel."

"Yes, Mark, that's what I think also."

They started to scrub. Barstein was still nowhere in sight. When they finished scrubbing their hands they walked into the theater, Dr. Feber first, then Mark, and Theo last, as per long established convention.

"Mark, I want you to open. Theo, you assist him and I will watch for now. Soon we shall see if we were right."

"Shall I make a mid-line incision, sir?" Mark asked and received the expected answer. "Yes, by all means. Who knows what we will have to do, and a midline incision will give us more room."

Mark made a swift incision in the mid-line below the navel. At this point Dr. Barstein looked in through the O.R. doors. Addressing Dr. Feber, he asked, "Do you want me to scrub in Hugo?"

Without turning around, Dr. Feber answered, "We have enough help here, why don't you wait in the lounge."

Mark quickly extended the incision through the muscle layers and opened the peritoneum, the thin layer that lines the abdominal cavity. There was a lot of murky fluid around the loops of bowel.

"Yes sir, we have a perforation. Let's see where." He felt around in the abdomen and then brought the cecum, the beginning of the large bowel, into view. "Yes, sir," he repeated, "there it is. The appendix stump has blown. The suture must have come off. Yuck, what a mess!"

Dr. Feber looked around in the abdomen, then he looked up at Mark. "Well, doctor, what are you going to do?"

"We can't just close the perforation in the cecum. With all this infection, it'll just break down again, but if we do any-thing else it means an ileostomy and later another operation to hook up the bowel again. That's not only a lot of surgery but also a lot of scars."

Dr. Feber persisted. "What are you going to do?"

Mark hesitated, the he seemed to have decided. "I'm going to resect part of the cecum and establish an ileostomy, which can be closed in six weeks or so. The other course is too risky."

Dr. Feber smiled. "I guess I have taught you something. The patient will be upset at first, but in the end she will thank you for saving her life." He turned to Theo. "You assist, I'm scrubbing out." He turned to leave then stopped and said to Mark, "I'll talk to Barstein."

Mark nodded and smiled. They understood each other. Dr. Feber would 'advise' Dr. Barstein gently and politely but firmly, and there would be no need for Mark to get involved in the discussion.

Chapter 41

Theo enjoyed surgery, but on some days everything just seemed to be hexed. It was Sunday, and Theo had been on call since Friday night. Actually, he had not been home since Friday morning, but nobody seemed to consider the work residents did during the day. Friday night had not been too bad and Theo got to bed around one a.m., but Saturday had been murder, and so far, Sunday was no picnic either. Emergency cases were pouring in all day. He just got out of the O.R. when his beeper went again. He was beginning to hate the damn thing.

He phoned central. "Dirks here, you paged?"

"You're wanted in emerg, stat."

"Okay." Theo also hated stat calls, they always indicated some urgent, unpleasant business. He hurried to the emergency. The head nurse, who already knew him, waved him over. "Dirks, this way. I think this one is trouble," she said as they walked to the resuscitation room.

Theo grimaced. "They are all trouble, Marg."

In the resuscitation room there was lots of activity. One nurse was starting an i.v., someone else was hooking up a cardiac monitor, while a resident was talking to the patient who was, surprisingly, quite conscious.

'That's a switch,' Theo thought. 'Usually they're out cold.' He walked over to the medical resident. "What's up, Mel?"

Mel looked up. "Oh, hi Theo. Came in with abdominal pain. It came on suddenly, no nausea or vomiting, slightly high pulse, normal ECG. I think he had an aortic aneurism fixed about four months ago."

Theo just about jumped out of his shoes. "What? Get out of my way." Then to the patient: "I'm the surgical resident, sir. May I examine you?" While he was talking he was already palpating the patient's abdomen. The abdomen was slightly distended but soft. A mass was easily palpable just below the umbilicus. When Theo pressed gently, the patient winced. Theo repeated the pressure—same thing.

"Cross match this man for six units of blood," he told the head nurse, "And move it!" Turning to the i.v. nurse, he said, "Start another i.v. in the other arm. Use a large needle, and I mean large!" Then to the patient. "You'll be fine, but we have to hurry, I will explain later."

The patient only nodded.

"Someone prep his abdomen, he's going to the O.R." Then he hurried to the phone. He quickly looked at the call roster. Dr. Bronski was on for vascular stuff. Theo called him. After identifying himself, he said, "I think we have an urgent one, a ruptured aortic graft. I have notified the O.R."

"You're sure then?"

Theo hesitated ever so briefly, "Yes sir, I'm sure."

After a moment, Bronski said, "Okay," and hung up.

'I better be right or he'll have me for breakfast,' Theo thought. He now had a few moments and went to discuss the situation with the patient who seemed to have already come to the same conclusion. Theo briefly outlined what needed to be done and the patient agreed. Theo then went to the nurses station to write a note on the chart and to write some orders, most of which he had already given orally, but protocol required that he now write them on the order sheet. As he was writing, Mel came to the desk. "Hey, Theo, what do you think is wrong with the guy?"

Theo was stunned. "You mean you don't know? He's ruptured his graft, it's obvious. Surely you must have thought of that!"

"No shit. Are you sure? It never occurred to me. No shit." Mel shook his head.

Bronski arrived in due course and they proceeded to the OR. When they opened the patient's abdomen they found a large purplish bulge in the area of the lower aorta.

"Look at that sucker, Theo, you were right. There is a separation where the graft was sutured to the aorta. It is only contained by the peritoneum. We have to open the peritoneum before we can get to the aorta. Get the vascular clamp ready."

Bronski made a quick incision through the thin layer, scooped away some clot, and then compressed the aorta. "Quickly, Theo, clamp the sucker, hurry up. That's my boy."

Theo had managed to get the large clamp across the aorta and, at least for the time being, the bleeding was under control.

"Now we have to see how we can fix this mess. What do you suggest, Theo?"

"Well, we could extend the graft by adding another piece to it."

"Yes, yes. That's what I thought too. Let's get at it."

They worked quickly and soon had the defect repaired.

"That's nice, Theo. You close while I go and have a cigar." Dr. Bronski took off his gloves. On his way out, he stopped and said to Theo, "You saved his life, you know."

Theo did not answer, but he had this warm glow in his chest. Sometimes it was all worth it.

Chapter 42

It was early summer. Theo and Laura were sitting on the bench in the back garden and watched the children play. How they had grown! It seemed that only yesterday Paul J. was a small baby and now he was a boy, and Sarah was almost a young lady.

"We have not heard from my mom for a while, Laura. You think we should phone her? You know how she gets."

"I sure do. In her last letter she asked if we still remembered where she lived. Better give her a call, but not too long, it's expensive you know."

Theo laughed. "Not that expensive, and soon you will be the wife of a rich doctor."

"Well, right now I am the wife of a dirt poor resident, so better make it short."

Theo went into the house. After he had phoned his mother, he reviewed his schedule for the coming year. July first he started with thoracic surgery, then short rotations through some other surgical specialties, such as urology and orthopoedics, and then six months of gynecology and obstetrics. His first year of residency had gone well and Theo had already decided that he would stay in general surgery, but he wanted to get at least some experience in obs and gyne. Thoracic and some minor rotations were part of the general surgery program, which he had to complete, but obstetrics and gynecology were optional.

As he had done previously, Theo went to the cardiac ward the day before he was due to start there to familiarize himself with the ward, and to briefly review the patient charts. When he arrived at the nurses' station, one nurse was sitting there doing her charts. Theo said hello and introduced himself but the nurse just nodded. 'Snobbish bitch,' Theo thought but then got engrossed in the charts and forgot her. About an hour later he left, the nurse was not there and he did not see her again until the next morning. As soon as he arrived at seven a.m., she greeted him with a smile. "You are Dr. Dirks, are you not?"

"Yes I am," Theo answered, surprised by her friendliness.

"I am to inform you that you have been selected to look after Dr. Cowan-Parker's patients. He will meet you when he is finished in the O.R."

"When will that be?" Theo wanted to know.

"Your guess is as good as mine." She smiled again. "By the way, I am Nancy Harper, I am the head nurse on this ward."

Theo bowed slightly. "Glad to know you." He was beginning to like this now pleasant and much more friendly nurse.

He did his rounds and other chores on the ward, then sat down to do some studying. By two o'clock Cowan-Parker had not yet arrived. He saw Nancy at the chart rack. "Say, Miss Harper, when can one expect Dr. Cowan-Parker to arrive?"

"I told you, your guess is as good as mine. And please call me Nancy." She gave him another one of her quick smiles.

At three-thirty Dr. Cowan-Parker arrived. Theo could hear him before he saw him. On arrival at the chart station, he bellowed out, "Where is my resident?"

Theo knew instinctively that the next two months would be tough; he knew he would not like Cowan-Parker. "I suppose you mean me, sir. I am Dr. Dirks."

"Are you the new resident? Well, then of course I mean you. Do you see anyone else around?" He started for the little classroom next to the station. "Come on Dirks, and bring the charts."

"What charts, sir?"

"Those of my patients, of course. I hope you're not always this dense."

Theo was about to answer but thought better of it. He grabbed some charts and followed into the classroom. Dr. Cowan-Parker was seated at the table. "Okay, give me a report, brief mind you."

Theo was lost. "A report of what, sir?"

"Christ, don't you know anything? I want to know about my patients, of course. Or do you have a report on the stock market?" He laughed uproariously.

Theo was glad he had come in the previous day. At least he could give a sketchy report of each patient. Surprisingly, that's all C-P, as he was often referred to, wanted. He gave Theo some curt instructions and left. Over his shoulder he called back, "I want you in the O.R. tomorrow."

Theo took the charts back to the nurses' station. Nancy was there. "Don't take it too hard, he's like that to all the residents."

Theo just grunted. "Great."

He assigned admission histories to the ever-complaining student-interns, checked the O.R. slate, and then found a quiet corner in the library to read up on cardiac bypass surgery. He expected that C-P would grill him in the O.R. and he wanted to have at least an idea what open heart surgery was all about.

Just as he was getting ready to leave, at around seven o'clock, there was an urgent call from the ward. One of the patients who had cardiac bypass surgery a few days ago was spiking a temperature, up to 39.5C. Theo examined him. There were some noises in the right lung, probably pneumonia, but aspiration during the anesthetic was a distinct possibility. Another worry was a possible embolus, a blood clot to the lungs. Theo felt he had to discuss this with Dr. Cowan-Parker. He found his home phone number in the hospital directory and called him. When C-P came to the phone, Theo explained the situation. To his surprise there was a virtual explosion at the other end of the phone line.

"Christ, Dirks, what kind of resident are you? Do you have to bother me at home with shit like that? You look after minor stuff like that, and if you can't do it find me another resident." Slam went the phone.

'Well,' Theo thought, 'well, well, now what?' He ordered a chest x-ray and some, what he thought appropriate, blood tests. He started the patient on an antibiotic, but he was not at all sure what he was treating. By the time he was finished it was after ten, and by the time he came home, Laura was already in bed and asleep.

The next morning he got up at six. Although he tried to be quiet, Laura woke up. "Are you leaving? What time is it?" She looked at the clock. "Do you have to leave so early?"

"Yes, dear." Theo gave her a quick kiss and left. He felt badly that he was away so much and that he had so little time for Laura and even less for the kids, but what could he do? He could not quit now.

At the hospital, he made quick rounds. The patient with the temperature was the same, the x-ray showed a consolidation at the base of the right lung. This could be either and embolus or pneumonia. Theo decided to order a lung scan. Then he hurried to the O.R.; thank goodness C-P wasn't there yet. Theo changed into O.R. greens and then had a quick cup of coffee in the doctor's lounge. No sooner had he sat down when Cowan-Parker arrived.

"Christ, Dirks, don't you ever do anything? Are they ready in the O.R.? Let's go." He rushed off and Theo trailed behind. While they scrubbed, C-P gave Theo instructions on what he expected from his assistants. "I know that you are green but I want you to be quick and with it, you know. Can you tie knots? Probably not very well. I like my knots square, you know. Well, I guess I'll have to teach you a few tricks."

They went into the O.R. and gowned. The operation was the removal of an aortic aneurysm, a dilated segment of the aorta, and insertion of a synthetic tube, a graft, to replace the damaged part of this large artery and not cardiac bypass surgery as Theo had expected, but he did not let on that he had seen this type of surgery before. C-P made a midline incision the full length of the abdomen. He obviously was not interested in appearance; the incision was not very straight and a bit ragged. There were moderate bleeders but P-C ignored them. When the abdomen was open, he inserted a large retractor.

Glancing at Theo he explained, "You need good exposure, you know. See there, it's a beaut." There was a large swelling in the abdominal aorta.

"Get a plastic bag and place the bowel in it." When Theo hesitated, he roughly pushed the bowel into the bag and moved it to the side of the incision. "You have to be gentle. I can see you have a lot to learn. Now pay attention and assist."

Theo knew it would be a long day. C-P clamped the aorta above the aneurysm, injected Heparin into the distal aorta to keep the blood from clotting in the legs, and then proceeded to remove the dilated part of the big vessel. Theo tried to anticipate and assist as best he could but C-P berated him constantly. When C-P misapplied a clamp and blood squirted all over the place from a small artery, he yelled at Theo and threw an instrument on the floor. Eventually the graft was in place and C-P stepped from the O.R. table. "Close up, Dirks, and mind do a good job. You residents are always so sloppy, but not with my patients, you hear?" 'I seem to have gone through this before,' Theo thought. He did not answer and continued to clean up bleeders inside the abdomen before closing the incision. After finishing with this first case, he assisted at two other smaller operations and then returned to the ward. Before he got home it was seven o'clock, and this was his night off. Laura had waited with supper. "Come, let's eat, the children are watching TV. They've eaten."

Although he felt a little guilty, Theo was glad for some time alone with Laura. He told her about his day, how miserable C-P had been. "I can't believe that a doctor can behave in that manner. I guess I'm naive, but I'm learning fast. God I'm tired. You don't mind if we go to bed early, do you?"

Laura did not mind, but she was surprised when Theo was asleep as soon as his head hit the pillow.

Chapter 43

Theo's short stint in cardiac surgery had gone by ever so quickly. In spite of some unpleasant experiences with Cowan-Parker, it had been a relatively good rotation and he had learned a lot. Urology, which he was just finishing, had also been worthwhile, but Theo looked forward to obstetrics and gynecology, especially the obstetric part where one dealt mostly with healthy young women. He knew that there could be problems, serious problems, but mostly it was straight forward, at least that's what Theo assumed. First, however, there was Christmas.

In a few weeks, Laura's mom and dad would arrive. It was amazing how excited Laura and the kids got just talking about it. Theo looked forward to their visit but mainly for Laura's sake, who had not seen her parents for some time. Theo knew that it would be a strain with four adults and two kids in a small house. Well, they had to make the best of it.

Laura's parents arrived two days before Christmas. Sarah and Paul were almost beside themselves with excitement. Not only because of the visit and Christmas, but they saw the parcels that Grandma unpacked and rightfully assumed they were presents. Laura had spent the last week cooking, baking, and cleaning. Theo had teased her about it, but she brushed him off. "Do you think I want my parents to think I can't manage?"

Theo had made a face. "Oh God no, not that!"

"Oh, stop teasing and help me get things ready. Paul will have to sleep in the living room on the couch, and Mom and Dad can have his room, which means we'll have to be in the kitchen if we want to stay up late and visit."

"Or we could go to bed early every night," Theo said with a grin on his face.

"Oh you, you're impossible."

When Laura's parents arrived, everything was ready. The house was clean, the kids were clean, the food was prepared, and the table was set. The approval on Laura's mother's face was evident.

It turned out to be a much better visit than Theo had expected. The lack of space was manageable and did not really present any significant problems. In any case, the pleasure the visit had brought to Laura and the kids far out-weighed any inconvenience.

Christmas Eve they spent at home; the kids unpacked their presents, the Grandparents told stories and gave the children extra candies when the parents where not looking, and Theo was busy preparing hot wine and coaxing every-one to try it. Laura's parents did usually not drink, but even they were persuaded to take a small amount. On Christmas day they all went to church, even Theo, who had managed to be off for three days. Overall, it was a very relaxing time. When Laura's parents left, her mother hugged everyone and assured Laura that they had a good time. One thing they missed though was a good old fashioned Mennonite Church. "It would have been much more festive with a solid

Mennonite church service," Laura's mom said, then she hugged Laura one more time.

The next morning Theo was in the hospital early. He had to finish off his urology rotation and get ready for obstetrics, which he was to start in a few days on the first of January. Before that he was on call for surgery on New Year's Eve and on New Year's Day—it would be busy.

As expected, the 31st was busy, but on New Year's Day all hell broke loose. First thing in the morning a young man with a smashed liver came in. It was obvious that he had internal bleeding and was becoming shocky. Two i.v.'s with large bore needles were started and blood cross-matching was ordered. When the i.v.'s were running the blood pressure stabilized and Theo made the necessary phone calls to the staff man, the O.R., and the anesthetist on call. The patient's blood pressure was falling again and Theo put a pressure pump on one of the i.v.'s to speed up the flow, knowing that saline only helped temporarily and that blood, large quantities most likely, would have to be used as soon as it was cross-matched. The final treatment was the surgery, which they would start when the blood was available.

In the OR, as soon as they entered the abdomen, blood welled out through the incision and spilled onto the floor. The anesthetist transfused blood as fast as he could but still the pressure was falling. Theo was glad that the staff man was Bronski. He was very competent and also managed to preserve an aura of calm in the O.R.

"Relax Bert," he said to the anesthetist, "in a few moments we have the bleeding stopped and then he will stabilize."

There was difficulty in getting a bleeder under the liver and both Theo and Bronski struggled a bit before the bleeding was stopped.

"All right, Bert, it's dry. Now do your magic before we proceed." Bronski stepped back from the O.R. table and flexed his fingers to get the stiffness out. "This surgery is damned hard work sometimes."

"Ah, you just want excuses for your outrageous fees," replied Bert, and a few minutes later, "He's stable now, you can continue."

They made sure that there was no further bleeding and also examined the rest of the abdominal cavity.

Bronski turned to Theo. "Well, Dr. Dirks, do you think you can manage now? I'll stay if you can't manage."

Theo flushed with pride. "Thank you, sir, I can manage."

"Sure?"

"Yes."

Bronski was showing great trust in Theo and everyone present knew it. Theo closed the incision and then wrote some orders. He looked at the clock; they had been in the O.R. over five hours. Strangely, he was not a bit tired.

By the time Theo was able to go home, around midnight, they had done several more emergency cases. Now he was tired, and the next morning he was starting in obstetrics. It would be tough.

Chapter 44

Theo arrived at the obstetric wing of Midwest Hospital at eight in the morning, as instructed. The other residents were already there and were preparing teaching rounds, which were held every Monday morning. Theo introduced himself to the chief resident. "I'm Theo Dirks. I'm to spend six months here."

"Ah, yes. I'm Mike Nelson. Just sit down. I will be giving out the assignments in a minute; you're starting off with obstetrics, right?"

Theo nodded.

The staff men started to arrive and at eight-thirty Mike began rounds. The junior residents presented some cases for discussion. The cases were interesting but not that unusual. 'I hope this rotation will not be too boring,' Theo thought. However, the next case, an obstetric patient who seemed to have developed every complication one could think of, changed his mind. The events were so unusual that Theo thought they must have been made-up just for rounds. There was vigorous discussion. One staff man in particular seemed to dispute almost everything the others said. Theo thought, 'oh no, not another one,' remembering his experiences in cardiology.

At the end of rounds, the chief resident asked the new residents to remain behind. First, he gave each resident a large envelope. "Read the stuff, especially the on-call list. If you want some changes let me know and I will see what I can do, but don't expect too much." Then he had a few comments about the consultant staff. "I don't have to tell you how to treat the staff men. It is to your benefit to be courteous and civil. They are the ones who teach you and let you do things. We have good consultants and not so good consultants, as every other specialty. You, however, have to be good or you'll get your ass kicked, and occasionally some resident gets kicked right out, so keep your noses clean. That's all."

After rounds, the residents all went for coffee. There was an easy cameraderie among them and Theo hoped he would fit in equally well.

Theo started on ward duty, which meant that he dealt mainly with women who were admitted to hospital with some problem associated with pregnancy. He visualized this as boring, routine drudgery and was disappointed that he could not start in the case room, where he perceived all the action to be.

Two days later, when he was on call, he found out how wrong his ideas about obstetrics had been. The day had started in the usual fashion with rounds and discussion of some cases that the instructor picked. The majority of patients on Theo's ward were admitted with blood pressure problems, so called PET, or Pre-Eclamtic Toxemia, to Theo so far a boring condition, requiring only bed rest for treatment. The rest of the day was also quiet and Theo looked forward to his first night on call when he also covered the case room. He was eating supper in the hospital cafeteria when his pager went off. It was the antenatal ward. A seven-year old in her seventh month of pregnancy had been admitted during the day. Theo had examined her about an hour after admission. Except for slightly brisk knee reflexes, he had found nothing abnormal, and he had been mildly critical of the consultant who had admitted her.

It seemed that the patient now was slightly anxious and her blood pressure was up a bit. 'Doesn't sound too serious,' Theo thought and advised the nurse that he would be there soon. He finished his meal and had a cup of coffee with another resident before returning to the ward. As soon as he entered the ward, he noticed the commotion down the corridor. He rushed over there and one of the nurses, coming out of the room, grabbed his arm. "Hurry, she's fitting, hurry."

Theo rushed into the room; it was the seventeen year old. It was obvious that she was having a Gran Mal seizure. 'O h God, eclampsia,' Theo thought. "Bring me ten of Valium," he yelled, and to another nurse, "We need to start an i.v., and get some magnesium sulphate. Someone call the attending and get the O.R. to stand by, and bring in the monitor."

While he was giving these orders, he had managed to get a tourniquet on one arm and when the Valium arrived he injected five milligrams. The seizure did not stop and he injected the other five. Within a minute, the girl stopped jerking and now seemed to be in a deep sleep. Her blood pressure was very high now, which caused Theo further worry, especially since he was not sure what medication was safe in pregnancy. He knew that magnesium sulphate was used to prevent further seizures and that sometimes it also lowered the blood pressure. He quickly established an i.v. and started to infuse the mag sulph. Fortunately, the attending consultant arrived at that point. Theo was greatly relieved to see him. Dr. Halley was a portly man in his mid fifties. He had obviously seen similar situations before as he seemed not a bit perturbed. He checked the i.v., the medication, the blood pressure, all the while muttering, "Hum, yes, mag sulph, not seizuring now, blood pressure slightly down. What about the fetal heart?" He looked at Theo.

Theo shrugged his shoulders. "I haven't had time to take it."

"What! In obstetrics you never forget that you have two patients, the baby and the mother. You never, never forget!" He turned to the nurse. "Get me a fetoscope, and move it!" He felt the mother's abdomen quickly to determine the position of the fetus. "Christ, it's a breech!" He placed the scope on the abdomen and listened for a few seconds. Theo prayed silently that the babe would be all right. Suddenly Dr. Halley became all action. "The damn heart rate is only eighty and irregular at that, we have to get the kid out now. Get the O.R. ready Dirks, and make it stat!"

When Theo informed him that the O.R. was standing by, Halley patted Theo on the shoulder. "Good boy. Let's go."

Turning to one of the nurses, Dr. Halley said, "Get somebody to talk to her parents, or whoever you can get for a consent if possible. If you can't find anyone then I will sign it."

When one of the nurses asked, "Shall we do a prep?" he yelled at her, "Are you crazy? This is an emergency, get the stretcher, now!" To Theo he said, "Stay here and help to get the patient to the O.R., and hurry. I'll go and get things ready there."

When Theo and two nurses brought the patient into the O.R., the anesthetist and O.R. team were already there. The patient, who now was awake, was quickly moved to the operating table, and in a few minutes was asleep and intubated. Some disinfectant was poured over her abdomen and sterile drapes hastily placed on her. Dr. Halley, who by now was gowned and gloved, made a four-inch long incision in the lower abdomen, while Theo assisted. In less than a minute, they had entered the abdomen and exposed the lower uterus.

"Because it's a breech I will make a vertical incision in the uterus," said Halley as he peeled down the bladder and then opened the uterus in the midline. Theo had never seen such bleeding. He tried to clamp some bleeders but Halley pushed his hand aside. "Get out of my way, I have to get the baby out!"

He reached into the uterus and through all the blood brought out first one foot and then the other. "Got it," he grunted as he pulled out the rest of the infant and clamped the cord. "Cut it," he snapped at Theo, who hastily obliged. He the handed the baby to the pediatrician, who had appeared in the theater unnoticed. To Theo the baby seemed dead, it was so limp, but he had no time to dwell on it as the patient was still bleeding.

"Got to stop the bleeding," Halley was grunting. To Theo it seemed that Dr. Halley's composure had been shaken just a bit. He removed the placenta from the uterus and looked at the side that had been attached to the uterine wall. It was covered with clot. "See that? She's had an abruptio, a premature separation of the placenta. That explains the baby's slow heart rate."

They were working frantically to get the incision in the uterus closed. Once they had achieved that, the bleeding stopped. Halley smiled at Theo. "Got it." His relief, however, was premature. While they were closing the incision in the abdominal wall, there was increased oozing. At first Dr. Halley looked perplexed, then, realizing what was happening, he swore under his breath. "Hell, she's developing DIC, micro clotting in the vessels. Now we're really in shit." He gave some quick instruction to the nurse. "Get clotting factors done stat, and get up some blood and fresh frozen plasma so we can start replacing her clotting factors."

Theo had read in some textbook that in DIC, one sometimes used Heparin to stop the micro-coagulation, which was using up all the clotting factors. Cautiously he asked, "Is Heparin indicated?"

Dr. Halley looked at him over his glasses. "Only if you want to kill the patient. That stuff only works in the textbooks. We'll be lucky if she pulls through as it is."

They finished closing the abdomen and placed a pressure dressing over the wound. The patient was still bleeding from the vagina, more than was usual after a delivery. She was also bleeding from the i.v. puncture wounds. They now had two i.v.'s going and were running in blood as fast as they could.

"All we can do is to try to keep ahead of the loss," muttered Halley. He turned to the nurse. "Where is that fresh frozen plasma? We need to give her some clotting factors, and soon. The next problem will be her platelets. Have the lab check them, and repeat the clotting factors, and keep track of her blood pressure and urine output."

Two hours later the oozing continued, they had already given twelve units of blood and four units of fresh frozen plasma. The anesthetist had put in a central venous pressure line to measure the pressure in the big veins near the heart. This gave a better measure of the blood pressure and was of help to prevent overload of the heart. The platelet count had been low and they were now also infusing platelets. Since there was nothing further to do at the moment but wait, Dr. Halley and Theo had gone for a cup of coffee. After a few minutes, Dr. Halley became restless. "Let's take the coffee and go back to the P.A.R., I need to know what's happening."

Well, Cindy Shore, the seventeen year-old, survived. In took thirty-three units of blood and about twenty units of platelets, but she did survive. In fact, she made a total recovery and went home with a normal healthy baby. Theo never again thought that obstetrics was boring or uncomplicated. For the rest of his life he approached obstetrics with a certain caution, although after his residency, he had to deal with obstetric patients only rarely.

Chapter 45

Theo was glad that his obstetric service was finished. He was certain now that delivering babies was not his cup of tea. Oh sure, lots of deliveries were a piece of cake, but when problems arose they could be doozers, and they could arise so fast and without warning. One would have to be daft to have that kind of stress all the time.

He was starting on the cancer ward today. His experiences in obstetrics had made him more cautious and he tried to approach this new service with an open mind. He could however not deny a certain apprehension. He had dealt with cancer patients on the surgical ward, but this was different. Many patients here on the cancer ward were terminal, their initial and subsequent treatments having failed. Many were patients who had recurrences of their disease and needed additional therapy, which really meant that most of them would sooner or latter die. Not many would live five years, the magic milestone that some academic had picked as a measure of success.

Theo had already gone through the usual introductions by the chief resident and the head of the service. He knew which beds were his responsibility and was now on his way to see who occupied those beds. He first went into 411, a four-bed ward. The first bed was occupied by a frail looking woman. She seemed not quite with it. Theo looked through her chart: Forty-six, cancer of the pancreas, previous treatment was surgical, but not all the cancer could be removed. Present plan of treatment: palliation, which meant she was dying. Present medication: large doses of Morphine when required. No wonder she seemed out of it, she was heavily doped. But even so, she still moaned with pain now and then. The last entry on the chart was by a neurosurgeon. Arrangements were being made to perform a chordotomy because of intractable pain. This meant that the pain fibers in her spinal chord were to be cut to afford her some relief from her pain.

Theo closed the chart and looked at the woman. He could not bring himself to talk to her. What could he say? How could he comfort her? No matter what anybody did or said, she would soon die. He stood there a few moments more and then went to the next bed.

Suddenly he heard his name called. He turned around and saw one of the oncologists standing in the doorway.

"Do you have time for a cup of coffee, Dr. Dirks?"

Theo was perplexed. "Why yes, I suppose so."

"I'm Dr. Barker, Brad to my friends. I thought you needed a psychological boost, or am I wrong?"

"Well I... " Theo gave a deep sigh, what the hell, " . . .yes, you're probably right. It's difficult to face dying patients."

They turned toward the cafeteria. Brad Barker was a large but well-proportioned man in his forties. He had been in this field for some time. "Is this how you see these patients, as someone who is dying? Why don't you look at them simply as one who needs some assistance, either physi-cal or mental? If death comes, so be it."

They found a table in the coffee shop and sat down. "Once you overcome your own hang-ups about illness and dying—and we all have those—then it will be easier, you'll see."

Theo began to like this man. Maybe he had been looking at these patients from the wrong point of view. "How do you help someone you know is dying? What do you say?"

Barker was quiet for a moment, then he looked Theo straight in the face. "The words will come once you deal with your own hangups about death; your own fears, your own beliefs. The difficulty is not with the patient, it's in you."

They continued the discussion for a while, then Theo went back to the ward to finish rounds.

Chapter 46

It was Theo's clinic day. For several weeks he had been working in the chemotherapy clinic at the Cancer Institute. In some ways, the work was depressing, but there were also rewards. He had just seen Beth Holland, what a delightful old lady. She had Multiple Myeloma, a cancer that arose in the bone marrow. She knew that there was no cure and that chemotherapy only slowed down the inevitable progression of the cancer, but she never complained, she always had a cheerful word for Theo, and would not fail to ask about his family.

Then there was Betsy Taylor, a twenty-nine-year-old mother of three, with stage three ovarian cancer. She seemed to be in total remission, but cures of stage three ovarian cancer were rare. Yet everyone was hoping she would be the one to be cured. Every time Theo saw her he could see the questions in her eyes, and the hidden fear; she so wanted to live.

At home, Theo would sometimes discuss cases with Laura, but not having a medical background, she at times did not appreciate the significance of a diagnosis or treatment, and not show enough interest. That's at least how Theo saw it. Maybe she only wanted him more involved in the family where she thought Theo did not show enough interest. They seemed to be more distant now and, probably without noticing it, Theo spent more and more time in the hospital.

One evening when he was on call and having a cup of coffee in the cafeteria, one of the nurses from the cancer ward joined him at his table. This in itself was nothing unusual except that Sandy Clarke, the nurse, had never talked to him before, except on the ward when it concerned patients. She placed her tray on the table, smiled, and asked, "You don't mind if I join you, do you?"

Theo jumped up. "No, no, sit down." No matter how hard he tried, he could not remember her name.

Fortunately, she did not expect that he would remember her and introduced herself. "I'm Sandy Clarke from the cancer ward."

For want of something better to say Theo mumbled, "Yes, I know Mrs. Clarke," which clearly was not so.

"Please call me Sandy, and I'm not a Mrs., at least not anymore."

Theo had noticed her on the ward before. She was a good-looking, slim woman in her forties with an outgoing personality, and she was a good nurse. Theo could not understand why he felt uncomfortable sitting with her. Fortunately, his pager beeped at that moment and he excused himself and left.

"I'll see you here tomorrow for coffee," Sandy called after him.

The next time Theo was on call he looked for Sandy but she was not on the ward, and when he went to the cafeteria, she was not there either. 'Guess she's off today,' he concluded and wondered why it should matter to him anyway.

He met her again the following day on the ward, just before morning rounds. She was in the nurses' room and he waved to her through the window. She waved back and gave him a big smile. As soon as rounds were finished, Sandy appeared at his side. "Hello, Dr. Dirks. Will you come and join me for coffee during my break?"

"Sorry, I can't, I have the students. But maybe when your shift finishes at four?"

"Oh, that would be nice." She smiled and rushed off to her work.

'Now why did I do that?' Theo mused as he went to meet his group of students.

At four o'clock Theo was looking through some charts on the ward when someone put a hand on his shoulder. When he looked around it was Sandy. She smiled at him. "Well, it's four o'clock. Are you ready? We have a coffee date, remember?"

"Hi, yes I remember, let's go." He put away the charts and got up. "It'll have to be the hospital cafeteria, I'm on call."

"Oh, that'll be fine, Dr. Dirks."

"I think you should stop this Dr. stuff. My name is Theo and if I'm to call you Sandy, you will have to call me Theo, don't you think?"

Sandy laughed. "Well, I guess you're right, Theo."

They both laughed. "See? It's easy."

The restaurant was crowded but they managed to find a table off to the side.

For a few moments they were quiet, drinking their coffee, then Sandy said "It's been a hectic day, I needed this," presumably referring to the coffee.

Theo felt distinctly uneasy. 'This is silly,' he thought, 'I'm only having coffee with her—but she is good looking.' Aloud he said, "Yes it's been busy. I hope the night will be quiet." For some reason he felt the need to tell her about Laura and his children. Sandy sat there and listened to him, occasionally smiling. When he stopped talking, she finished her coffee and got up. "Have to go. Thanks for the coffee and the company."

Theo got up. "Yes, I have to finish the charts. See you." He would have liked her to stay longer, but he wasn't quite sure why. He watched her walk through the cafeteria and leave through the far door. 'Nice back too,' he thought.

A few days later he met Sandy as he was leaving the hospital. He had the impression that she had been waiting for him.

She wore her usual smile and waved, then walked down the steps toward him. She was smartly dressed in a blouse and skirt and had a purse over her shoulder. She came up to him and put a hand on his arm. "Hi."

"Hi. Working late are you?"

She blushed slightly. "Well, I visited someone in the hospital. You know how it is?"

"Yes, I know," he said, thinking, 'what idiotic conversation.' They started walking down the street towards the parking lot. Nancy hooked her hand under his arm as if it was the natural thing to do. "Do you have to go?"

"I, ah, parents' night at the school, you know."

"Ah yes, parents' night." She let his arm go. "I'll see you tomorrow?"

"Yes, yes, tomorrow. I'm not busy tomorrow."

She smiled at him. "That's nice. Until tomorrow."

Chapter 47

The next day Sandy stopped him in the corridor of the ward. "No parents' night today?"

Although Theo was in a hurry, he stopped for a few minutes. "No, no parents' night today."

Sandy gave him a quick smile. "Well, maybe you can walk me home after work?"

"Yes maybe. See you later. I have to get things ready for rounds."

'Why did I agree to that?' Theo asked himself. 'I must be off my rocker.' He tried to put Sandy out of his mind and concentrate on his work, but it was difficult.

Rounds were uneventful, for which Theo was thankful, and the rest of the day was easy. He was finishing some charts on the ward when somebody put a hand on his shoulder. When he turned around he looked into Sandy's smiling face. "Ready to go?"

"Go? Oh yes, I am walking you home, right?"

"You've got it."

"Well, a few minutes. I have to finish these charts."

"Okay, I'll wait for you out front."

Theo watched Sandy walk down the hall, hips swinging, erect posture, slim figure. 'Very sexy,' he thought. 'Do I want to get involved?' He did not want to but seemed unable to resist.

He took his time with the charts and then put on his coat and walked down the corridor. Sandy was waiting near the front door. "You must have had a lot of charts left, but I forgive you." She again hooked her arm through his as if it was the thing to do.

Theo felt a bit awkward but did not know what to do about it. "I'm sorry if I kept you waiting. Where are we going?"

"Oh, just down the street a few blocks, to my flat." She tugged his arm and smiled up at him. "You don't mind, do you?"

"No, no, that's fine. I'll walk you home."

"You could come in for a cup of coffee, couldn't you?"

"Well, I, well yes, I suppose so," Theo stammered.

Sandy laughed. "Don't sound so enthusiastic now."

Theo was going to say something but then just smiled. A few seconds later they arrived at an apartment building with and elegant entrance and went in.

Sandy's flat was on the fourth floor. It was stylish and clean. Theo walked to the window. He saw the mountains over the roofs of the houses. Sandy disappeared through a door, and soon Theo could smell fresh coffee. He felt intensely out of place but at the same time excited. 'What am I doing here?' he asked himself, but had no answer, at least none that he wanted to admit to.

"Hey, dreamer, come get your coffee." Sandy stood in the door to the kitchen with a cup of coffee. "Let's sit in the kitchen." She stepped aside to let Theo through. There was another cup of coffee standing on the table and Theo sat down.

"Nice place," he remarked to make conversation.

Sandy smiled. "Yes, I like it." She put a hand on his. "Try the coffee, you'll like it."

Theo sipped his coffee and after a few minutes got up. "I have to go."

"Aw, already? Well, we'll make it longer next time."

Theo only nodded and then left. 'Why did I even go in?' he wondered.

A couple of days later Sandy was again waiting for him near the front exit. "Hi there, stranger. Long time no see. Walk me home?"

Theo did hot want to go but could not think of a reason to say no. He only nodded as Sandy again hooked her arm through his. When they were in her flat, she turned to him and kissed him hard on the mouth, then disappeared through a door. Theo was totally rattled but had not resisted. 'I should leave right now,' he thought, but did not.

A few minutes later Sandy re-appeared. She had changed and now was wearing only a housecoat. As she came close to him the housecoat fell open; she had nothing on underneath. She put her arm around him as Theo just stood there.

"Come lover, do you like what you see?" She kissed him on the mouth. Theo could feel her heat as she pressed against him. He seemed at first unable to resist, but then he pushed her firmly away. "Sorry, Nancy. I can't. I just can't. My wife, you see . . ."

"Oh, fuck your wife! You jerk! Why did you come up here? Did you think we were going to play tiddlywinks, or what? Why don't you get the hell out of here!" She ran into the bedroom.

Theo stood there a second and then quietly left the apartment. On the street he paused for a few minutes, took several deep breaths, and then walked back to the hospital parking lot and drove home.

The next day Theo came to the hospital early as usual. The day progressed uneventfully until early afternoon when he was called to the resident program director's office. Dr. Erdig invited him to sit down. "There is something I need to discuss with you, Dr. Dirks. In fact it is something serious."

Theo was perplexed, and a little scared. 'I hope it is not something that will affect my residency,' he thought.

Dr. Erdig went on. "There has been a charge against you, a charge of sexual harassment."

"What!" Theo just about fell off the chair. "Who would do that?"

"Well, it's actually one of the nurses on your ward. Let's see…" he shuffled among some papers, "Yes, a Ms. Sandra Hughes."

"Sandy! Why that's preposterous!" Theo shook his head. How could he have been so stupid. "This is incredible. I guess I better tell you the whole story."

Dr. Erdig listened attentively and when Theo was finished, took of his glasses and cleaned them carefully. After a while he said, "It's an interesting case, but I want to tell you that this is serious, and so far it's her word against yours. Difficult indeed. We will have to investigate further. Thank you for coming, Dr. Dirks."

Theo left in a daze. How could she do this? What had he done to her? He obviously did not understand the rage of a woman scorned. To clear his head he walked around the block before returning to the ward. He decided he had to discuss this with somebody and get some advice. At once he thought of Dr. Barker. Brad had helped him before; maybe he could do so again. In any case, there was nothing to lose. When he had finished the immediate needs on the ward, he phoned Dr. Barker and arranged a time to meet him. It was not until the next day, but that would have to do.

Dr. Barker scratched his chin, cleared his throat a few times, sat up straighter, and then looked at Theo for a few seconds. "You did nothing to provoke this?"

"Nothing is probably not quite correct. I did not do anything that could, even remotely, be construed as sexual harassment, but I was friendly towards her. I had coffee with her in the cafeteria several times, I went to her apartment, but she was the one that made the sexual advances and I left when I realized what her intentions were."

Dr. Barker was drumming his hands lightly on the table. "It's your word against hers; very difficult. What do you expect from me?"

Theo sat there staring at the floor. "I don't know. Maybe some advice. I don't know. I don't want to lose everything I've worked for. It's not fair, it just is not fair."

"I sympathize with you, Theo, but you will just have to wait until Dr. Erdig has finished his investigation. Don't do anything rash or foolish now, just stick to your work."

A few days later, Dr. Erdig called Theo into his office. "Things don't look so good, Dr. Dirks. We could not find anything that supports your word. We might have to consider suspending you until this mess is cleared up."

Theo was aghast. "But I did not do anything. Am I not innocent until proven guilty?"

"Don't quote me the law, Dr. Dirks. This is not a court procedure. We will discuss the case at committee tomorrow and in a day or two you will have the decision. That is all, Dr. Dirks."

Theo left the office and went back to the ward. His world was falling appart and there seemed to be nothing that he could do. The head nurse found him sitting there with his hands over his face. "What's the matter, Dr. Dirks? Headache?"

Theo looked up at her. "I wish it was only that." He thought for a few minutes and then the whole story came pouring out, right to the bitter end. "Do you realize that I am about to lose everything that I have struggled so hard to achieve, everything? What will Laura think? She has skimped and done without and now it's all down the drain, all gone." His eyes grew moist and he turned away and blew his nose.

"Now Dr. Dirks, I would not be so ready to give up. I thought you were a fighter, and here you are, ready to throw in the towel. No Dr. Dirks, let's not give up yet. Why don't you go home now and we will talk some more in the morning."

The next morning started very busy. One of the post-operative patients had developed separation of his incision and had to be taken to the operating room. Then Theo had to finish seeing the patients and have a teaching session with the students. When he finally had a chance to sit down at the nurses station to complete some charts he was called to the phone. "Dr. Dirks, it's Dr. Erdig."

'Oh God,' Theo thought. 'This is it, so soon.' He took the phone from the ward clerk. "Hello, this is Dr. Dirks."

"Theo, this is Erdig." Strange, thought Theo, he always called me Dr. before. "If you can make it I would like to see you in my office."

Theo stuttered. "Now? Right now? I mean . . ."

"Yes, if you can come."

"Oh, yes, of course, as you say." He hung up the phone, put away the charts, and walked down the corridor. He could hardly move his feet. They must have had the meeting sooner and had reached a decision. He could think of no other reason why Dr. Erdig would want to see him. So this was it, this was the end of his medical career, the end of his dream. He felt totally drained. What would he tell Laura? She had worked so hard to help him through his medical studies. He did not know how he could face her. When he reached Dr. Erdig's door, he knocked and then entered. As soon as he had opened the door, he stopped. What were these people doing here? Dr. Barker was sitting on a chair beside the desk, with Dr. Erdig behind the desk and Mrs. Harper, the head nurse and another nurse standing beside the window. Everyone was smiling. What was going on? Theo just stood there.

Dr. Erdig waved his hand. "Come in, come in, Theo. For a change I have some good news. It seems that Mrs. Hughes has, ah, how shall I say, been after other doctors before. She seems to have gone this route at another hospital and has been observed to, shall we say, make eyes at other residents from time to time. These good people," he motioned towards the nurses, "have convinced me that the charge against you is false, and I was not that easily convinced. But they had some very compelling arguments, so for now you are cleared. We will have to clear up some final details, but I would doubt that there will be a change in the decision. I must say, I am glad of this outcome. I have always considered you one of our better residents."

"Thank you, thank you, sir." Theo stumbled out of the room and closed the door behind him. He walked a few steps down the corridor and then leaned against the wall. Tears were running down his cheeks. He quickly ducked into the washroom and washed his face; it would not do for the students to see their resident crying.

Chapter 48

Theo finished what needed to be done on the ward and left the hospital. For once, he wanted to be home early to see Laura and the kids. Was it guilt, was it relief, was it happiness? He didn't know, he just knew that he had to be home. When he arrived, Laura was in the kitchen, preparing supper. She smiled when she saw him come in. "Hi, home early, huh?"

Theo kissed her on the cheek. "Yes, they let me out today, but I'll probably have to make it up tomorrow."

"Well, enjoy today," she glanced at him searchingly. "You look beat. Bad day?"

"Well, sort of."

"Anything special?"

'Yea, fooling around with nurses,' Theo thought. Aloud he said, "No, just the usual, it's busy." He felt an urgent need to hug Laura and tell her the whole lousy mess, but what would that achieve? It would not undo anything, and who knows how she would take it, and what was there to tell? In the end, he did not say anything.

Laura poured him a cup of coffee. "Here, this might perk you up. The children are watching TV, why don't you join them and relax." Theo noted a hint of anxiety in Laura's

259

voice; he had not spent much time with Sarah and Paul lately. He took the coffee and went into the living room. "Hi kids."

They glanced up. "Hi Dad," then continued watching TV. Theo observed them: Paul, ten years old now, a typical thin lanky boy; and Sarah, slim but showing signs of early womanhood. 'How soon they grow up,' Theo thought. He remembered his own childhood, his own father. He missed him. It was strange that one could miss someone after such a long time. It seemed to him that he now remembered more of the good times and that the negatives were getting less severe and much less important.

He went and sat on the chesterfield between his children. After a while, Paul moved closer and leaned against him, but continued to watch TV. Theo put his arm around him and gave him a gentle squeeze. He glanced at Sarah, she was totally absorbed in the TV show. 'Paul has always been the more affectionate of the two,' Theo thought.

When the program was over, they both jumped up. "We have to do our homework," they cried.

"Yes, me too," Theo said. He kissed both of them on the forehead and left. He did have a lot of studying to do. His last year of residency was coming to an end and he had to be ready for the exams. Failure was totally out of the question, for it would mean that, at best, he would have to wait a year to repeat the exams, and at worst, that his whole residency had been wasted. No, failure was out of the question, he had to make sure that he passed.

Chapter 49

In the end, the exams proved not too difficult for Theo, but two of the six residents that wrote the exams with him failed. The oral exams had been a strain, not only mentally, but also financially, as the registration fee, travel to Montreal, and the cost of staying there amounted to more money than Theo had, and he had once again gone to the bank and borrowed money.

Although Theo had done well in his exams, he soon found out that his former disagreements with some of the staff, notably Dr. Brooks, now made it unlikely that he would obtain an appointment to Midwest. She seemed to be determined to prevent his acceptance there. Theo talked to the chief of surgery and other staff, but in the end he realized that he would have to look elsewhere.

There was a pressing need for Theo to find work and an income soon, because they were deeply in debt. An opportunity presented itself in a smallish town in Minnesota. Fortunately, he had done his State Board exams when he finished medical school and should have no problems with a U.S. work permit, as northern Minnesota was an under-doctored area. Wheaton was a small town with a seventy-bed hospital and one general surgeon who desperately needed a holiday. Immediate income was assured.

Laura was not too keen on moving to the United States but Theo assured her it would only be temporary. So it came about that Theo, at age thirty-nine, started his surgical career in a small U.S. town. He had always thought of working in a university hospital in Canada, of teaching students and residents, of doing some research; this, however, was not to be. He wished he had been more careful to avoid disagreements with the staff, but if he was honest with himself, he had to admit that Dr. Brooks had not liked him from the beginning, and as for Parker-Cowan, the guy was a bungler. Who wanted to work with him anyway?

Theo threw himself into his work with determination; he would do the best he could. Even if he wasn't at a university, he was still doing surgery. The first two weeks were quite routine, he was not too busy, but there was enough work. But on the fourth of July weekend things began to pop. First he had a serious burn when a teenager mishandled a fire cracker; then there was a motor vehicle accident, again teenagers. Three were seriously injured, one of these critical. There were internal injuries and urgent surgery was needed. After four hours, Theo came out of the O.R.; he had removed the ruptured spleen, had repaired tears in the liver, and had removed some torn bowel, altogether not a bad day's work. On top of that the patient was in reasonable shape afterwards and had a good chance of recovering completely.

One of the other teenagers also required some surgery, but of a lesser nature. When Theo went home near midnight, he was very tired, but had this very satisfying feeling of having done something very worthwhile.

He was surprised to find Laura still up, but it was comforting to have someone to talk to, as he was still to wound up for sleep. He told her about his day at the hospital, the surgery, the good results. Suddenly he noticed that Laura had said hardly a word.

"What's up honey, you haven't said a word, are you sick?"

"Oh, Theo, can't you see anything? We are far away from any friends and relatives, and I have not seen my parents for nearly two years. You have not seen your mother for a long time either. It's fine to be dedicated, but look at us! We are among strangers, in a strange land. What about me, what about the children?" It was the longest speech Laura had made in a long time.

Theo was totally dumbfounded. "But you never said anything."

"Did you want me to upset your studies? Now that you are finished you should consider us to."

"Laura, I have always considered you and the kids. I'm doing this for you and them, don't you see that?"

"If you considered us, why did you move here?"

"Because we needed money, and this was one place where I could make quite a bit quickly. It's only a locum and we can leave when Noel returns from his holidays. Of course, we will have to find a place to go to, but I am sure there will be need for a surgeon somewhere in Canada. That's where you want to go to, isn't it?"

Laura looked at him sadly. "It's B.C. I want to live in, or near Vancouver, where my relatives and friends are, you know that." She had tears in her eyes.

Theo hugged her. "I know Laura, I know. You are lonely, I'm sorry." He pressed her close and with one finger wiped away her tears. "How would you like to visit your mother for a few weeks? I think it would be a good change for you, don't you think?"

"Oh Theo, you know I can't go. The children are in school, and what would you do?"

"I will manage, I'm a big boy, and the kids are doing well in school. If they miss a few days that won't matter at all, they can go with you."

Laura wasn't at all sure, but she very much wanted to see her parents. In the end arrangements were made, the children's continuing education was arranged, and homework assigned, piles of food were prepared for Theo, and they were off.

Chapter 50

The weather had worsened. It was snowing and there was a light wind, which caused the snow to drift across the road. At first Theo worried that the adverse weather would affect Laura's flight, but soon his whole attention was needed just to keep the car on the road. There was now a stronger crosswind, the road had patches of ice, and visibility was poor. He reached the border crossing without difficulty. The guard there recognized him. "Hi Doc. Terrible weather, better be careful, the driving is getting tricky."

"Hi Cliff. You're right, I'll be careful. Just dropped the wife off at the airport in Winnipeg."

The customs officer waved him on. "Carry on." He leaned out of his window as Theo was leaving and shouted after him. "Be careful!"

The driving was now quite difficult and Theo had slowed to a crawl. It was beginning to get dark. After about thirty minutes, Theo was wondering whether he would make it home. The wind was now almost a gale, driving the snow through the air in a whirl of white clouds. Suddenly he saw a dark object in front of him. It looked like a car. Why would a car be standing here in this snow storm? They must have trouble. Theo came to a careful stop, buttoned up his coat, and got out. He could not see anyone. Bracing himself against the wind and shielding his face, he made it to the car. He could not see anybody but the windows were partly frozen and, in the dark, he could not see the inside well. As he started to open the door, the back of his head suddenly felt as if it were exploding and everything went black.

The first thing that he noticed as he came to was the incredible cold. His hands were stiff, his feet felt like pieces of ice, his whole body was numb. Then he noticed the pain as he became more awake. The whole back of his head was one incredible ache. He felt it with his stiff fingers and there was a large lump. Slowly Theo realized that he had been mugged. He turned around, his car was gone. The other car was next to him and actually shielded him from the wind. 'Small luck,' Theo thought, but as he got up he noticed how much colder it was in the wind. He opened the car door and looked through the car. It was an old beat-up Chev. The keys were in the ignition. He got behind the wheel but, as he had suspected, the battery was dead and there was no response. He sat there for a while but the cold was getting to him. 'Have to get moving,' he thought. There was an old blanket on the back seat. Theo took it and wrapped it around his head and upper body, then got out of the car and started walking.

It was slow going. The wind was blowing across the road and Theo had difficulty keeping his balance on the slippery road. He moved to the side of the road, into the snow where balance was easier but walking was harder. It continued to snow and visibility was poor. Fortunately, there were poles marking the edge of the road for the snow plows so that he had something to keep him from wandering off into the fields.

Leaning into the wind, he kept moving. It was incredibly cold and his head was throbbing but he knew that he could not stop. He started to count his steps just to occupy his mind, but he kept getting the numbers mixed up. He remembered the war. There had been times then too when he had been cold, very cold, but he had survived. Would he survive now? He thought of Trudy. He still missed him after all these years! He began to imagine how it would be if he died and met Trudy. Was there a hereafter? Suddenly he saw a light—it must be a car. Should he hide? Was his assailant returning? Before he could decide, a car stopped beside him. There were voices and shouts. Somebody grabbed Theo's arm and led him to the car.

Theo could not remember how he got to the hospital or why he was in a hospital bed with his hands and one foot bandaged, or why he had a king-sized headache. He lay there with his eyes closed, trying to remember, but there were only bits. He remembered driving in the storm, them he remembered walking. Why was he walking? He opened his eyes. There was a nurse standing beside his bed. She smiled. "Hello there, Dr. Dirks. You are awake."

Theo could only whisper, "What happened?" His lips were stiff and dry.

The nurse smiled again. "I'll get the doctor."

She soon returned with one of Theo's colleagues, one of the local GPs, Paul Gregg. Paul pulled up a chair and sat down. "Hi there."

Theo motioned with his hand.

Paul leaned toward him. "You've had quite an experience. We still don't know exactly what happened. Why were you walking? And what happened with your car?"

"Got mugged. Car stolen. My hands, how are my hands?"

Paul looked sympathetic. "Frost bite." He took Theo's bandaged hand and squeezed it lightly.

Theo became quite agitated. "My hands, how are my hands? Surgery?"

Dr. Gregg beckoned to the nurse who gave Theo a shot to sedate him and Theo was soon asleep. Paul stood there a while and looked at Theo then turned around and walked out of the room.

Theo woke up in the middle of the night. The door to his room was ajar and there was a light on in the hallway, keeping the room from being totally dark. He raised his bandaged hands. In the semidarkness they looked like clubs. How badly were they injured? Would he be able to return to his work? What would he do if he could not operate? His thoughts turned to Laura. With a start, he thought that someone might have notified her, but that was unlikely as nobody knew exactly where she was. He became aware of the throbbing pain in his hands. His right foot ached too. He had forgotten about his foot, probably because it was not as important to him as his hands. His pain increased and he pulled the cord to call the nurse who came almost immediately. "Yes, Dr. Dirks?"

"My hands, how bad? I mean, is it serious, will I be able to work?" He became quite agitated again.

The nurse hesitated. "I, I don't know. I'm sure you'll be all right. Would you like something for pain?"

Theo nodded. Nurses were instructed not to discuss the patient's condition. Being a patient, Theo now realized that that was not always the right thing to do, but he had given the same instructions on many occasions. The patient's perception was that things were really bad, otherwise why would the nurse be so evasive? The nurse went out and quickly returned and gave Theo a shot and he soon fell asleep.

Chapter 51

Theo was struggling but he could not free himself. Somebody was holding him down. He pushed harder… Suddenly he was awake, the nurse was shaking him by the shoulder. "Wake up Dr. Dirks, wake up. You must have had a bad dream, you were shouting and struggling. Are you awake now?"

Theo nodded. "I'm awake."

It had been a bad dream: He was lying on the street in Warsaw, only a few feet away from Trudy, who's guts were bulging out from his abdomen. Theo was desperately trying to get to Trudy but there was something wrong with his hands and he could not move himself forward. No matter how hard he tried, he could not get to him. 'I have to save him, I have to, no matter what!' He tried to move his legs but something was holding him down. Somehow, Theo did not think that unusual, but what was wrong with his hands? They just did not work, and there was Trudy, dying with his guts out. He had to get there. This time he would put everything into it, he pushed with his hands and feet. There was this tremendous pain and he screamed. . .

"That must have been a doozer of a dream, the way you struggled and yelled. You okay now?" The nurse looked concerned.

"Yes, I'm fine. Thank you, nurse. It was a bad dream."

It was funny how he always remembered Trudy when he was down, even in his dreams. It seemed only yesterday that he had been in the war and saw Trudy die. He still missed him. 'I wonder if that ever goes away,' he thought. His hands ached but he decided against another shot, he did not need any more bad dreams.

His thoughts turned to Laura.He had to get in touch, he had waited too long already. She would be so shocked, and she would want to return immediately. He had to work out a plan before he called her. To do that he would have to know how his hands were.

When Paul Gregg made rounds in the morning, Theo asked about his condition. "Paul, I have to know what's what. How are my hands? Will I recover? Will there be permanent damage? What about my work?"

Paul pulled up a chair and sat down. He gave Theo a long look. "Well, we have to discuss this sooner or later, it might as well be now. You have serious frostbite to some of your fingers, not all the same. Your right index finger is the worst."

"How bad?"

"Well, that's hard to say at this time. You will probably need some surgery?"

"Could I lose the finger?"

"Not all of it but you could loose the distal part, it's hard to say now."

"How long do I have to stay in the hospital?"

"You could go home now, if there is somebody to look after you."

Theo thought for a moment. "Could I travel to Vancouver?"

"That's about three hours by plane; I would think so."

"Then that's what I want to do, go to Vancouver." Then, as if he needed to explain, "My mother lives there, and my family is there now."

He took the flight from Minneapolis to Seattle the next day. From there he would take the shuttle to Vancouver.

The flight was smooth. The weather was clear over the Rockies and the view fantastic, but Theo's mind was not on the scenery. He was happy to return to Vancouver, although he would have been happier if the circumstances had been different. He had been away almost ten years; four of medical school, five years of internship and residency, and a few months of private practice. What did the future hold? He had to believe that he would again be able to operate. He could not imagine a life otherwise. There had been times in his life before when everything had seemed hopeless, but there had always been some solution. He leaned back in his seat and closed his eyes. 'Oh God,' he thought, 'let my hands recover so that I can do my work again.' Then he remembered that he had not prayed for a long time, and he could not even remember when he had been to church the last time. 'You're a fine one to ask God for help now,' he thought. Then he remembered his home: His father reading the bible, praying before meals. He had not attended church as a child as the soviets had closed all the churches, but there had been occasional secret meetings in various houses.

The pilot's voice announcing the imminent landing brought Theo back to the present. His hands ached but he had decided not to take any pain killers unless it became unbearable, and so far it had not been.

With the help of the airline personnel, he transferred to a shuttle for Vancouver and soon saw the familiar north-shore mountains and city sky line.

Chapter 52

It was good to be home again. Peet had picked him up at the airport and taken him to his mother's house. The kid had become a fully grown, handsome man. Theo kept looking at him—God, how he had changed. Theo had hardly recognized him. His manner also was so different. At first Theo could not quite tell what he did not like about Peet's manner, but then it suddenly struck him: the kid had become a snob. He could not believe it, a real snob!

"Well, Theo, now that you are back, I suppose you will be head of the family."

"What on earth are you talking about, Peet?"

"You know, the oldest male, that's biblical. That's how God has arranged it. Until now I was head."

"I don't know what God has arranged, but what you are saying is utter rot. What does Mom say about that?"

Peet's face tightened and he became very serious. "I suspected that you are not a Christian, not born again. You should change your ways and wander in the ways of the Lord, otherwise you shall surely be lost."

"Now listen Peet, I am here because I had a serious injury. I need time to recover. I do not need either preaching from you, nor this type of conversion. I will not stay here any longer than I have to. In the meantime, if you want to think I am a damn heathen, please do so, but spare me your overbearing religiosity."

Theo was happy that they had arrived at the house, ending the unpleasant discusion. Their mother was waiting on the porch; how she had aged. Theo got out quickly to avoid any further discussion and walked up the steps. He could see the horror in his mother's eyes when she saw his thickly bandaged hands. "It's okay, Mom, they're not that bad." He put both arms around her and hugged her.

She had tears in her eyes. "Oh Theo, I had pictured your homecoming differently. How bad are they? Will… will you be able… I mean, the surgery?"

"Well, we will have to find out, but I will give it a damn good try."

Peet walked up the stairs with the suitcase. "That sort of language is not used in this house. It is not pleasing to the Lord."

"You have become a real religious nut, haven't you Peet?" When he saw his mother's face he regretted his words. "It's okay, Mom, I will restrain myself."

Laura was driving over from her parents and had not yet arrived. They all went into the house where Jutta had piles of food ready. Theo was hungry and ready to dig in but Peet stopped him short. "Let us pray and give thanks to the Lord for his guidance and blessings." They prayed. Before they could start eating, Sonja arrived with her husband and three children. They stormed into the house. "Are you our uncle? Are you the doctor? What happened to your hands?"

Sonja shooed them away. "Don't ask so many questions. Give the poor man a chance." She hugged Theo. "Oh, it's so nice to see you again. Come, sit down and tell me all about you. Never mind my kids, they're always like a storm, but they're good kids." She gave them a loving glance.

Theo looked longingly at the food, but Sonja did not notice. Fortunately, Laura arrived shortly after and Theo was rescued.

Laura rushed over and embraced him. "You should have called me right away. I have been so worried since you called."

Theo smiled. "That's exactly why I did not call; you would have only worried more. And don't look so worried now, you're worse than Mom. I'm okay, but I'm terribly hungry. Could we eat?"

They sat down again. Laura helped Theo with his food in spite of his protestations. He had to admit, it felt good to be looked after.

There was lively discussion at the table. Sonja's children wanted to know what it was like to be a surgeon. How did he injure his hands? Did it hurt? They were very animated and Theo liked them. When lunch was finished, the children went to play and the adults had coffee.

"What are your plans, Theo?" Jutta asked.

"I need to see a plastic surgeon in Vancouver, so we will need to stay somewhere for a while."

"Why a plastic surgeon?" Laura looked very serious. "Is it that bad? What needs to be done?"

"Oh, it's just minor stuff," Theo lied. What was the use upsetting her? She would find out soon enough, and he was not sure himself what needed to be done.

Laura interrupted his thoughts. "We can stay at my parents' place. They have lots of room, and I have already talked to them."

Theo was not sure whether to be happy or not, but since their finances were low, as usual, he did not have that much choice. He did not want to stay at his mother's, not with Peet living here. God, what a prig his brother had become. 'I must be more tolerant,' Theo thought, 'maybe he's not so bad.' "I have to make some calls. Can I use your phone, Mom?"

"Sure, it's in the kitchen."

Theo phoned Hank Rubens, a plastic surgeon he had heard about, and made an appointment. Laura had followed him into the kitchen. "You know, Laura, I'm tired, and I haven't seen you and the kids for a while. Let's go to your parents. I hope we have a room of our own there, do we?"

"Of course, silly. Let's go."

Laura had come in her parent's car. Peet helped with Theo's luggage and, after good byes, they left. They soon arrived at Laura's parents' house. Mr. and Mrs. Elias were friendly but reserved as usual. They visited for a while, then Theo and Laura went up to their room as it was getting late.

"I have missed you so, Theo," Laura's voice was husky.

"Me too, love, me too." They hugged and just stood there for a while. Then they undressed and went to bed. Their lovemaking was unhurried, ardent, and pleasant. Theo felt relaxed after. They talked for a while and then fell asleep.

The next day Theo drove to Vancouver to see Dr. Hank Rubens. After the nurse had taken the necessary information, Theo was ushered into a nice, but not ostentatious office. Hank Rubens entered a few minutes later. "I'm Dr. Rubens, sorry for the wait."

Theo liked him instantly. Hank Rubens was tallish, slim, and had an open, pleasant manner. "There was no wait. I'm Theo Dirks, I wish I could say I am happy to meet you. I would have been if I were not the patient."

"Ah, you're the surgeon. Yes, yes. Well, it could have been under better circumstances, yes. Tell me what happened."

Theo gave a quick summery of the attack, his treatments so far, and his worries. Dr. Rubens listened quietly.

"Well, yes. Nasty business, I suppose you are lucky to be alive. Let's see those hands." He took off the bandages and looked at the left hand. "Some loss of skin, might need some skin grafting, but nothing major. Should get a good result functionally. Now the right." He looked at both surfaces, then all the fingers individually, then the palm again, then the fingers again. "Not quite the same, is it?"

He looked up at Theo. "No use me mollycoddling you. You're a surgeon, I'm sure you now the score." He paused.

Theo swallowed once. "It's the index finger?"

Rubens nodded.

"What will you have to do?" Then, after a short pause, "How much will I lose, Dr. Rubens?"

"Please call me Hank. The distal phalanx will have to go. Maybe just a little more. Plus some skin grafts here and there."

"How will it function?"

"Reasonably well."

"What about surgery?" Theo's chest felt tight in anticipation and fear.

"You know," Hank Rubens rubbed his chin, "that's probably more dependent on your mental attitude than on anything else. There will be some physical impairment, to be sure, and I don't want to minimize that, but I have seen people overcome worse impairments."

"Don't worry about that. If I can get back to surgery, I'll do anything. When?"

Hank smiled. "I believe you would do anything. A typical surgeon, eh? I'll set it up and let you know; probably at the end of the week." He explained in detail what would be done, but like most patients, Theo only heard half of it. His mind was racing. There was a chance that he would be able to work again. A good chance, at least a reasonable chance. He was happy with that. Suddenly he could not wait to get back and tell Laura. He would eventually be able to provide for his family. What a joy!

Now they had to decide where to live and work. Laura wanted to stay in Vancouver but Theo convinced her that it would take too long for him to become established there. A surgeon was needed in Fremont, a small city with a nice hospital, not far from Vancouver. There would be lots of work and in addition there was a Mennonite church. After some discussion they agreed that Theo should apply for the vacant position.

Chapter 53

Theo was sitting in his new office. The office was not exactly new, but new for him. He had been lucky; someone had gone broke and Theo had come along just at the right time, had found it, and had been able to lease it for a reasonable rate. To be sure, some renovations had been required to make it fit for a surgeon's office. Now it was perfect, just the right size, located on the fourth floor right next to the elevator, and the view was magnificent. From his office he could see the lake with its steep banks on either side, and the snow-capped mountains in the distance. Theo sat there and looked out. Such a tranquil picture; he could look at it for hours.

Only six months ago he had his operation. The results, in the end, were good, but a second operation had been required. His right index finger had become infected. Not only had he lost the distal joint, but the middle joint had become stiff. However, with the slight bend that Dr. Rubens had left the finger in, the right hand was quite functional. Theo still felt a little awkward with some of the instruments, but Hank Rubens had assured him that he would soon adjust to it. He looked at his right hand. The scars were still red and prominent, but there was no pain. How strange to look at one's hand and to see part of it missing, even if it was only a little part.

After the operation they had lived with Laura's parents. Boy, was Theo glad that time was over! Not that her parents were particularly bad, but Laura's father had gotten on Theo's nerves by constantly knocking doctors. It seemed that doctors, in his view, could not do anything right. They always screwed up, especially the surgeons: they always operated without a good reason; they were greedy; and on and on. Doctor bashing seemed to be a popular past-time generally. It was quite okay for actors, sports persons, artists, and many others to have a good income, but not for doctors. It was strange. After all, doctors, especially surgeons, *were* artists. Not only did a surgeon need skilled hands, he also required good judgment, lots of knowledge, and lots of stamina to survive the night calls. Yet there seemed to be this strange opinion around that anybody could be a doctor. All one had to do was attend medical school. And that was another thing: did these people know what medical school and residency were like? Theo was sure most did not have a clue. Ah well, what could one do?

Theo got up and walked through the office, past the two examining rooms, the small supply room, the waiting room, and the front reception area. Not big, but quite satisfactory.

The hospital, Fremont Memorial, or FMH as it was most commonly referred to, was not big, but adequate. It had three nice OR's, good lab and x-ray units, and a nice surgical ward. The fact that he was the only general surgeon in town had both advantages and disadvantages. Most of the business would be flowing his way, or so he thought. On the other hand, he was on call all the time. Well, time would tell.

Tomorrow was his first official day in the office, and he was eager to get started.

The sun was setting behind the snowcapped mountains and Theo decided it was time to go home. He locked the door and took the stairs to the main floor. He needed the exercise. He drove the short distance to the house they had rented in the car that was also rented. Ah well, soon there would be some income, and if his luck held things should improve.

Chapter 54

As he was driving, his thoughts turned to Laura. They seemed to have become much closer during the last year. Maybe it was all the adversity they had to face, he thought. God, he loved this woman. Why could he not express it? He swore he would try harder.

When he got home Laura was in the front yard. "Oh good, you're home, we can eat. Paul, Sarah—dinner." She hurried off to the kitchen.

Theo went to the bedroom and took off his tie and shoes. Laura made it hard for him to talk to her, he thought, as she was always busy. But, he had to admit to himself, he could have stopped her. He washed up and went downstairs. The children came running and hugged him. How affectionate they were, and without inhibitions. He had a lump in his throat—how lucky he was. He went into the kitchen and hugged Laura.

"What was that for?"

"Oh, I just felt like it." Why did he not say, 'Because I love you'? He did not know.

Laura patted his back. "Let's go and eat."

They sat down and Laura said grace. This was as natural for her as eating. They had just started when the phone rang.

Theo jumped up. "I'll get it, it's probably for me." It was. There had been an accident and at least two people were injured. Theo was needed.

"Sorry, Laura, I have to go. I'll have my dinner later." He grabbed his jacket and rushed out.

It only took a few minutes to get to the hospital. He walked over to the emergency where one of the local GP's was on duty. "What have you got for me?" Then, remembering that he was not yet known, "I'm Dr. Dirks, Theo Dirks."

The GP shook his hand. "I'm Robert McQuinn, some call me Bob, and I'm sure glad to see you." He walked over to stretcher seven. "Young fellow, the driver, hit the steering wheel hard, probably has internal bleeding. Pulse is increasing, blood pressure is still stable. Looks pale."

They walked through the curtain that enclosed the bed on which lay a very pale young man. Theo was introduced. After a few questions, he examined the patient. The abdomen was slightly distended and there was tenderness, especially on the right side. Theo completed his examination, checking the chest, head and neck, the limbs, and the neurological system—no other apparent injuries.

"I think you could be right, in fact, I'm quite sure he has internal bleeding. We should arrange for the OR now so we don't lose any time and then we can check a few other things to make sure. I take it he is crossmatched?" Theo looked at the nurse but Dr. McQuinn answered. "Done. Also a chest X-ray and flat plate of the abdomen. Both normal."

The OR staff was still in the hospital doing an urgent orthopedic case but were just about finished. They could be ready in about one half hour. Theo nodded. "That gives us time for an abdominal tap. If there is free blood, we have a diagnosis." He turned to the nurse. "I will need a Verres needle and something for a prep."

The nurse nodded and disappeared to return a few minutes later with a small tray. Theo washed off a small area of the abdomen with antiseptic solution, injected some anesthetic, made a small incision, and pushed the needle through the abdominal wall into the abdominal cavity. When he sucked back, blood easily welled into the syringe. "We have our diagnosis," he said to no one in particular, and as an afterthought, "There is a lot of blood, we'd better hurry."

Dr. McQuinn and Theo walked over to the OR. There was some coffee in the doctor's lounge and Theo poured two cups. "We have a few minutes and might as well relax. Any others in the accident?"

Robert McQuin took a quick sip of his coffee. "Two more, nothing serious."

Theo was a bit nervous. This was his first case in this OR. He had a tour earlier and knew the layout but this was different. He got up. "I'll just check to make sure they have the right set-up."

The patient was just being transferred to the OR table. The anesthetist was there. Theo put on a mask and walked into the OR. "I think I have met most of you already but I'm afraid I can't remember any names. I am Dr. Dirks." He turned to the anesthetist. "Theo, Theo Dirks."

The anesthetist smiled. "I'm Jack Dale. We'll be ready in a few minutes. Might as well scrub." He turned his attention to the patient, who now had two IV's going, one in each arm. On one side, blood was being administered.

Theo turned to the patient. "As I explained downstairs, we have to operate." The patient only nodded.

Theo called Robert and they began their scrub. Although Theo appeared outwardly calm, he felt somewhat anxious as a lot of surgeons do before and during operations. Numerous possibilities, all of them bad, crowded Theo's mind. What if he had made the wrong diagnosis? What if the liver was badly damaged? Was he up to the surgery? What if, what if . . . He heard but did not pay much attention to Robert's chatter.

They went into the OR, dried their hands, gowned, gloved, and were ready to start. Theo made an incision in the middline of the upper abdomen, then extended it down past the umbilicus for more room. He worked quickly, being only hampered by Dr. McQuinn's poor assistance; the man seemed inexperienced or disinterested, Theo could not tell which. McQuinn did not do anything on his own and Theo had to direct his every move. It was frustrating.

When they entered the abdominal cavity, they found a lot of blood. Theo's actions became faster. He inserted a retractor and directed his assistant to hold it a certain way. "Don't pull too hard, just hold it this way." To the nurse: "Suction." He began to remove the blood in the abdomen. "Just a little more, then we can see what's up. Tilt the retractor more this way, Robert. A little more, that's fine." Theo could now see the spleen, which had a large tear on its upper surface. Theo placed a couple of sponges against the spleen and directed Robert's hand to them. "Put pressure on the spleen to stop the bleeding, I want to have a look around first to see if there is other damage." When Robert had the pressure right, Theo examined the liver as best he could. He then removed some more blood and clot and looked at the large blood vessels on the posterior wall. They were intact; there was some blood behind the posterior lining of the abdomen, near the right kidney, but not enough to worry about.

"Looks okay. Let's take out the spleen and then we will have another look."

By now Robert seemed to have tired as the retractor had slipped. Theo replaced it. "You will have to give me some good exposure. We have to tie off some of the gastric vessels on the upper side of the spleen first." There was some further bleeding and Theo also got the nurse to help. "Take the suction and try to keep this area dry." He quickly clamped, tied, and divided a number of blood vessels, then he inserted his hand for more exposure and with the scissors freed the spleen further. Just as was clearing the large splenic artery and vein, there was a sudden gush of blood. Theo found the vascular pedicle, more by feel that anything, and compressed it.

"Suck here, quickly," he directed the nurse.

"Give me a vascular clamp. No, larger! Yes, that's it! Retract more, Robert, a little more." Theo placed the clamp. He held out his hand. "Another, same size." He placed it then slowly released the pedicle. There was no noticeable bleeding. He let out a sigh of relief. "Got it, should be okay now."

The rest of the splenectomy was uneventful. Theo again examined the rest of the abdomen and, having found no other significant trauma, proceeded to close. Dr. McQuinn seemed to be getting restless. Theo glanced at him. "Would you like to go? We can manage now."

McQuinn seemed relieved. "Good, fine work there, doc. See you." And he was gone.

On his way home, Theo went over the case in his mind. He felt good about the surgery. A good outcome was to be expected, unless some complication ensued. Suddenly his pager went off. Theo had to think for a second what the beeping noise was before he realized it was his pager. He looked at the number, it was the hospital. His first thought was that something had gone wrong with the patient he had just operated on. What to do? Go home and phone or turn around and go to the hospital? He decided to turn around. A few minutes later the pager went off again—must be urgent. He stepped on the gas. When he arrived at the hospital, the switchboard operator waved him over. "The caseroom wants you in a hurry."

Theo was not sure whether he was relieved or not. He was not an obstetrician—the caseroom could be trouble, but at least it was not about his patient. He hurried to the second floor where the delivery suite was located. A nurse pointed him to a door. "Caseroom two, Dr. Dirks."

Theo looked in through the door. There was a woman on the delivery table in stirrups. Someone in OR greens and a mask was sitting at the bottom end, a nurse was giving the patient oxygen, and another nurse was listening to the fetal heart with some sort of stethoscope. The man in the OR greens turned to the door with a questioning look.

"I'm Dr. Dirks," Theo explained. "Somebody called me?" Then as an explanation: "I'm a general surgeon."

The man's face brightened, he got up and came to the door. "Lets go out."

They stepped back into the hall where the man introduced himself. "I'm Dr. Bright, Hal Bright. This is her first pregnancy and there is some irregularity of the fetal heart and she is not fully dilated, so I can't deliver the baby. If things get worse we will have to do something."

Theo was perplexed. "Don't you want an obstetrician?"

"Well, you see, we only have one and he is away today, so you're it. You have done C-Sections I hope?"

"Yes, I've done C-Sections," Theo replied hesitantly, "but I'm not an Obstetrician and I would find it difficult to assess the patient as to her labor and progress."

Dr. Bright pulled down his mask and rose to his fullest hight. "Oh, that's no problem. I'll tell you when a section is indicated."

Theo thought, 'Great, another Einstein of medicine.' At that moment one of the nurses yanked open the door. "Dr. Bright, quick, the fetal heart—it's way down, quick!"

"I think now is the time, Dr. Dirks. Arrange a CS." Bright said to Theo as he disappeared into the caseroom.

Theo hesitated a second and then with a shrug of his shoulders went to the phone. First he phoned the anesthetist on call, it was Jack Dale. 'At least one piece of luck,' Theo thought.

"Hi, Jack, we have an emergency. C Section, can you come?"

"Be right there," Jack answered and hung up.

Theo was thankful. At least someone who trusted him, some anesthetists would have wanted the whole history so that they could make the decision as to urgency in order not appear to be 'just a technician' as one anesthetist had put it to Theo in Wheaton. He next phoned the OR. The evening shift was still on and could be ready quickly.

Dr. Bright came out of the caseroom. "The fetal heart is staying low but steady, and there is some persistent abdominal pain. I think there is some separation of the placenta, an abruptio, I have already cross matched some blood."

Theo was thankful. Maybe this doc was better than Theo had first thought. After arranging the transfer of the patient to the OR they walked over there and changed into OR strip. To Theo's amazement, the anesthetist was already there and the OR was set up.

"You gents might as well scrub. As soon as she gets here I'll do a crash induction and you can start almost immediately," Jack said as he was getting his medications ready.

While they scrubbed, the patient was wheeled into the room. Theo was going over his last C-Section in his mind, trying to remember all the important steps. His pulse had quickened and his worry must have been evident, for Dr. Bright said, "Relax, Theo. May I call you Theo? Call me Hal." Without waiting for an answer he went on, "You'll be okay, it's just surgery, same as an appendix. Of course there is the baby to consider."

Theo was not sure whether to be reassured or more worried. They went into the room and gowned. Jack was just injecting the Pentothal. The patient was already draped. As soon as the Pentothal was in, Jack said, "Okay, go ahead."

Theo hesitated a second. "What, no intubation?"

"I'll do that while you start. You want a live baby, don't you?"

That jolted Theo into action. He was not used to worrying about another patient in the patient's belly. He quickly made a midline incision in the lower abdomen, noting in passing Dr. Bright's skilled assistance. He entered the abdomen, quickly dissected the bladder from the lower uterus, and made a short transverse incision. For just a fleeting moment, he had been tempted to make a vertical incision in the uterus, but decided against it. He extended the incision in the uterus by producing some lateral traction with his fingers. He could feel the baby's head through the membranes. He fumbled a bit as he tried to break the membranes with his fingers, then grabbed the scissors and cut them. There was a flood of bloody fluid but Theo ignored it and tried to get his right hand under the baby's head. At first he did not succeed as the head was wedged tightly into the pelvis, but then he managed and after a few seconds had brought the head out of the pelvis. By now Theo was sweating. It seemed to him that he was taking much too long. He delivered the rest of the baby as Dr. Bright suctioned out the baby's mouth. Suddenly the baby made a noise and then began to cry. Theo had never heard a sweeter sound, but there was no time to relax as there was now quite a bit of bleeding from the uterus. Theo reached in and removed the placenta and a large amount of clot while Dr. Bright, who had cut the cord, handed the baby to the nurse and then turned back to help Theo. Seeing the large clot he remarked, "Abruptio, all right."

After massaging the uterus and getting it to contract, Theo quickly sutured the incision in two layers as he had been taught many years ago and then relaxed a little. He let his hand rest on the abdomen to hide its slight tremor.

Hal smiled at him. "Nice baby. We were lucky."

Theo regretted his earlier unkind thoughts about Dr. Bright and resolved to avoid snap assessments in the future. Hal had been a good assistant and had also given good moral support. Theo was grateful. The rest of the operation was routine and Theo was soon on his way home. His feeling of satisfaction was now quite pronounced; two difficult cases, both with satisfactory outcomes—a good start.

When he got home it was almost midnight but Laura was still up. "I waited for you, thought you might need some support." She grinned.

Theo gave her a hug, a rare event. "You know, Laura, I think I will like it here. It's a nice place. Some good people."

Laura hugged him back. "I'm glad, it's time we settled down somewhere. I've met our neighbors. Nice people too. I like it here also.

Chapter 55

Life settled into a routine and Theo soon was busy. He was well accepted by both the hospital staff and his colleagues, and took an active part in hospital activities. It was now spring of 1967; they had been in Freemont just over a year. A month ago they had bought a house in a nice area of Freemont and were getting ready to move in. Paul was now twelve; he was in grade seven and was doing very well indeed. Next year he would start junior high. Theo could hardly believe it! How time flew.

Sarah was already a young lady of fifteen and very beautiful, at least in Theo's mind, and he was sure he was right. Sarah had decided that she also wanted to become a doctor, but not a surgeon. Surgery she thought was too gruesome. "All that blood!" Her specialty would be kids. She and Theo argued endlessly as to the merits of the different specialties, until Laura told them to stop it and talk about 'civilized things'.

Laura's parents had visited several times already, and Theo's mother was with them now. She had become quite old but her health was still good. She worried about things as mothers tend to do. One of her main concerns was her youngest son Peet. Theo could not understand this. "I thought he was your pride and joy—so pious, so virtuous. Isn't that what mothers want?"

"Don't joke about it! You don't understand things. It's difficult for Peet. His wife has persuaded him to join this very charismatic church. They seem to be totally crazy, and not at all like a normal Mennonite Church."

"You're right, Mom, I don't understand it. I don't even know what charismatic means exactly. What do they do, roll on the floor, or what?"

Laura intervened. "Theo, stop it! Can't you see that your mother is distressed?" She put the tray she was carrying on the table. "Let's have tea."

They discussed other family matters: Sonja's, Theo's sister's, children; Theo's children; the house; but carefully avoided Peet and his family so that Theo never did learn what exactly Peet's problems, and his mother's concerns, were.

Jutta left a few days later and Theo forgot the discussion until about a month later when his mother phoned. She seemed almost hysterical. "Theo, we need help. I want you to come right away!" She was sobbing and could hardly speak.

"Please Mother, settle down. Tell me what happened."

"Don't tell me to settle down! I am settled. We need help and all you can do is to tell me what to do." His mother blurted out between sobs.

"Is that not what you want, for me to tell you what to do?"

"No! I want you to come!"

Theo sighed. "All right, all right, I will try to get away tomorrow."

"Can't you come today? You are always busy with your surgery."

"That's my job, Mother. I am a surgeon, I have patients, and I can't just leave them. I will see you tomorrow." Theo hung up. 'What a mess,' he thought. 'I wonder what it is this time.' He began to make arrangements for two days off.

The next morning he left early and arrived in Vancouver before lunch. His mother was happy to see him but seemed very nervous.

"Come into the house, I have coffee ready."

"What's the big emergency anyway? Why am I here?"

"Come into the house. We'll have coffee and talk."

Theo followed his mother into the house. "Don't stall, Mom. What is this all about?"

Jutta poured the coffee and sat down. She had tears in her eyes. "It's terrible, just terrible! Peety is in jail."

"What?!" Theo could not believe his ears. "In jail . . . What did he do? Is he okay?"

Jutta wiped her eyes. "Yes, yes, he's fine. The police put him in jail. They just put him in jail like a criminal, just like a criminal." She was crying again.

"Now Mother, tell me what happened from the beginning."

"Ja, well, it was at the abortion clinic."

"The abortion clinic! What was he . . ." Suddenly Theo knew. "Was he protesting, Mother?"

Jutta nodded.

"Did he refuse to listen to the police?"

Jutta nodded again, still crying.

Theo was incensed. "And you got me here for THAT?" He could not believe it. "What do you expect me to do about it? He broke the law. He should be in jail, the crazy fool!"

"He's your brother, you should help him." Jutta brought forth between sobs.

"Look Mom, he can help himself. This is hardly a major issue."

"You don't understand. They are killing babies in there. Killing babies," and after a few sobs, "He punched a policeman."

"Mom, they are not killing babies. They perform abortions; that's not the same thing. It's a legal procedure. One can try to change the law peacefully, but one can't take the law into one's hands. I can't help him, nor do I want to." He got up. "I have some things to do in town. When I'm done I'll stop by before I go home."

His mother remained silent, and after a few moments, Theo left.

After his business in town was finished, Theo left for Fremont. He just wanted to get home. He would call his mother tomorrow, but he just could not face her accusing eyes today. How could she condone what Peet had done? How could she support him? Theo did not particularly like abortions, but there was no way he would support the drastic actions his brother seemed to favor.

While driving home he began to regret leaving without stopping by at his mother's as he had promised, but what could he do? Peet, the fool, had not only blocked access to the clinic, he had hit a policeman! Not exactly a pacifist action. How could he justify that? In the end, Theo decided he had done the right thing. After all, what could he do? Maybe this would smarten Peet up and make him realize that it was not a good idea to take part in illegal actions.

Theo parked the car in the garage when he got home and went into the house. Laura greeted him in the foyer. "I thought you would stay overnight, but I'm glad you're home. I have some supper for you in the oven, come and eat."

"If you thought I was staying in town, why would you keep supper warm?

Laura smiled. "I sort of knew that you wouldn't stay."

Theo hugged her. "You're getting too smart, and I'm glad I'm home." Suddenly he was hungry. While he ate, Laura asked questions, which he answered between bites of food, so that when he was finished eating Laura had the whole story.

"Theo, you should not blame them. After all, abortion is an evil thing and they are only trying to stop it. Isn't that a good thing?"

"Don't you start too!" Theo was getting a bit agitated. "Abortion is legal in this country and hitting a policeman isn't. It's as simple as that, and Peet deserves what he is getting. I hope they keep him in jail for a while. Maybe it'll smarten the idiot up."

"Theo! Don't talk like that. After all, he's your brother and you have to stand by him."

"Oh no, I will not! Don't you understand? He broke the law. You know, the way criminals do. He deserves to be in jail!"

They argued back and forth and in the end agreed to disagree, but there was no animosity between them, as they could both understand the other's position.

Theo resumed his work in the office and the hospital. He was now quite busy. In fact, he was thinking of bringing in another surgeon. The other surgical specialties had also added consultants and there were two orthopedic surgeons in Fremont, two eye surgeons, and one urologist. Very welcome from Theo's point of view were the two obstetricians, one of whom had come this year. Theo had always been apprehensive about doing C-Sections and now it was unlikely that he would be called to do one.

Theo's mother did not phone for a month, and when she did, she spoke to Laura to inform her that Peet was out of jail and that his court date was in three months. When Laura told Theo he only shrugged his shoulders. "I have not done anything wrong, and if she does not want to talk to me, that is her business."

Chapter 56

Theo sat at his desk and looked at the mountains. He took in this view and enjoyed it whenever he could. Lately that had not been often as he was very busy, despite having brought another surgeon into the community. How the time had gone! He came to Fremont only five years ago. His practice had flourished and he was well liked, both in the community and in the hospital. This year he was head of the department of surgery. It was a dubious honor as there was no salary attached to the position. It was strictly voluntary, even though it required a fair bit of time and dedication.

At home things progressed as they should, Theo thought. Sarah was now in college and doing very well indeed. Her top marks should have a good chance to getting her into medical school. 'Wonder why she was so preoccupied during her visit home last weekend' Theo thought. She had not been her usual bubbly self. In fact, there was something about her lately that Theo did not like, but he could not exactly define what it was. Probably some stresses with her college work. After all, it was quite a change from going to high school and living at home, a lot more responsibility now.

Theo turned his thoughts to his work and forgot about Sarah.

The next day, in the middle of a busy office, Sarah phoned. "Dad, I need to talk to you."

"Can I call you back later, Sarah? I'm in the middle of a very full office."

"Well, could you come and see me? It's important."

"I'll call you as soon as I'm finished here."

As usual, the office took longer than expected and when Theo called back, Sarah seemed quite anxious. "Can you come to see me, Dad? Soon please. But please don't say anything to Mom, she'll just be upset."

"Upset about what, Sarah?" Theo could not keep a hint of irritation out of his voice.

"Dad! Please, just come, just you. Today?"

Obviously it was something important. "Okay, Sarah, I'll be there in a couple of hours. Shall I come to your dorm?"

"No!" Sarah answered quickly. "You know the coffee shop near the entrance of the university? I'll meet you there."

Theo sat a few minutes and tapped his fingers on the desk. What could it be? Nothing came to mind. He made a phone call to his colleague to advise him that he would be out of town and then called Laura and told her that something had come up and he had to go to an urgent meeting. He would try to be home early.

Driving to Vancouver, he tried to imagine what was troubling Sarah. It couldn't be academic; she was an excellent student. Was it financial? Not likely but possible. Was she sick? Highly unlikely. What else? Finally Theo turned on a tape, but could not concentrate on the music either.

He drove to the coffee shop at the university entrance where he had agreed to meet Sarah. She was already there, looking very anxious. It was obvious that she had been crying. Theo sat down across the table from her. "Hi, Sarah. You don't look so good. Are you sick?"

Sarah started crying. "Oh Daddy, I wasn't going to cry and look at me now. I'm so sorry."

"What are you sorry about? What's wrong?"

"Oh Daddy, I'm… I'm pregnant."

Theo could not believe his ears. "What! You can't be! How can you be? I don't understand!"

Sarah was crying quietly. "I'm just pregnant. I can't have a baby, I can't. Oh Daddy, what am I going to do?" She took his hand. "Please Daddy, what am I going to do?"

Theo sat there and stared at her, totally stunned. "This can't be. What . . . how . . . this can't be, you can't have a baby, it will ruin your carreer. Your mother, what about your mother?"

Sarah tried to dry her face with an already wet handkerchief. "I, I know. She must not know. She mustn't. I… I was thinking . . . I was . . . I am g-going to have an abortion."

"What? You can't! What will your mother say? It will kill her. You can't!"

Sarah cried harder. "What am I going to do? I'll kill myself!"

"Now listen, young lady," Theo was visibly angry. "No daughter of mine is that stupid. There is always a way." He threw five dollars on the table. "Let's get out of here, let's walk."

At first they walked silently, then Theo asked, "Have you talked to anyone about an abortion?"

"No, not really."

"How far are you?"

"About seven weeks, I think."

"Well," Theo took a deep breath, then, typically a surgeon, he attacked the problem head-on. "You can't have a baby. Therefore, the only other course is an abortion. Your mother must never find out, never. Do you understand? Never. I know some of the gynecologists, I'm sure Saul Klein would agree to do it. Do you want me to talk to him? You must be sure you want this, very sure. Are you?"

Sarah nodded. "Yes, yes. Oh Daddy." She cried again as she gave him a big hug. "Thank you, thank you so much. I knew you would understand."

"I don't understand anything. I don't understand how or why or who, but now is not the time. Someday you can explain it to me." He put his arm around his daughter's shoulder. "Let's go back. I have to get home or your mother will wonder where I am. Remember, not a word to her."

The next morning he phoned Saul and arranged an appointment for his daughter. Theo could not come to grips with this problem, although he had reacted instinctively when making the arrangements. He was not violently against abortion, but now that the chips were down, he knew that he disliked it more than he had realized. Had he been too hard on his brother? No! Definitely not, his brother was a fanatic and acted irrationally. But still...

Theo turned to his work and started to dictate the histories he had left undone yesterday. Then he drove to the hospital to make rounds and have lunch. In the afternoon he had two cases in the O.R. It was good that the two operations were simple, for Theo's mind kept wandering and he found himself thinking about Sarah and abortions several times. He was glad when the cases were done without a hitch. He wrote the post-operative orders and then left the hospital.

Unfortunately, he still had patients to see in the office, but the variety of work made him forget Sarah at least for a while, and at the end of the office Theo felt more relaxed. He phoned Saul again. "Hi Saul. Have you seen my . . . Have you seen Sarah?"

"Yes Theo, earlier this afternoon. Nice girl."

"What do you think?"

"What's to think? She's pregnant and does not want a baby. She needs an abortion."

"Just like that?"

"Theo, you're her father. I understand, but she can't have a baby at this time. She's early, it'll be easy."

"Yes, I know, but an abortion?"

"Theo. What are you, a pro-lifer yet? Be realistic, she can't do anything else."

"I know Saul. It's just . . . Well, thanks. When?"

"Next Monday. Someone should pick her up around three."

"I'll be there. Thanks. Goodbye." Theo hung up and leaned back in his chair. The mountains were particularly beautiful today. Theo remembered looking out a window in another city, a long time ago. In his mind he saw Trudy, lying on the street, his guts hanging out. Irrationally he thought, 'I could fix that, now that I'm a surgeon.' He shook his head as if to chase away thoughts of the past. It was already after six, he might as well go home.

Chapter 57

"Yes Henry, I'm on my way. Oh, make sure he's crossmatched, four units, and try for fresh blood. Thanks."

Theo dressed quickly, trying to get fully awake. These multiple injury MVAs were always difficult. This one seemed to have internal injuries and a head injury, at least according to the emergency physician, and Henry was usually right. Well, he would see when he examined the patient.

Theo parked in the doctor's parking lot and went to the emergency. It was quite busy, the usual evening rush. He walked to the nurses' station and looked at the chart and then went to see the patient. Fast but regular pulse, blood pressure fluctuating, pale face, conscious but drowsy; obviously the patient had bled, and was probably still bleeding somewhere. There was no visible bleeding, therefore bleeding in the abdominal cavity was strongly suggested by the clinical picture. What about a head injury? Possible but not likely in view of the patient's level of consciousness, but not ruled out. What to do? Theo decided quickly. "We are going to the OR now, get things going," he said to the nurse next to him. "I'm going to talk to the family. He is still bleeding internally, so there is need for hurry."

Theo went to the nurses' station where Henry was doing his charts. "Are there any relatives, Henry?"

"Why, yes. His wife, she was also in the car, not seriously injured, just some bruises. I believe she's sitting in the waiting area, let's go and look."

They found a thin, anxious woman with some bruises on her face. Henry approached her. "Mrs. Fedder?"

The woman looked up. "Yes?" Her face was puffy, either from crying or the bruises, or both.

"This is Dr. Dirks," Henry continued. "He is a surgeon and would like to talk to you. He has just examined your husband."

Mrs. Fedder raised her hand to her mouth as if to stifle a cry, she had a fearful expression on her face. "Is… is it bad?"

Theo took over. "Your husband has internal injuries and is likely still bleeding. We have to take him to the OR now. He may also have other injuries, but time is of the essence and we can't delay to do other investigations."

"Oh no, don't waste time. Do what you have to. As long as Bill will be okay. He will, won't he?" Again the fearful pleading look. There was no point in scaring this poor woman even further. "Of course he will be all right," Theo said, although he was not certain at all. "We will have to go now, Mrs. Fedder. I will come and talk to you after. Will you stay here?"

"Oh yes, I will be right here."

Theo turned to Henry. "Are you assisting?"

"Yes."

"Well then, let's go."

The patient was already in the OR and the anesthetist was getting ready to put him to sleep. While scrubbing, Theo went through his mental checklist as was his habit before major operations: What incision to make, the systematic check of the abdominal contents, etc.

Henry broke into his thoughts. "What do you expect, Theo?"

"Who knows. There must be some substantial bleeding, probably liver or spleen, but anything is possible. We will have to look at everything."

They went into the OR. The patient was anesthetized. Two i.v.'s were running, one in each arm. Through one, blood was being given. Theo and Henry gowned and gloved. The patient was being draped by the nurse and Theo helped, to speed things up. He turned to the anesthetist. "Ready, John?"

"Go ahead. He's as stable as he is going to be."

Theo took the scalpel and made an incision from just below the sternum to a point two inches below the umbilicus. He quickly deepened the incision and entered the abdominal cavity. As soon as the inner layer, the peritoneum, was opened, blood welled up. Theo went into quick action. "Suction. Scissors. Retractor. Here Henry, hold this."

As soon as the suction tip was introduced into the abdominal cavity, blood started pouring into the suction bottle. Large clots were also filling the abdominal cavity and Theo started to scoop them out through the incision he had enlarged with the scissors.

Henry was pulling on the retractor. "Christ, there is a lot of blood. Where is it coming from?"

"Don't know yet, we'll have to clear out this mess first." Suddenly there was an awful smell. "Shit, there is ruptured bowel, colon most likely. This is an awful mess!" Slowly he managed to remove most of the blood and started to look around. "Might as well look at the colon first and find the hole." The laceration in the colon was easily found. It was irregular and would require resection of part of the bowel. Theo put a clamp, covered with rubber tubing to protect the bowel, on either side of the laceration. "There, that should stop further leakage. Now let's look at the liver and spleen."

The liver had several lacerations, not large, and not bleeding anymore. The spleen was not injured. They looked at the rest of the bowel and stomach and found minor bruising only. Where had all that blood come from? Theo remembered that a lot of clot had been in the pelvis. He examined the back of the abdominal cavity. Some bruising, but nothing that would go with the large amount of blood they had found in the abdomen. What to do?

Theo looked back at the sigmoid colon where the hole in the bowel was. Where the lower clamp was applied an area of bloody tissue, a hematoma was visible. Could the bleeding have been where he put the clamp? He slowly took it off, sure enough, some bleeding again started. On closer inspection, there was a lacerated vein in the mesentery, the sheet of tissue that anchors the bowel to the back of the abdominal cavity. Theo carefully isolated the ends of the vein and tied them off. He then resected the torn bowel and brought the ends out as a colostomy, to be hooked up at a later date when everything had healed. He again inspected everything; no bleeding, everything looked fine. "I guess that's it, Henry. You want to go?"

"If you're okay, I wouldn't mind."

"Sure, I only have to close. You might as well leave. Thanks."

The rest of the operation was routine and quickly done. 'I've been lucky again,' Theo thought, 'it could have been a lot worse.' He washed the abdominal cavity out with copious amounts of saline and then closed the incision. When he was finished he thanked the nursing staff, as was his habit, and went to the lounge and had a cup of coffee. It helped to relax him a bit and let his adrenaline level return to normal.

Theo was glad that there now were more surgeons on staff at FMH and he could take more time off.

Chapter 58

'Serves me right,' Theo thought. It was annoying though. Because he was chief of surgery, it was now up to him to unravel the mess that one of the surgeons had got himself into. People not in the medical field did not understand how the peer review process worked, how doctors could police themselves, but most of the time the process actually worked very well. 'Sometimes it does not work,' Theo thought. According to some, it worked until the courts, human rights commissions, medical appeal boards, and others interfered.

It was already eight o'clock at night and Theo was still not finished reviewing the chart. He was determined to finish this task today so that he did not have to start all over tomorrow. He would give the whole matter some more thought in the morning, before sending the report to the MAC, the medical advisory committee, that made recommendations to the hospital board.

It seemed that Dr. Kurt Frazer had operated on a forty-eight year old male who had been involved in a traffic accident. Internal injuries had been suspected and a laparotomy performed. A small incision—too small in Theo's opinion—had been made and the abdominal contents examined. A laceration of the liver had been found and sutured and the abdomen closed. Almost from the start, the patient's course had been stormy. He developed a distended abdomen, a high temperature and chills, and had finally gone into septic shock and died. The autopsy had shown two lacerations in the bowel and extensive peritonitis.

Why had Kurt not done a more careful examination during the laparotomy? Why had he not re-operated when there was obviously an acute abdomen? Why? Why? This man had not needed to die. But he had, nothing could change that, and now Theo had to assess the case and recommend some sort of action to the MAC. What action? Could this have happened to him? Theo hoped not, he was always super careful, and yet, everyone could make a mistake. What to do? Theo made a few more notes and closed the chart. Best to sleep on things and write the report tomorrow.

The next morning, after further deliberation, Theo decided to turn the matter over to the audit committee for further investigation. After all, it was up to audit to investigate cases such as this, and it spread the responsibility. This way no one could say that he had not followed proper procedure or that he had not been objective because he was also a surgeon, and in the end the final decision would still be made by the MAC and ultimately by the board.

Feeling better, Theo drove to the hospital and set the appropriate wheels in motion. It would be weeks before the audit committee would issue a report of their own, so Theo tried to put the case out of his mind. Other cases, where the outcome had not been favorable, came into his mind. Was there reluctance by doctors to discipline their own? He had to admit there was. It was always difficult to find the line between honest human error and neglect, but too often there was great reluctance to assign blame. The more Theo thought about it, the more cases came to mind: Doctors not being available when they were supposedly on call, not responding to pagers, not returning calls. Sometimes the resultant delays had disastrous consequences. Incompetent doctors were also more common than the profession would care to admit. Even when a doctor was brought before the college for incompetence, a smart lawyer could often get him or her off, if not at the college hearing, then on the subsequent and inevitable appeal. Hospitals had very little clout in dealing with doctors who, either by neglect or error, provided substandard care. They could suspend a doctor but, unless they had a very strong case, the medical appeal board would often reverse this decision. 'Well, I can't do anything about that,' Theo thought, but the nagging thoughts did not go away.

After a while, Theo forgot about the case, as his daily activities, hospital rounds, a consult in the emergency, administrative maters regarding the department of surgery, and his private office demanded his attention. But in the evening while driving home, the case was again on his mind. Was he shirking his duty by referring the case to audit? Was he being too judgmental? No, it was better that audit investigate first. He would still have a chance to voice his opinion if necessary at the MAC meeting.

When he got home Laura greeted him at the door. "Hi, nice to see you at home so early. I guess you remembered that we are going to your Mom's for dinner."

'Thank God for small mercies,' Theo thought. He had totally forgotten.

Chapter 59

"What's this I hear of the board taking some type of action against Kurt, Theo?"

Theo was sitting in the OR doctor's lounge having a cup of coffee. Brad Harris, a local GP, had just finished assisting him with a very routine gallbladder. "What did you say, Brad? What did the board do?"

"You mean you don't know? But you're the chief of surgery, how can you not know?" It was obvious that Brad was skeptical.

"Brad, tell me exactly what you know, and how you know it." It was quite obvious that Theo was quite agitated, maybe he doesn't know, Brad thought. "Well, I don't have anything definite, only that the board had an extraordinary meeting to discuss Kurt, and they're thinking of suspending him."

"That can't be! You must be mistaken. The case is before the audit committee, surely the board would not go without a recommendation from the MAC, they never have before."

There had to be some mistake. The board would not act in medical matters without the advice of the medical side. He could not leave now as he had two more surgical cases but as soon as he was finished he would contact the chief of staff and get the facts straight. Brad probably had it all garbled up.

On the way to administration, Theo remembered that Clarence Hock, the chief of staff, was only in his office Tuesdays and Thursdays, and today was Wednesday. He would have to wait until tomorrow. It was probably just as well; at least he would be calmer by then. Might as well go directly to the office, it would be busy today and he was late already.

When he arrived at the office several patients were in the waiting room, the nurse was already ushering the first patient into the examining room. She closed the door behind the patient and turned to Theo. "It's Mr. Block. He's here for the removal of stitches."

Theo nodded. She was a jewel; quick, always friendly, and very perceptive. 'I'm lucky to have her,' he thought as he put on his white coat and went to see Mr. Block.

The office was busy as expected, but things had gone smoothly and Theo finished on time. When he was finished with the charts, Theo decided to phone Clarence, as he could not get this business with Kurt out of his mind.

Luck was with him and Clarence answered the phone. "Hello?" Theo recognized his voice. "Hello, Clarence, this is Theo. Sorry to bother you at home."

"That's okay Theo, what can I do for you? I guess you know I'm not on call today."

"Yes, I know. This is not work, at least not patient work. I, eh, want to ask you about Kurt."

There was a considerable pause before Clarence answered. "Ah, yes, Kurt. It's a nasty business that. You know that his mistake caused a man's life?"

"Come on, Clarence, that's not been established. Or have you had a report from the audit committee?"

"Well, no, but it's obvious, isn't it?"

"Shit Clarence, this is too serious a business to jump to conclusions and go off half cocked. The whole thing will blow up in the board's face if this is not dealt with by the book. What the hell is your hurry?"

"Don't get your tail in a knot, Theo. In any case, the board has decided and I would suggest that you leave it at that. Bye."

Before Theo could say anything further, Dr. Hock had hung up. 'What an ass,' Theo thought, but immediately realized that Clarence was not a voting member of the board, although he attended board meetings, and therefore was not party to the decision to suspend Kurt Frazer. Nevertheless, Theo suspected that Clarence had given the board some advice.

Theo looked over his schedule for the next day, finished off some reports, and went home.

Chapter 60

"Theo, are you coming to church with us tomorrow?" Laura asked, even though she knew the answer. She asked every weekend and the answer was always the same. "Not this time, Laura." Since they had moved to Fremont twelve years ago, Laura and the children had attended the local Mennonite Church, but Theo had so far not been. He told Laura that he had no need to go. It wasn't that he was an atheist, he did not like, nor need, all the trappings of the church, he said. He was fond of pointing out all the bad things that church-going people did. Laura never pressured him nor argued, but it was an ongoing worry for her. She was deeply religious, but one of those rare people who did not feel the need to impose her view on others. Nevertheless, it bothered her when Theo criticized the church and its members.

It was actually not quite true to say that he had never been to church. He had never attended a regular church service, but he did go when his children were baptized. The friendly greetings of many of the congregation he dismissed as false. "They don't know me, why should they like me?" he had remarked to Laura, who, in a rare moment of irritation had answered, "Don't flatter yourself, just because they are friendly doesn't mean they like you."

Sarah was away at university and Paul had gone hiking with friends, so Laura had no choice but to go alone. She did not like to go alone. She hated to admit it but she also did not like it when she was asked about her husband at church. Whether there was any hidden meaning behind the questions was doubtful, but Laura always felt a pang of guilt, as if there was some shortcoming on her part, as if she was responsible that her husband did not attend church.

When Laura had gone, Theo made himself a cup of coffee and settled down to watch American football, an admitted weakness of his. The 49ers, his favorite team, were playing the Cowboys—it had promise of a good match.

During a commercial, Theo's thoughts drifted. Sarah was in first year medicine. There had been no problems with her acceptance as she had maintained excellent grades. She now had a more or less steady boyfriend and seemed to have totally recovered from her ordeal a few years ago. Paul was now a tall very athletic young man of nineteen, in his first year of college, on the tennis team, and with no idea what he wanted to do with his life. The last was of concern to Theo, but Paul did not share these worries. "Why do you worry, Pops? When I need to, I will decide. Relax."

Theo's thoughts drifted to his mother. She had not been well lately but when Theo had suggested that she move into an apartment she had become downright hostile. Well, Theo knew when to keep quiet, especially where his mother was concerned. Eventually even she would realize that she could not look after the house.

The phone rang. It was the OR. "But I'm not on call," Theo protested. The OR nurse explained that Phil Trang, their newest general surgeon, and the one on call, requested help. "I'll be right there," Theo said, turning off the TV. Too bad, it was a good and exiting game.

On arriving at the hospital he rushed to the OR, changed and entered the OR area. "Theater three," the nurse at the front desk answered in response to his questioning look. Theo donned a mask and looked into the OR. Two doctors were bent over the patient. Their gloves and lower sleeves were bloody, a pile of blood soaked swabs were in a container on the floor, there was an i.v. in each arm and blood was being administered with pressure cuffs on each side. It all added up to trouble. Theo scrubbed less than the usual time and went in quickly. Phil Trang looked up. "Am I glad to see you! We have significant bleeding and can't stop it. I don't know exactly where it is coming from." His face was covered with beads of perspiration.

Theo stepped up to the OR table next to the assistant. "What were you doing?"

"A gallbladder."

"A gallbladder! Nothing else?" Theo was stunned. He was already packing away bowel and adjusting the retractors. "Here, suck in this area, Phil. Keep it clear. What happened?"

"Nothing. The bleeding just started."

"From where?" Theo was working furiously trying to see something, trying to find the source of bleeding.

The anesthetist suddenly became very active. "You gays better hurry, his pressure is falling. He's getting lots of... oh Christ... he's arresting... he has!"

The drapes were pulled off the chest. Sterile procedure was not of major importance when a patient was dying. Theo initiated cardiac massage and the anesthetist administered medications through the i.v. and kept ventilation going, but the patient could not be resuscitated and after a while was pronounced dead.

Theo was numb, he had never seen a patient die on the table, at least not during elective surgery. He muttered, "Oh shit," took of his gloves and gown, and walked out of the OR. In the corridor, he leaned against the wall and closed his eyes. What a disaster, and he still did not know why. There had to be an investigation. Theo opened the OR door. "Don't remove anything. Phil, notify the coroner. Nancy, leave all the instruments and swabs where they are. Don't move the body until the coroner instructs you to do so." He then went and changed and drove home. Even though it was not his patient, he was quite shook up and slept poorly that night.

When he arrived at the hospital the next morning, the first person he met was Kurt Frazer, who, with a grin on his face said, "Lost one on the table, eh?"

Theo could not immediately find words to reply, he was too surprised. By the time he regained his composure, Kurt was out the front door. On first impulse Theo wanted to follow him, but then thought better of it and went to do his rounds. He went and discussed the case with the hospital administrator and then went to his office.

No sooner had he arrived at the office than Clarence Hock phoned. "What's this I hear, Theo? You lost a patient in surgery?"

Theo was trying not to show his anger. "Who is spreading this nonsense?"

"Not nonsense, Theo. Phil tells me that you were in charge of the case when the patient died."

"Why that scumball, he called me in after he messed up. When I came in it was already too late, there was nothing I could do."

Theo could hear the smugness in Clarence's voice. "Nevertheless, you were in charge."

"That's bullshit, Clarence, I was never in charge. I was asked to come and help."

"Well, we shall see. Bye."

Theo sat there a few minutes. How could anybody suggest that it was his fault? The patient had died within minutes of his arrival; there had not been time to do anything. Who had said that he was in charge? He phoned Dr. Tran.

"Say, Phil, there is this thing going around that I was in charge when the patient died, what is your perception?"

"Well, ah, well, you had taken over. . . I think."

"I see." Theo's voice was ice. After a moment, he hung up. That bastard was trying to shift the blame. Theo was determined that would not happen. Above all, he had to maintain his cool. He contacted the CMPA, the Canadian doctor's insurance, and reported the case and stated his involvement.

Chapter 61

The autopsy had shown a large, two centimetre laceration in the portal vein, a vein not usually in danger during gallbladder surgery. How it was injured was not clear. The coroner ruled death through surgical misadventure and recommended an inquest. The relatives had already contacted a lawyer and both the hospital and the doctors involved had received writs. It would be a messy affair. A lawyer acting for the CMPA had contacted Theo and had instructed him on what to do.

In the meantime, the business with Dr. Frazer was still in the wings. Kurt's suspension had taken effect three days after the death of Dr. Tran's patient in the OR. Kurt had immediately asked for a hearing before the hospital board, but this had, for mysterious reasons, been refused and he had taken the case to the medical appeal board. A hearing was scheduled for the fifth of October, two weeks from now. Theo had been asked to attend.

The audit committee had completed its investigation and in typical protect-your-own fashion stated that: 'Yes, there had been complications, but this could happen to anybody and therefore Dr. Frazer should not be punished'. This, after the board had already decided on the suspension.

The medical appeal board hearings were held in the courthouse in Vancouver. Theo had booked the whole day off and arrived there before nine a.m. He was finally called in at one p.m. At his request, he was allowed to affirm rather than swear. He was not sure why he had not wanted to swear. 'It must be my Mennonite background,' he thought.

He was informed that the medical appeal board functioned as a court, but there were some differences. Theo was not quite sure what the differences were but was not about to ask.

One of the members of the appeal board asked how he was involved in the case.

Theo was not sure that he was involved at all. "Well, sir, I guess as head of the Department of Surgery I had to review the case. Otherwise, I am not involved."

"Did you recommend to the hospital board that Dr. Frazer be suspended?"

"I had no discussion with the board, sir."

"You mean that you did not recommend suspension?"

"I had no discussion with the board, sir."

"Did you recommend suspension? Please answer yes or no."

'Silly bugger,' Theo thought as he answered. "No."

"You mean you did not recommend suspension? Is it not up to the chief of surgery to make those recommendations to the board?" The tone was sarcastic.

Theo had to remind himself to stay calm. "No sir, that's the MAC's job."

"You did, however, review the incident involving Dr. Frazer. What did you do then?"

"I sent it to the audit committee for review."

"So you recommended a review. Did you not state earlier that you made no recommendation?"

"That was to the hospital board. In fact, I did not make any recommendations to anybody. All I did was to request audit to look over the case."

"Hm, it seems you are a bit fuzzy as to what you did do, Dr. Dirks, aren't you?"

"No, I'm not," Theo blurted out.

"Dr. Dirks, let me remind you that this hearing has the same powers as a court and contempt will not be tolerated. I would suggest that you cooperate and answer more concisely." He turned to his neighbor. "All yours, Fred. Hope he's more cooperative with you."

Fred, the person referred to, was a middle-aged man who seemed to have more medical knowledge and asked more reasonable questions, or so it seemed to Theo. Presumably he was a doctor, at least he seemed to have a lot of medical knowledge. The other members of the board also asked a number of questions and then Theo was dismissed. The first questioner, who seemed to be in charge, said when Theo had already stood up and was starting to leave, "Just a reminder, Dr. Dirks, we may call you back, so I want you to be available. It would help if you could refresh your memory in the meantime so that you could give more precise answers should we need you again." He waved his hand indicating that Theo could go.

'You stupid old bastard,' Theo thought, but managed to keep quiet. Once outside, he could only shake his head. Why had the old guy been so rough on him? It was almost as if he was trying to get Kurt Frazer off. By this time, Theo did not care which way the hearing went. He had never been for suspension anyway, at least not permanent suspension. On his way home he went over the events since the operation that got Dr. Frazer into this mess. The hospital board had acted prematurely and had not followed the usual course; The audit had found that Kurt was not negligent but had been unfortunate; The coroner had found surgical misadventure, a term that did not necessarily imply blame; and the inquest, held two weeks ago, had agreed with the coroner and had recommended that the Council of Surgeons investigate. All in all, it was rather a confusing mess and Theo was glad it was in the medical appeal board's hands rather than his. With all this confusion, it was an even bet that Kurt would get off.

For several days now, Theo noticed that he got a somewhat cool reception by some of the medical staff. His office was also less busy, indicating fewer referrals. At first he thought it was just one of those things that sometimes occur without a good or evident reason, but after a few more days he was certain that his referrals had decreased. Something was going on. Theo decided to speak to the chief of staff, even though Clarance Hock was not exactly his busom buddy.

He walked over to administration and as luck would have it, Dr. Hock was in. The door was open and Theo walked in. "Say, Clarance, would you have a few minutes for me?"

Clarance looked up and in a distinctly cool voice invited him in. "Sure Theo, sit down. How can I help you?"

'Why do I feed he wants to do just the opposite?' Theo thought. Aloud he said, "Well Clarance, it's a difficult business. I'm not even sure there is anything, but I have the impression that some of the medical staff have recently treated me differently, you know, they seem cool and reserved, nothing obvious. Do you have any idea why?"

Dr. Hock looked at him with surprise. "You must be kidding! After you stabbed Kurt in the back and then screwed up in the OR, you don't know? What does it take, a brick on the head? Come on."

Theo could not believe his ears. "Why you rotten son of a bitch. You have always had it in for me, haven't you? I will take this to the hospital board and you can repeat your accusations there." Theo was furious.

Clarance smiled. "You must think I'm stupid. Go to the board? I'll deny I ever said anything. A few well placed words with some of the medical staff are much more effective, don't you think?" There was a nasty smirk on his face.

Theo had regained control somewhat. "You always were a scumbag, Clarance. I should have known you are behind this, you would not miss an opportunity like this."

"You're damn right I wouldn't. You can now forget your ambitions of becoming chief of staff."

Theo gasped. "You thought I wanted..." He started to laugh and was still laughing when he was halfway down the hall.

The next day, thinking more rationally, Theo sent a letter to the head of the audit committee requesting an audit on the case. As chief of surgery, he was entitled to do that, but to be on the safe side he also sent copies of the letter to the chief of staff, the board, and the MAC. The results were almost immediate. Within a short time the chief of staff's secretary phoned wanting Theo to come for a meeting. Theo declined. Then the chair of the board asked to speak with Theo and a meeting was arranged. Over a cup of coffee,

Theo explained his position and an agreement was reached to explore things further once the audit committee had submitted their report.

The MAC chair talked to Theo a few days after and again it was agreed to wait for the audit report. Theo was satisfied, he had set the appropriate wheels in motion and he fully expected a satisfactory resolution.

He concentrated on his work again. His office was still relatively busy and he still had the same surgery days. His colleagues at the hospital, with some exceptions, again treated him with the usual friendliness and things seemed almost normal again—until Theo received a letter from the Council of Surgeons to attend a hearing into his conduct. He was baffled, as he could not think of anything that would be of interest to the council.

At the Council of Surggeons, he found out that a doctor Phillip Trang had complained that he, Dr. Dirks, had made disparaging remarks about Dr. Trang that were racist in nature. Theo was dumfounded. Fortunately, he managed to keep his cool. He requested a complete investigation by the council, and on his way home decided that it was time to involve a lawyer.

The next day he contacted Abe Franklin, a respected lawyer and a former patient of Theo's. After their first meeting, Theo was more worried than before. Abe had advised him not to discuss anything even remotely connected with the case with anyone unless he, Abe Franklin, was present. He also warned Theo not to take this matter to lightly as racially complicated cases often took a strange course.

ESCAPE TO PARADISE

It is interesting how events sometimes proceed in completely unexpected ways. For a few weeks nothing much happened, and then one morning the hospital was buzzing with rumor. The first thing that Theo heard was that Dr. Hock was resigning as chief of staff, then that he had been asked to resign, and one rumor had it that Clarance Hock had been fired by the board. Nobody knew why this should have occurred and Theo left the hospital to go to the office, doubting that any of it was true.

As more and more information became available, the full story evolved. It seemed that Clarance Hock had not agreed with the findings of the audit committee, who had found Theo innocent, and Dr. Trang, if not negligent, at least careless. At first, Dr. Hock had tried to influence the audit committee and change its findings and then, when that did not work, to suppress the report. The hospital board had found this out and had simply dismissed him.

The medical staff was in an uproar. Those that were pro-Hock were upset by the board's actions and those that were anti-Hock were shocked that he would try something so underhanded. Everyone, however, now seemed to agree that Theo had acted appropriately.

Theo now assumed that the investigation into his conduct started by the Council of Surgeons would be stopped, but to his surprise he found out that this was not so. When he inquired, he was informed that the council regarded matters 'of a racial nature' quite seriously and was still investigating.

Chapter 62

Driving home, Theo felt pleased with events as they had unfolded so far. The council matter was still a pain but he was certain that nothing much would come of it. After all, the charges were unfounded and he had many who would testify as to his good conduct in the past. He was sure this matter would not be a problem.

On arriving home, he parked his car in the garage and entered the house through the back door. When he did not see anyone in the kitchen or the family room he called out, "Hello, I'm home, where is everybody?"

"I'm up here," Laura called from the bedroom, "I'll be down in a minute."

Theo went into the kitchen. There was a pile of mail on the counter and he glanced through it; nothing important, a few bills, some advertising, a catalogue.

Laura came down the stairs. "Anything there?"

"Nah, just junk," Theo turned to Laura to give here a kiss. He noticed how pale she looked. "You okay?"

"Yes." She turned away to get a cup out of the cupboard. Facing away from Theo, she remarked in a casual manner, "I was in town today to see Saul."

Theo's instincts perked up. "You mean Saul Klein, the gynecologist?"

Still in a casual tone. "Yes, your friend."

"Why? What problems do you have? You never said anything to me. What about Jerry Ward? Why did you not see him?" Dr. Ward had been the family's GP for a number of years.

"Oh, I did see him, he sent me to Saul."

Now Theo became really worried. GP's did not send patients to specialists without reason. Cautiously he asked, "Why did Jerry find it necessary to send you to see Saul?"

"Well, he thinks there is a, what do you call it, a mass, that's it, a mass."

Now Theo knew this was something important. "Tell me, what made you go to the doctor in the first place?"

"Well, ah, well, I thought there might be something wrong. Yes that was it, I thought there was something wrong."

"Laura, don't play games with me. I am a doctor too, a surgeon at that. A mass, in the pelvis I presume as you saw a gynecologist, can be a serious problem. Have you had pain? Why did you not tell me anything? What did Saul tell you?"

"That's a lot of questions, Theo. I'll answer the last first. Saul said he would review the scan and then talk to me again."

"Why did he not talk to me?"

"Because I asked him not to."

"But why?"

"Because I did not want to worry you, because you had other worries, but mainly because I am the patient, I am competent, and he should not talk to anyone about me without my permission."

"But Laura..."

"No more buts, Theo. Let's have dinner."

"But I am worried."

"I know, so am I. Let's go and eat."

"Laura, don't play games with me. What did Saul say?"

"I see that you are not going to give up. Well, he does not know yet, but he thinks I will need a laparotomy. I will ask him to talk to you. Now, will you come and eat?"

They ate in silence at first, but Theo could not hold back. "You should have told me, Laura. I will call Saul tomorrow from the office. I hope you won't mind, but I have to know what's what."

"No, I will not mind, but don't worry. If God wants me to go through this then there must be a reason and I am willing to accept it, and you should too."

Theo was going to respond and then thought better of it. How could one argue with God?

When he went to sleep, Theo tossed restlessly before falling asleep and during the night, he dreamt again of Trudy. He could see him quite clearly, his belly ripped open, he thought he saw a hand reaching out for help but that could not be, Trudy had been dead. Theo woke up drenched in sweat and shaking. He got up and went into the kitchen for a glass of milk, but it took a while before he could go back to bed.

The next morning he phoned Saul and eventually located him in the hospital. "Hi Saul, what's this with my wife?"

"Theo? Oh, you know that Laura asked me not to call you, don't you?"

"Yes, she told me. She also said it was okay for me to call you. What gives?"

"Well, it's one of those things, Theo,. It could be malignant but it also could be benign. It needs to come out."

"What is your guess?"

"Come on, Theo! You're a surgeon, you know guesses don't mean a thing. I have booked her for next Friday, then we'll see."

"Guess you're right Saul, but I'm worried."

"Of course you are, it wouldn't be normal if you did not worry. I'll do my best."

"Yes, I know. Thanks. See you." Theo was no further ahead but he had known that Saul could not tell him anything more. It would be a long week.

Chapter 63

The business with the council raised its ugly head again. A hearing was set for the following Friday, a bad day for Theo, but he arranged to have someone cover him for any calls in the hospital. He just wanted to get this business over with. In the meantime, he tried to concentrate on his work but it wasn't easy. He often found himself thinking about Laura, hoping that the mass would be benign, but fearing the worst. A few more days and she would be in the hospital, have her operation, and then he would know. 'Know what?' he asked himself, 'that she will die?' And then what? He wished now that he would have spent more time with her, that he had been more attentive, more loving, but instinctively he knew that he could not have done that. He marveled at his difficulty in expressing affection. Why was he this way? He didn't think it was his upbringing. Was it genetic? He gave up and made himself concentrate on his work. His patients had a right to expect that, he told himself.

In spite of Theo's worries and impatience, Friday came very quickly. 'It'll be an eventful day,' Theo thought. Laura was having her operation at about the time of his hearing before the council. Theo hoped he could keep his mind on the business at hand and not think too much about Laura, but he knew it would be difficult.

He arrived for the hearing more than a half hour early. He tried to read but could not concentrate. Finally, he went to find a phone and called the hospital. Saul was still in the operating room. Theo slowly walked back to the waiting area. Eventually someone called. "Dr. Dirks, please come in."

To Theo's surprise and relief, his lawyer was there. "Hello Fred."

"Hello Theo." He shook Theo's hand. "Don't worry, this will be over soon."

There was a longish desk at one end of the room with three men and one woman sitting behind it. One of the men said, "Sit down, Dr. Dirks. I think you know everyone here." Theo didn't, but did not think it mattered. "We would like to clear up this unpleasant matter quickly, and I am sure you would too."

Theo nodded but kept quiet. He glanced at his lawyer beside him who gave him an encouraging smile.

The man behind the desk continued. "I understand that you made some unfortunate remarks to Dr. Tran, is that correct?"

Mr. Franklin, the lawyer spoke up. "No, that is not correct. Allegations have been made, but they are false."

The woman then spoke. Theo thought he recognized her and was certain she was a doctor. "Do you deny having made those remarks, Dr. Dirks?"

Theo looked at his lawyer, who nodded. "I don't know what remarks you are referring to Dr. . ." the woman helped out: "Pearse, Dr. Pearse."

"Thank you, Dr. Pearse. No one has ever told me what I was supposed to have said."

Dr. Pearse looked genuinely surprised. "How can that be? You must know what you are accused of."

"That, Dr. Pearse," Mr. Franklin turned to the others, "gentlemen, is the understatement of the day. I would think this negligence on the part of the council is enough for a dismissal, but let's hear what Theo, Dr. Dirks, is accused of."

The man who had spoken first, presumably the chairman, spoke again. "That sounds reasonable. Dr. Dirks is accused of calling Dr. Trang a miserable, little, yellowbellied liar."

Mr. Franklin could not keep from laughing:. "You mean . . ." He laughed. "You mean that's all?"

The man at the end of the table spoke up. "Calling someone yellow is quite a slur with degrading racial overtones. It promotes hatred and must be stamped out."

Theo was about to speak but the lawyer put his hand on Theo's shoulder and stood up. "You must be kidding! Yellowbellied is not a racial slur; it usually implies cowardice and has been so used for centuries. My client and I are leaving and you ladies and gentlemen should have a serious discussion and then let me know what you decide. Let me assure you that further harassment of my client will have significant consequences. Good day." He pulled on Theo's arm. "Come, Theo, we are finished here for now—and likely for good."

When they were outside, Theo stopped. "What was that all about? You were quite rough in there."

"Aw, they had it coming to come up with such nonsense. Even if you said that stuff, it doesn't matter, provided Tran *was* lying. Was he?"

"Yes, he was. That's easy to prove."

"Then we have nothing to worry about. Everybody knows that yellowbelly is an old English word that refers to a coward of whatever race and can hardly be taken as being a racial slur." He shook Theo's hand. "Don't worry, this is probably the last you will hear of this. Bye."

"Bye Abe, and thanks." Theo turned and walked to his car. He was eager to get to the hospital.

The surgery had finished some time ago and Laura was in the recovery room. The nurses let him in for a few minutes, although it was against regulations. Theo was grateful, but as Laura was still too drowsy to talk to him, he just stood there a few minutes and held her hand. Dr. Klein had been called to the case room in the maternity hospital a few blocks away. Theo called there but was told that Dr. Klein was in the OR. What to do?

'Might as well go over to my mom's place,' he thought. 'No use wasting time here.'

His mother was at home. She had become quite old and did not leave the house much. Sometimes she did not even go to church, much to her regret. "My back won't let me sit that long," she had explained.

Theo knocked and to his surprise, Peety opened the door. "What, you here? I thought you'd be protesting somewhere." He instantly regretted his words and tried to make up. "Hi, Peete, how are you?"

"Oh, I'm quite well, thank you." There did not seem to be any rancor in his voice, which made Theo feel even worse.

They went in and Theo gave Jutta a kiss on her cheek. "Hello Mom. How are you?" 'She looks old,' he thought.

"It's nice to see you after all this time. Has Laura had her operation?"

"About an hour ago. I know it's been a long time, Mom, but I have been very busy. I think it will slow down now."

Jutta placed a book she had been holding on the table. Theo noticed how her hand was shaking. He also noticed the swelling of her legs. 'Must be some heart failure,' he thought. Not that unexpected. After all, his mother was getting close to ninety. Theo sat down.

"I saw Laura briefly, she seemed fine. How are you keeping, anything new in town?" Theo tried to keep the conversation light. There was no point in worrying his mother with his own recent problems. They talked of this and that, everyone obviously trying to avoid controversy. Theo was happy that both Peet and his mother were in a conciliatory mood, as he himself was tired of arguing.

On his way home, he again thought of his mother's appearance. She was not well. Should he contact her doctor? And then what? He decided not to do anything for now. After he had left the city, he remembered that he also wanted to see Laura's parents. Well, he was not going back, so tomorrow would have to do.

Since he arrived in Fremont early, he stopped at the hospital to check on a few things. Everything was in order. He drove home. The house seemed empty; he did not know what to do. Now he knew how much Laura meant to him, how much he missed her already. He resolved to tell her tomorrow and to also tell her that he loved her, but he knew that he wouldn't. He wandered through the house aimlessly and finally decided to go to a restaurant rather than cook a meal at home. Before he could leave, Sarah called. "Hi Dad. I phoned the hospital but they only gave me sketchy information. How's Mom?"

"Mother is fine, Sarah, and to anticipate your next question, no, I don't know yet what it is. Sorry I did not call, I have a lot on my mind just now. I will keep you informed, I promise, and oh . . . before I go . . . could you call Paul? Tell him what you know and tell him I'll call tomorrow. Bye."

Theo remained sitting for a few minutes. He reflected on the changes that had occurred over the last few years. Both Sarah and Paul were now away from home, both doing well, both quite independent. He should be happy, but somehow it made him sad. There did not seem any need of him anymore. 'Don't be silly,' he told himself. 'Laura needs me now more than ever, and there are the patients and colleagues, and the kids still need some help and advice even if they are adults.' He got up and walked to the nearest coffee shop. The walk cleared his head and when he arrived, he felt refreshed and hungry.

The next day Theo only made rounds in the hospital and saw a few urgent cases in his office before driving to town to visit Laura. He found her surprisingly alert and looking almost her normal self.

"Hi," he placed the flowers he had bought on the night table at her bedside. "I hope you like these, there was not much time to shop."

Laura smiled. "You know I will love them, but you should not spend that much just for me."

Theo hugged her. "I am so happy to see you so well. How did you sleep? Has Saul been here? Has he any results yet?"

They chatted away, comfortable in each other's presence, until Saul walked in. "I'm glad to catch you here Theo. Maybe we can go for coffee after, there is something I need to talk to you about." Then, seeing the questioning look on Laura's face, "I'm sorry, Laura, I did not mean to exclude you. It's something to do with work. I wasn't going to discuss you."

He checked the chart and briefly examined Laura. "You are doing very well," he smiled. "A few days and you're out of here." Turning to Theo, he said, "Let's go to the hospital cafeteria, the coffee isn't fantastic but it's okay."

"Sure Saul." Theo gave Laura a quick peck on the cheek. "I'll be back shortly."

They walked to the cafeteria silently and picked a table that allowed for privacy.

"Well Saul, what is the news you have for me? The results must be bad if you want to discuss them with me first."

"The results? Oh, I see. You think I was not telling the truth up in the room? Well relax. What I want to discuss has nothing to do with Laura. You had a hearing at the Council of Surgeons, remember?"

Theo was baffled. "Why yes, but what has that got to do with you? Are they not finished with that shit? It makes me mad that . . ."

Saul interrupted him. "Simmer down, Theo. Hear me out. Again you are jumping to the wrong conclusions. You seem to do that a lot lately." Saul paused a moment, stirring his coffee. "It seems that the council has had a moment of enlightenment. They want me and Tim Lee, the general surgeon from the north shore, I think you know him, to do a review of Dr. Trang's practice. After checking with the OR staff, the anesthetist, and his assistant, someone has come to the conclusion that what you said was the truth after all. What I want from you is some advice and assistance. What do you think of Dr. Trang?"

It was Theo's turn to smile. "Things sometimes take strange turns. I am surprised that the council has opted for a complete review. I doubt that you will find anything significant. This case was unusual; Trang got into deep water and did not realize it in time. It's one of those things. Generally he's a good surgeon. What I objected to was that he tried to get out of it by blaming me." Theo sighed. "It's tough. What do you want me to do?"

"Nothing right now, but I would appreciate some help in getting the records at your hospital."

"Got it. Now tell me about Laura, about the path report."

Saul sighed. "You're as bad as other patients. No, worse! As a surgeon you know how long it takes to get the slides processed and reported. I said I'll phone you when I have the report." He went and got a refill of coffee. "How's life been in general, Theo?"

"Oh, you know, it's this business with our colleagues that makes things unpleasant sometimes. We have some strange birds in our profession, Saul, some real weirdoes. I sometimes think that in spite of the long training they get, doctors are poorly educated."

"Oh, that's absolutely true. Others have commented on that also. No doubt about it, in some areas doctors are absolute ignoramuses—but they think they are experts at everything. That's one reason why doctors do so poorly with investments; they don't listen to good advice. It's surprising how many doctors also suffer from feelings of inferiority. All that blustering often is a cover for insecurity."

"You could be right. Well, I don't know about you, but I have a few things to do."

"Yes, me too. Bye Theo."

"Bye Saul."

Theo went upstairs and stayed with Laura for a while and then drove home. The house felt empty and cold. God he missed Laura!

Chapter 64

Laura recovered uneventfully and came home, somewhat weak, but otherwise fine. The path report did show cancer of low malignant potential. It was a type that was very unlikely to return, but nevertheless it was cancer. All they could do now was to hope for the best. Saul assured Theo that no further treatment was indicated.

At the hospital, life resumed its normal course. Saul had been there and had completed the assessment of Dr. Trang. As Theo predicted, no other problems had been uncovered. The council now had the dilemma of deciding what to do with Dr. Trang. They procrastinated a while and then, in what seemed to Theo a condescending attitude, sent a letter of reprimand to Dr. Trang.

Theo was beginning to feel very relaxed and complacent when two events very seriously disturbed his equilibrium. In the middle of the night, Peet phoned to inform Theo that his mother had suffered a serious stroke. Theo immediately drove to Vancouver. When he arrived his mother was dead—she had not regained consciousness.

Then, just a few days after the funeral, Paul was involved in a serious accident. A car, driven by a drunk, had come across the midline and hit Paul's car head on. Paul had suffered injury to his head, fractures of his left arm, right leg, and several ribs, and multiple abrasions and bruises. When Theo saw him, Paul was unconscious and no one could predict when, if ever, he would wake up. Theo was beside himself. Not only had the sudden death of his mother shaken him deeply, but now this. He did not know how to handle these two tragedies and went into a deep depression. He carried on with his work in a fashion, but he became forgetful and on several occasions missed patients in the hospital while making rounds. He missed meetings and then resigned as chief of surgery.

Laura did not know what to do. She put aside her own problems in an attempt to help Theo, but it was as if he was in another world and nobody could get there. Even when Paul started to improve and eventually came out of his coma, Theo did not change. Laura became frantic. She talked to Theo's friends, she talked to a psychiatrist, she pleaded with Theo, to no avail. Unless Theo wanted and asked for help, there was apparently nothing that anybody could do.

To Theo it seemed as if his world had been turned upside-down. He felt imprisoned in a cage created by his mind. The periods of hopelessness he experienced were often more that he thought he could bear, but somehow he did muddle through from day to day. He went to work, he operated, he talked to patients and examined them. In fact, it was the daily routine that helped him cope, it gave him something to hang on to. Work, at least for part of the day, kept his mind busy and displaced the dark cloud that encroached on his thoughts when his mind was not otherwise occupied. The nights were the worst. He could not sleep, and when he got up he could not relax. It seemed that his mind was going a mile a minute and yet he felt as if everything was progressing in slow motion. The worst was the utter despair. It actually hurt, as if someone was squeezing his brain in a vise.

In his despair, Theo had actually prayed for deliverance, but then had despised himself for being such a hypocrite. 'First I discard and ignore God, and then I go begging when things don't go right.' In spite of his realization that not all was okay, he would not seek professional help. He could not explain why, he just knew that he could not see a psychiatrist, and that nobody could help him. Lately thoughts of suicide had entered his mind, but he had immediately rejected them. It was strange, but at times it seemed to him as if someone else had suggested that kind of solution.

This state dragged on without much change until Laura brought things to a head. One day at supper, she confronted Theo. "I think this business has gone far enough, Theo. I am not willing to let this marriage nor you go to the dogs. I have made an appointment with Dr. Jarowski, Stephan Jarowski, for both of us." She held up a hand when Theo attempted to say something, then continued. "Wait until I am finished. As I said, I am not willing to let things deteriorate further. You either come with me and be part of the solution or you can carry on without me. I have daily prayed for a solution but I think God helps those that make at least some effort, and I think the time has come for you to do just that. So, I am done now, you can say your piece, but believe me, I meant every word." She sat back. Her face was slightly flushed, her heart was racing, but she tried hard not to show how upset she was.

Theo looked at her for a few moments, then he spoke quietly. "I did not realize how affected you are by this, this . . ." he could not find the right word. "Of course I will go with you. You know that I love you."

And so it was that Theo became acquainted with Stephan Jarowski, the psychiatrist. For the first two visits, Laura accompanied Theo, but after that he went on his own. It was difficult for Theo to bare his soul, so too speak, but Dr. Jarowski was patient and soon a good relationship developed, which allowed Theo to talk more freely. Medication was suggested but rejected by Theo. He was willing to continue the visits but inwardly remained skeptical. He made a conscious attempt to act more normal towards others but inwardly the dispair remained, until the day Paul came home. Although the fractures had healed and he had undergone intense rehabilitation, he still was far from what he had been before the accident. Seeing Paul daily seemed to bring Theo's problems to a climax and one early morning after lying awake for a while, he got up and went into the study. In a locked drawer he found a Luger, a war souvenir, and a clip of ammunition. He put both in his pocket and quietly left the house.

Chapter 65

As Theo stood near the large fir and looked into the valley, the day was just dawning, a mist swirled over the fields and gave everything a mysterious, surrealistic quality. The sky was still gray and there was just a hint of the sunrise over the mountains in the distance. It promised to be a fine day, but Theo did not see any of this, his mind was far away. He was thinking of a small village in the Ukraine where he had been a boy, where he had grown up, where his parents had been born, where they had worshipped and had both enjoyed life and endured hardship. Theo marveled at the strength and steadfastness of his father. Where had that come from? The answer came immediately to Theo. It was from his father's strong belief and commitment to God. How fortunate his father had been, Theo thought, that he had such a strong faith. Theo had always been full of doubts and had often questioned not only religion, but the existence of God. He never had noticed any uncertainty in his father's faith. Then Theo remembered the war, his friends: Wanjka, Horst, others, but especially Trudy. Ah yes, Trudy. It was strange, but he still missed him after all these years. Theo again saw Trudy on the street of Warshaw, in the dirt, with his guts hanging out. 'Oh Trudy,' he thought. 'Why could I not help you? Why did you die?'

Theo looked at the gun in his hand. Why had he taken it? Did he really want to commit suicide? The idea suddenly seemed absurd. He looked into the valley. How beautiful it was. The sun was shining brightly, the mist was thinning and the bright green meadows came into view. Theo felt as if a heavy weight was being lifted from him, and he suddenly saw things in a different light. Suddenly he knew what had been missing, and he felt that he had to do something quite urgently. He quickly removed the clip from the Luger, put the gun and the clip in his pocket, and went inside.

Laura was in the kitchen making coffee. Theo felt a lump in his throat. Laura had always been the stable element in their family. She had loved him without question, without conditions, without judgment. Her whole life had been her family, and her faith. Yes, that was it, her faith. 'How often have I failed her,' Theo thought with a deep sense of regret. He walked up to her and gave her a hug. "I love you, Laura. I have always loved you. But I think you have always known that. I am so glad that I have been able to tell you so now. I have not been easy to live with lately. It's as if I have been away. I would like to change that, with your help. Would you like it if I came to church with you today? I would like to make my peace with God."

CPSIA information can be obtained at www.ICGtesting.com
Printed in the USA
LVOW06s0735200815

450656LV00019B/270/P